VAL'S LAST SECOND CHANCE

A Sweet Small Town, Secret Baby Romance

A GLEN FALLS ROMANCE
BOOK 1

BECKE TURNER

CHAPTER ONE

G<small>LEN</small> F<small>ALLS</small>, M<small>ISSOURI</small>

V<small>AL</small> R<small>EESER</small> <small>SWORE</small> she'd never come back to Glen Falls. Leaving had crushed her, but staying had never been a choice. No matter how much she'd loved Tate Carver—since middle school, since the first time he'd looked at her like she was the only girl in the world—there had always been a gap too wide to bridge.

The Reesers were blue-collar, the kind of family that worked hard for everything they had. The Carvers? Pillars of the community. Owners of the most powerful law firm in three counties. Earl Carver II had carved out a path for his son, and Tate had followed it. Although Tate had told her he wanted her and a music career, in the end, like always, his father won.

Still, walking away had nearly destroyed her.

Then she found out she was pregnant.

Glen Falls was a small town. An unwed pregnancy would have ruined her family's reputation, maybe even cost them the business her father had built with his bare hands. So she'd done what she thought was right. She'd left.

And Gabby Stanford? The best friend she'd shared secrets, heartbreak, and laughter with since they were kids? She'd lost her too.

Now, ten months later—plus a month of waiting for the test results that had rocked her world—she was back.

For her daughter.

For Tate.

For the truth.

Heart slamming against her ribs, she climbed out of the car, her legs weak after the eleven-hour drive. Exhaustion clung to her like a second skin, but it didn't matter. Not when every second counted.

She crossed the porch and knocked. Hard.

The door opened. Not just to Tate. To Gabby.

Val's breath caught.

She hadn't thought this through. She'd imagined facing Tate, but both of them?

Gabby's eyes widened before narrowing into a glare that cut straight through Val's ribs. "You've got to be kidding me."

Tate stepped forward, his expression unreadable, but the tension in his jaw, the way his hands curled into fists at his sides—those weren't blank. Those were fire and betrayal.

Val swallowed hard. "I need to talk to Tate. Alone."

Gabby let out a sharp laugh, arms crossing over her chest. "Oh, now you want a private conversation?"

"Gabby." Tate's voice held a warning, but his gaze stayed locked on Val.

Val clenched her fists, forcing herself to hold it together. "This isn't about the past," she forced out. "This is about something bigger. Something that can't wait."

Tate's brows pulled together. "What does that mean?"

She inhaled a shaky breath, bracing herself. "You have a

daughter, Tate. And she has MCADD. It's an inherited condition. She has two recessive genes. That means you have one too. You don't need a test to prove it. You just need to accept the truth."

Tate blinked at her, his mouth parting, but no words came. Gabby sucked in a sharp breath.

Val held out the paper, the one she'd stared at for weeks, memorizing every line. "Her newborn screening flagged it. The results didn't come back right away, but when they did... she was already a month old."

"Stop." Tate's voice lashed through the air, slicing her words clean in half. "You're telling me..." He shook his head, like he could erase the words. "I have a kid?"

Val's breath hitched. "Yes."

"And you kept her from me?" he said, punctuating each word.

Gabby stepped back like Val had physically struck her. "How could you?"

The betrayal in her best friend's voice stung worse than anything Tate could throw at her.

Tate swayed, his expression shifting from shock to something darker, something dangerous. "You knew and you still walked away?"

Tears burned behind Val's eyes. "I was trying to do the right thing."

Tate let out a hollow laugh, one without humor. "And now? What, you finally grew a conscience?"

"I came back because I had to!" She shook her head, chest rising and falling too fast. Her nails dug into her palms, but nothing could hold her together. "Because every day I wake up terrified something will happen to her. Because I heard you were getting married and I couldn't let another baby go through what I have. I couldn't—"

Her voice cracked.

Tate's hands flexed at his sides, his breaths shallow. "You don't get to decide what's best for me. For us. You don't get to drop this at my feet like some afterthought. And just where is this phantom baby?"

Gabby's throat bobbed, her arms tightening around herself. "I trusted you."

Val pressed her lips together, her entire body shaking. She had known this moment would be brutal. She just hadn't realized how much it would cost.

"I'm sorry," she whispered.

"Yeah," Tate said. "So am I."

His jaw tightened, and for a second, she thought—hoped—he might say something else. Instead, he shut the door in her face.

The resounding thud rattled the porch light fixture overhead. Val shivered, the cold morning air biting into her skin. But it was nothing compared to the weight pressing harder on her shoulders. Tate hated her. Gabby hated her.

Worse, this was her first stop. Now, she had to warn her own family. So far, Brett had healthy children, but the next birth? And Ruger? She'd give anything, do anything, to save them from this heartbreak. But she couldn't stay silent. Not now. Not ever again.

Val's tires crunched over the gravel lot behind the Reeser Garage, her father's pride and joy. The metal-sided building stood just as she remembered—sturdy, no-nonsense, a staple of Glen Falls.

When she stepped from her Honda, the scent of oil and cut steel hung thick in the morning air, familiar, grounding. Maybe it would be okay—after she explained what had happened, explained how much she missed them, how she wanted to protect them from her shame and the potential fallout against their business.

She'd always held a special bond with her papa, Paul

Reeser. She prayed their connection could sustain this blow, that despite her betrayal, he'd see her, really see her, and understand. She imagined him pulling her into a hug like he used to after a long day in the shop, when grease covered their hands, and he'd say, "You're my girl, Val. Best welder I've ever had."

But she wasn't his girl anymore.

Not after what she'd done.

Through the open bay doors, the overhead lights flickered against the morning dim, casting long shadows. Her brothers' voices carried from inside, low murmurs mixed with the clang of metal on metal.

Papa was always first to arrive, always the last to leave.

Val wiped her palms on her jeans and forced herself forward.

The moment she stepped inside, Brett looked up from under the hood of a truck, a grease rag draped over his shoulder. He froze, his mouth parting slightly, his dark brown eyes —Papa's eyes—widening in shock.

A loud clang rang out and Ruger, her younger brother, stooped to retrieve the wrench he'd dropped onto the concrete.

"Look who finally showed up," Ruger muttered, his expression unreadable.

Val swallowed against the dryness in her throat. "Where's Papa?"

"You got a lot of nerve asking that," he said.

Brett's jaw tightened, and for a second, she thought— hoped—her oldest brother might step in, bridge the gap between them. But then the office door creaked open, and a shadow filled the doorway.

Papa had never been a man to waste words, and when he did speak, his voice carried the weight of a man who'd built something from nothing. His dark gaze landed on her, sharp as a welding torch, and for the first time since she'd arrived in Glen Falls, fear slithered through her.

Papa stepped forward, each booted footfall deliberate, slow. His lined face—older than she remembered—didn't crack. Didn't soften. Didn't welcome.

"I told your momma you were gone," he said.

The words struck like a hammer to the ribs.

Tell him. But Val couldn't produce the words.

Papa's expression never wavered. "She cried for months. We all did. And now you think you can walk in here like none of that mattered?"

She shook her head, panic clawing at her throat. "I never wanted to hurt you—"

"But you did," he cut in, voice firm as forged steel. "You broke your momma's heart. Broke our family."

A lump lodged in her throat. "Papa, please—"

"No." His tone was final. "You chose this. You left without a word. You let us think—" His voice cracked before he swallowed it down, his anger returning full force. "I don't know why you're here, but you don't belong anymore."

Pain shot through her, but she forced herself to stand her ground. "I had a baby," she said, her voice barely above a whisper.

Papa's nostrils flared, but he said nothing.

"She's sick," Val pressed on. "She has MCADD. It's genetic, which means—"

"I don't want to hear it."

The finality in his tone sliced deep.

She reeled back, barely able to breathe. "Papa, you—"

"You're not my daughter." His voice never wavered. "The daughter I raised wouldn't have done this to us."

The garage spun.

Ruger exhaled sharply, but he didn't say anything. Brett's

jaw twitched like he wanted to speak, but he kept his mouth shut.

Papa's gaze bored into hers, unrelenting. "You need to go."

She had known this would be hard, had prepared herself for anger, but this? This was a funeral. Her hands curled into fists. She wanted to scream, to make him listen, to explain why she had done what she did. But there was nothing left to say.

She turned on shaky legs, walking away, the garage doors looming before her like the gates of a place she'd never be welcome again.

She'd lost Tate.

She'd lost Gabby.

And now, she'd lost her family.

She had nothing left—except her daughter.

And Val would fight for her with everything she had.

Even if it meant doing it alone.

CHAPTER TWO

AND HE'D BEEN CONVINCED IT WAS ALL A LIE!
The test results trembled in Tate's hands.

PROBABILITY OF PATERNITY: 99.99%.

HE BLINKED, but the numbers didn't fade. It was true. He'd fathered a child. Somewhere in North Carolina, Val was raising his daughter—alone.

Why? What had happened to the love of his life?

She'd broken his heart, his pride, everything he'd believed about his future, in a single act of abandonment. And he still didn't have answers.

He'd gone over every detail of their final night together. They'd laid out a simple no-muss, no-fuss plan, just like the woman he loved. He'd appease his parents and attend his University of Virginia graduation ceremonies. After the pomp and circumstance, he'd drive home to Glen Falls and pick up Val for the drive to Branson. They'd have a simple ceremony under the trees in Dogwood Canyon Nature Park and start their lives together.

Except he'd come home and she was gone.

Until last month. Then, his life switched from chaotic to bizarre. He still couldn't wrap his head around the events. Val showing up at his door. A genetic condition he'd never heard of. A near hysterical explanation. Like who does that? He had lived it and still didn't understand the message. Except for the test results. He got those—loud and clear. Now it was time to act.

The door to Senior's office loomed ahead. Using the title Dad or Father had never felt right, so Tate had chosen to call him Senior. His father had earned his title in more ways than one. Today's news wouldn't change that fact. Tate didn't hesitate. He knocked once, his knuckles grazing the heavy wood, and entered.

Inside his father's expansive office, the scent of polished wood and aged leather filled his senses. The room, lined with floor-to-ceiling mahogany bookcases, carried an air of opulence. Yet nothing overshadowed Senior's presence. Earl Tatum Carver II stood at the bar, pouring scotch into a crystal glass.

"Sit down," Senior said, barely looking up. "Robert and I were just discussing your grandmother's cottage on Spruce."

Tate's uncle sat casually in one of the leather chairs, his easygoing demeanor a stark contrast to Senior's stiff formality.

With the latest news galloping through his bloodstream like a wild animal, Tate ignored Senior's instructions and remained rooted to the expensive rug, the paper gripped in his fingers.

"I just got the results of my paternity test." He extended the sheet toward his father. "Ninety-nine-point-nine percent."

Senior froze, the glass of scotch halfway to his lips. His

gaze locked on Tate, a flicker of disbelief quickly replaced by the hard edge of calculation.

"Is it anyone we know? How much does she want?"

"Hold on, Earl." Although his voice sounded calm, Rob's expression carried a warning. "Give him a chance to speak."

"It's Val. She showed up at the house a month ago wanting to talk about a genetic disorder." Tate cringed with the memory. "I wasn't exactly receptive."

Senior set his glass down with a thud. "The mechanic's daughter? After what, a year, she reappears? She must need money. It always brings them back."

"It's not about money." Tate's jaw tightened. Val hadn't made a lot of sense, but money had never been mentioned. If anything, his family money had been a problem for her.

"Her daughter...my daughter..." Even the words came with difficulty. "...has MCADD, a genetic condition. That's why Val came back. She wanted us to get tested to see if we were carriers."

"So she knows you're engaged to Gabriella and still has the nerve to come forward. Did Gabriella agree to this testing?" Senior asked, his tone razor-sharp.

"She did," Tate said. "The odds of her carrying the recessive gene were low. But Glen Falls is a small community. Lots of people here are related. Gabby's not a carrier, but I am. And Val..."

Senior always looked for the worst in people.

"As long as she doesn't come back to Glen Falls, I don't see a problem," Senior said.

"It's still a lot to process," Rob said, leaning back. "I've got to meet with my agent in Nashville, but you're welcome to use the cabin. Why don't you take a few days to clear your head and decide what you want to do?"

"What's to decide? Max can handle the legal documents." Senior huffed out a breath. "It's not an optimum situation.

Your future father-in-law gets to draft your Child Support Agreement." Senior cursed under his breath. "If this doesn't test our partnership, I don't know what will. But the kid's a Carver, and we Carvers own up to our responsibilities."

"She." Tate rocked on his heels, his voice steady. "The baby's a girl. She's my daughter. I want to see her. I have to know her."

Senior's cold laugh sent a chill down Tate's spine.

"You want to see her?" He waved his hand like Tate's daughter was little more than a nuisance. "That's not necessary. Don't complicate your life with this. We'll pay for whatever she needs because the Carver name means something in this town. But don't you jeopardize our name again. Your decisions, or in this case lack thereof, affect the firm, me, your mother, Gabriella, and Max."

Defiance tightened Tate's chest. "Even if Val doesn't move back, people are going to find out. Val's family is here. She'll bring the baby home to visit her parents."

Senior slammed his hands against the desk. "This is the first any of us has heard about an illegitimate baby."

"She's my daughter!" Tate struggled to modulate his tone. Although he disliked Senior's approach, he'd always treated him with respect. But if Senior didn't dial it down, he'd demand the same respect for his child and her mother.

"Court's adjourned," Rob said, pushing to his feet. His steady grip and empathetic gaze eased the anger bubbling in Tate's gut. "You've got some big decisions in front of you."

"Mind-blowing decisions," Tate muttered.

"It's going to be hard for Gabby too," Rob said. "She deserves your honesty."

Senior jammed the receiver back into his desk phone's base. "Well, this has all been heartwarming—my little brother comforting my son after his biggest screwup ever. But you'd better figure it out fast," Senior said, jabbing his finger at

Tate. "That was Karen, my admin. Gabby's waiting in your office."

Tate rubbed the back of his neck. "I'll need to take a few weeks off. Can you cover my cases for me?"

"No," Senior said. "Your mother has our Switzerland vacation booked. And I wouldn't even if I was in town and loafing. You made this mess. You can clean it up *and* handle your business responsibilities. And don't consider slacking off. I can fire you just like any other associate. Might be a little tough to pay child support without a job."

"Enjoy your trip," Tate said, struggling to keep the sarcasm from his tone. For once, he'd like Senior to do something besides criticize him. "I'll finish the Johnson case and then clear my schedule."

Still aggravated, Tate stepped into the hallway, welcoming the cooler air against his skin. Although he'd studied the law more out of obligation, the work steadied him. And man, did he need a simple repetitive task to get him through *this* day.

When a hand grabbed his arm, he tensed and then relaxed. Uncle Rob had always supported him—far more than Senior.

"I can't help you with your caseload," Rob said, "but I can cancel my Nashville trip. If you need a place—or someone to listen, I'll be there."

Tate shook his head, his tongue thick with the weight of his dilemma. "Don't change your appointment for me. I'm okay."

"You sure?" Rob's grip tightened. "This is not some small bump in the road."

Tate half-laughed, half-snorted. "Right now, I wish I was going to Tennessee with you. If I'd taken your advice and gotten my undergrad in music from the University of Memphis, things might be different."

"Whoa!" Rob's brows disappeared beneath his too tousled

hair. "Talk about going way back. You sure you don't want me to stay? It would be just the two of us. We could hike or night fish."

"I'll be okay," Tate said, lowering his voice. "But days like today make me question my choices."

"Well just for the record, I didn't tell you to pick Memphis," Rob said, his smile easy. "I told you to follow your heart. Big difference."

"Senior drives a hard bargain, but he was right on careers. I couldn't make a living with music. That was a little boy's dream."

"Music's worked for me." Rob canted his chin toward Senior's office door. "Based on the way my big brother rants and raves, the law hasn't been a great option for him."

The bubble of laughter escaped Tate's mouth before he recognized it was building. "Don't let him hear you say that."

Rob's smile faded. "No worries. He couldn't hear it, anyway. Never could."

"I was trying to make them happy by choosing law and working in the family firm."

"Hey?" Rob cuffed his shoulder. "They're proud of you. But that's not the issue. Piece of advice? Focus on what's ahead, not on what's behind you."

Karen appeared at the end of the hall and tapped her wristwatch.

Tate swallowed and turned toward his office door. "Gabby's waiting and I don't even know where to start."

"Start with the truth," Rob said. "She loves you. You'll get through this."

"I've always been truthful with her," Tate said—but he couldn't say the same about being honest with himself. Maybe it was time to start.

Uncle Rob waved and Tate sucked in a steadying breath. Time to face the music.

Unlike Senior's office—where everything shouted money —he'd kept his smaller space simple with clean lines and muted tones. While Senior enjoyed heavy, expensive furnishings, Tate had selected a functional moderately priced desk, matching bookshelves, a credenza and two comfortable leather guest chairs, where his fiancé awaited.

Tension arced through the air. Gabby, always elegant and perfectly turned out, sat too straight, her hands clasped so tight, they were nearly chalk-white against her navy business suit.

At the soft click of the door, she turned, her gaze steady. "Are you ready to tell me what's going on?"

Bracing for the onslaught of guilt, he crossed the room and dropped into the chair opposite her. "Yes."

Her small smile vanished. "You sound as solemn as a judge delivering a death sentence."

"It's serious." Ignoring the adrenaline rush compelling him to race through his delivery, he rested his elbows on his knees and laced his fingers together. "You remember when Val came to the house talking about MCADD?"

"How could I forget?" A crease formed between her brows. "Although I didn't think it was necessary for me to get tested, I did it anyway. I guess out of respect for the friendship I once shared with Val. I'm not a carrier. But honestly? Val wasn't making a lot of sense that day. She came off like a scared, desperate woman—not the person we'd been friends with."

Tate drew in a breath. "I'm sorry I didn't say something before. But I had them run a paternity test on me."

A tiny v formed between Gabby's brows. "That was weeks ago. Why didn't you tell me?"

Tate lifted his hands and then returned them to his knees. "I don't have a valid excuse for not talking to you about my decision. I didn't believe her. Like you said, she wasn't herself." And he hadn't wanted to believe her. "MCADD only develops when the baby gets a recessive gene from both parents."

She stiffened with realization.

He nodded, swallowing so he could speak past his dry throat. "Val and I both are carriers. I'm the father of her child."

Gabby's lips parted, her eyes searching his face. "What?" The word came out as a whisper, disbelief thick in her tone. "That doesn't make sense. You said you always used protection."

"I did." But he'd also been young, inexperienced—and stuff happened—had happened. He forced his jaw to unclench. "The paternity test came back this morning. Ninety-nine-point-nine percent. I'm the father."

Gabby shot to her feet, her hands clenching at her sides. "No. That's not true. She's lying. She must be lying."

"She's not lying, Gabby." Tate suppressed the urge to stand, comfort her. But that wouldn't help him finish what he had to say. "The test doesn't lie either. Val and I have a daughter."

Gabby turned toward the window, her arms folding across her chest. What did a guy do in this situation? Go to her? Remind her he'd chosen her for his wife? She didn't deserve this.

"This doesn't have to change anything." Her tone sharpened. "You can meet your financial responsibilities through a trust. Father can set it up. That will provide the child everything it needs without turning your life—and ours—upside-down."

It? He straightened. What was wrong with him? He'd just delivered a terrible blow and he had the audacity to criticize Gabby? His daughter wasn't an it. She was a human who hadn't asked to come into this situation. That was on him.

"This isn't about money," he said, every word caring more weight. "This is about a child. My child."

Gabby spun to face him, her eyes glistening. "We don't have to be involved. We can still live our lives without getting dragged into Val's drama. That's what this is—drama. You saw her, spoke to her. She's not the person we knew. She's *not* our friend."

"Sure it's drama, but it's my drama. This little girl is part of me, Gabby." The truth of his words settled into his core. "She's not an obligation I can ignore."

Gabby's shoulders sagged, her arms falling to her sides. "This feels like a rerun of our high school days. It was always the three of us—me, you, and Val. And when you two got together, I was the outsider, the extra."

"Gabby—"

Her hand shot forward. "It's happening again. This time, it's your daughter. You and Val created this child," she said, her voice trembling. "So don't tell me this isn't about Val, because it is. I'm just the extra. Again."

Tate hesitated, waiting for his anger and resentment to cool and allow reason to come forward. The denial train had left the station without him. Time for honesty with Gabby and himself.

"That's not what I want for you—or for us," he said taking her chilled hands in his. "But this little girl is my responsibility. I can't abandon her and forget she exists. She's a part of me and she needs me to figure this out."

Gabby's fingers gripped his. "What about me? Us? I've always been by your side—even after Val abandoned you and my friendship. I was here after she broke your heart. We were building something real; at least I thought so."

Her words echoed in his head, bumping from side to side like rocks in an empty can. Did he have something real with

Gabby? Because right now, nothing felt real. It felt broken, except for one thing.

"For now, I must focus on my daughter. She has to come first."

Gabby pulled away and reached for her bag, her knuckles white around the strap. "I'll wait because I love you. But I'm not going to build a life in second place—not this time. So think long and hard about your priorities and about who has staying power. Because it's not Val."

Her words hung in the air long after the door clicked shut behind her. Tate dropped into his chair. Gabby was right. He couldn't have two firsts in his life. Right now, his daughter occupied the spot, no matter how much it cost him.

CHAPTER THREE

SUNBERRY, NORTH CAROLINA

VAL LEANED against the apartment door, letting her eyes close for just a second. Libby's fine. Her blood sugar was stable. Her precious daughter had survived Val's first day of work far better than her mother.

Unsure if her wobbly knees could support her, Val slid down the door until her bottom rested on the stained wood floors. She hadn't anticipated it would be so hard to leave Libby.

Her first shift back had rivaled her first day on the job. But this time it was worse. This time she'd been forced to leave Libby. Sure, it was with her friend Sarina and she'd been only one short stair flight away. But proximity hadn't chilled her overactive imagination. Every time she'd taken an order, she'd checked Libby's blood sugar on the app. Every time a child entered the diner, her thoughts had gone to Libby. Did her daughter miss her? Feel abandoned?

Thank goodness, Sarina had anticipated her fear and sent

text messages throughout the day. One after another they'd pinged her phone like tiny lifelines. Libby's fine. She had a good nap. We're playing now. That one had landed just moments before she'd abandoned a party of ten and dashed up the stairs.

A shaky breath escaped her, but it wasn't the gasping kind of relief she'd grown used to over the past year. This one didn't leave her shaking, unable to think. Nothing had gone wrong. Libby was safe, the bills were paid, and somehow, she was making her life work for her and Libby. But leaving her baby—even for six hours had been torture.

"I did it," she whispered.

Her lips twitched. She could work and manage her baby. Libby would be okay, just like the thousands of other children in single-family homes. Their little apartment wasn't big and fancy, but it was hers. The cozy collection of mismatched furniture and cluttered counters created a home.

Her stomach growled. Dinner needed to happen before her little dumpling awakened from her nap. Just because she'd gone to work didn't mean the household chores were on hold. Val stood, turned on her playlist, placed leftovers in the oven to warm, and peeled a sweet potato to Taylor's folk-country vibe.

Tap, tap, tap!

She turned toward the front door, her hand frozen mid-swipe. She wasn't expecting company. Wiping her hands on a kitchen towel, she pulled open the front door.

"Tate!" Her hoarse whisper reverberated, a loop stuck on repeat, pulsing in time to the frantic beat of her heart.

He stood there, looking like he'd walked straight out of her memories—the same confident stance, the same intense blue gaze. Her hand cramped, reminding her of her death grip around the doorknob.

"I got the test results," he said, his voice quiet but sure.

Val blinked, her mind scrambling to connect the sound of his voice to the interpretation of his words.

"Test results?" Her voice came out strangled. "Why...why are you here?"

"Can we talk?" He shifted his weight, his hands resting at his sides.

The sickening memory of the last time she'd stood face-to-face rushed over her. She'd left her baby to warn him. He'd shut her out, slammed the door on her.

"I don't have anything to say to you," she said, forcing the words out.

"Please, Val." His voice softened. "Give me ten minutes."

Something in his tone tugged at her resolve. This was Tate, Libby's father. With a sigh, she stepped back and opened the door wider. "Ten minutes."

The apartment felt even smaller with him in it. Although he'd once fit into her life, now his presence sent a jittery feeling under her skin.

She swiped at her phone, checking Libby's monitor. The little number glowed green—still safe. Her lips twitched into a small smile. She was really doing this. With her friend's child-sitting swap, she could provide for her daughter.

A small, unfamiliar sound pulled her to present. Tate. In her house. Staring at her. She bristled and returned to dinner preparations.

When he followed her to the kitchen, she motioned toward the cluttered dinette set. Well heck, she usually ate standing at the counter or on the sofa and Libby ate in her highchair.

She pushed the box of diapers and wipes to the side. "Sit if you want."

Tate hesitated but eventually lowered himself onto the plain ladder-back chair, his long legs stretching into the living area. From his position, the sofa littered with a pile of clean linens and the bookshelf lined with toys and pictures were in clear view.

Tough. She returned to the sweet potato, chopping it into small chunks with more force than necessary. Single working moms didn't have the luxury of tidy homes. Shoot, her sheets hadn't been changed in two weeks.

"I came to see her," he said, his voice tentative, his gaze roving the photos.

Ignoring the vise circling her chest, Val dropped the potato chunks into a pan of water and placed the pot on the burner. "Why now?"

"I had to process...everything."

Process? Good for him. She'd be thrilled for a moment to *process* her life. But it wasn't going to happen soon. However, she didn't want to argue with him. She wanted him to say what he needed to say and leave her in peace. Because today was not the day to push her—not even an inch.

She dropped her gaze to his fingers, which worked like he was playing notes on a guitar. Funny how some things didn't change. When he looked up, she refocused on the stovetop. The gas burner clicked and then ignited.

"It was a lot to take in," he said. "But she's my daughter. I need to know her."

Val turned away to set the timer on her phone, but she couldn't pretend his audacity hadn't stunned her. She'd expected this moment, but not so soon.

"Libby and I are doing fine." She focused on each word, careful to hide her emotions. "She's happy and healthy— considering her condition. We have a good routine. I have friends who help. You don't need to worry about us."

"That's not the point," he said, his voice firm. "She's a part of me. I want to be here for her."

She jerked open the oven door, rattling the burners. Now he shows up—after he's had time to process! Isn't that special? Where was he on the nights she spent awake watching Libby's tiny chest rise and fall? Where was he when her heart gripped with the kind of fear she wouldn't wish on anyone?

Her anger shriveled like her overdone dinner. She'd gone to Glen Falls to protect him from that gut-ripping fear, to save him from the heartbreak of feeling powerless against the fragility of their daughter's life.

"She's her own person," she said, easing the oven closed. "She doesn't know who you are."

"I want to change that."

"Waaah!"

Libby's cry broke through the baby monitor, soft at first then growing in urgency. Val tapped the phone app and released a breath. Blood sugar still holding steady, but Libby needed to eat soon.

"I'll bring her out," she said. "Make yourself useful. Keep an eye on those sweet potatoes. Don't let them boil over."

If he was offended by her rude behavior, he could just get over it. He wasn't a guest in her house. If he wanted to visit, he could pitch in and help.

The moment she opened the nursery door, Libby's tiny hands wiggled for her. Worries about leaving her, about her first day of work and Tate's unexpected arrival, evaporated.

"Hey, sweet girl." She scooped Libby into her arms, smoothing away her tears. "Mommy's here. Did you have a good nap?"

Val rubbed her cheek against Libby's silky curls and then placed her on the changing table.

"I missed you too," she said, removing the soiled diaper. "But Mommy's home and you're clean and dry. Now, we're going to have a nice evening, just you and—"

And Tate, who she'd delegated to baby chef.

"He'll get over it," she whispered, settling into the rocker. "If he doesn't, that's okay too. We're doing fine, you and me."

Although her words were meant more for her than her daughter, Libby hiccupped and rested her head on Val's shoulder, her tiny fingers curling into Val's shirt.

She smoothed Libby's curls, her heart aching with both love and fear. "I love you."

Snuggled with Libby, Val's eyes drifted closed and then snapped open with a start. She'd almost fallen asleep—with Tate in her kitchen—waiting.

"Someone's here to meet you, sweetheart."

So much for dreaming this wouldn't happen for like twenty years.

CHAPTER FOUR

"You bet, Carver!" Tate muttered. "This is going about as smooth as cross-examining a hostile witness without a strategy."

Like he even had a strategy. He rotated the wooden spoon around the pot, splashing boiling water onto his hand.

"Ow!" He shook off the sting.

Nothing worse than feeling inept— fumbling, out of his depth, and unsure of his place. And cooking? Geez, cooking was as new to him as parenting. Both required skills he didn't have, but he'd learn. He had to.

The timer on Val's phone ticked down, though he couldn't remember what it was for. So what did he expect? Coming to North Carolina had been impulsive, unlike the careful planning he prided himself on. One test result had shredded his methodical nature. No analysis, no strategy— just a hastily packed bag and the miles rolling under his wheels.

And here he was standing in Val's tiny apartment kitchen like some ill-prepared loser. How was he going to bridge the chasm between them? She'd kept him in the dark for fourteen months. Yet all he could think about was how much she must have struggled while he'd substituted Val for Gabby and continued with his life. Talk about messed up.

Static crackled in the silence. Tate's gaze bounced from the baby monitor to the living room, landing on the scattered baby items— a play mat with bright jungle animals, a bouncer, and a pile of soft toys shaped like elephants and giraffes.

"Take a good look, buddy," he muttered.

These weren't just signs of Val's life. They were his too, if she let him in.

He turned back to the stove, but a sound from the hallway caught his attention.

Val stood there, holding a wide-eyed, chubby-cheeked baby—his daughter.

Tate's stomach tightened. The room blurred at the edges while his focus zeroed in on the tiny figure in Val's arms.

"Val?" Was that his voice? His knees wobbled. He fumbled to turn off the burner and then stepped forward. But he couldn't stop looking at the tiny person in Val's arms.

"Tate, this is Liberty Madeline Reeser," Val said. "I call her Libby."

"She's..." He swallowed. "She's like a little angel."

Val's lips twitched, but her expression remained guarded.

"You wouldn't have thought so five minutes ago. She was letting the whole world know she needed a clean diaper."

Big blue eyes tracked him. He blinked. She didn't. His eyes, but bigger. Brighter. Now, mere inches separated them, but he didn't know if he'd moved or Val had. He touched a soft blonde curl, fine as silk. Her skin? Smooth as a peach with the faintest blush of pink, like a watercolor painting brought to life.

"Can..." His body refused to obey his commands. "Will... will she let me hold her?"

Unlike his daughter's wide-eyed curiosity, Val's gaze

narrowed, her scrutiny burning into him. Yeah, he was acting weird. He felt weird. Felt like he couldn't master his own body. Something tickled his cheek. When he forced his frozen hand to move, he discovered a tear. His.

Crazy thing was, he didn't feel embarrassed. He felt awed, like he'd witnessed a miracle. With trembling arms, he lifted his hands, waiting for Val's permission to take her.

"She's pretty good about going to strangers," Val said. "I guess it's because of the doctor visits. I thought she'd be afraid of them, but she isn't. At least not yet."

The way Val's voice sped up at the end stopped him cold. Was she nervous? Afraid he'd drop Libby? His hands brushed Val's before wrapping around Libby's tiny ribcage. The little jolt overshadowed by a sudden feeling he couldn't name. Wow! Just wow. She felt so light in his arms—like an egg he was scared to crack.

"Hey, Libby," he whispered, his voice rasping with emotion. "I'm your... daddy."

She waved a tiny fist at his face, brushing his nose. He laughed, the sound breaking free before he could stop it. Another tear slid down his cheek. This time he didn't bother wiping it away.

"Got it." A big, sappy smile slid over his face. "You're a girl who likes to see what's going on."

Although he stood six feet, two inches, he'd never considered himself big and never awkward—until this moment. But this was Libby, his beautiful baby girl.

It didn't look hard. He'd seen countless women cradle an infant. However, with her tiny body and his clumsy hands, positioning her back and bum in the crook of his arm felt like running a marathon.

Perspiration trickled along his hairline and down the sides of his torso. During the entire process, all he could think about was his baby girl slipping from his grasp. Man!

More thoughts like that and he'd need to find a cardi-ologist.

Did she have a fever? He glanced at Val and put that idea out of his head. If he made one wrong move, she'd pounce and take Libby away. The thought made his breath catch. Look at the way she snuggled against him, just like she knew who he was. He could hold her just like this forever. Just him and his little angel taking on the big wide world. No way would he give her up so soon. He might not ever give her up. Yeah, like Val would get on board with that.

But she was so warm—like holding onto a heating pad—a very soft, sweet one.

Wow!

That was going to be his new earworm word. A chuckle leaked from his throat. How long had he been holding her, two minutes? Three at most, and he was tipsy on his new daughter. She smelled good too. Who knew the faint scent of baby lotion and formula could affect him like this? Expensive perfumes had nothing on his little girl.

She blinked huge blue eyes at him. Man, she was gorgeous already. He'd have to be on his guard when she hit her teen years. Tate shuddered.

"You've got a lot to take in, don't you?" he murmured. "Everything is new to you in this bright and wonderful world." *And I'm in charge of ensuring nothing happens to you.* The thought frightened and thrilled him.

Val returned to the kitchen counter and her phone. "I hope she's a hungry girl."

"You keep looking at that." Tate nodded toward the screen. "Are you checking her sugar?"

A shadow crossed Val's face, forcing his thoughts away from Libby. His little girl seemed healthy, but her mother? Mom looked like she could use a nap—a long one.

"She's stable." Val adjusted the tray on the highchair with

a quick, practiced motion, then returned to the mixing bowl and attacked the sides with loud rhythmic thuds. "Today's her first taste of sweet potatoes."

"Yummy! Need some help?" Tate bounced Libby, amazed at the way her giggle did crazy things to his insides. "Mommy's beating up that bowl. I think she's going to win." Libby giggled louder, but Val's spoon almost drowned out the sound.

"This," *thud*, "is not," *thud*, "working for me!"

Tate turned toward Libby, his voice dropping to a whisper. "Mommy's mad, Button. I think it's my fault."

Val frowned. "Why are you whispering?"

"I don't want her to think we're fighting," Tate said, keeping his voice soft. "I hated it when my parents argued in front of me. I'd sit there, feeling like I'd done something wrong, even when it wasn't about me."

Val blinked, her expression shifting from frustration to surprise.

"She just turned five months old. She's not going to remember."

"Maybe not." Nothing Val said would make him change his mind. "But I will, and I don't want her to hear anything to make her feel threatened. Not now, not ever."

Val released the spoon and her shoulders sagged. "That's... a good point."

"Glad we agree." See there. He could learn this daddy thing. He probably looked like a fool, but he couldn't stop smiling at Libby. A miniature pink tongue appeared, and she leaned toward the tray.

"Bring on those sweet potatoes, Mom," he said, "before she decides we're starving her."

Val brought over a bowl with elephants circling it and hovered near his elbow.

"I thought I'd feed her," he said, cringing at the embarrassing petulant edge to his voice.

Val raised an eyebrow, her lips quirking.

"Forget I said that." He cleared his throat. "Apparently, spending five minutes with my daughter has me baby-talking and whining like a toddler."

A small laugh escaped Val before she covered her mouth.

"Here." She slid the bowl and a tiny spoon toward him. "Make sure you smile so she thinks whatever you're eating is tasty."

Tate frowned. Okay, no more fun and games. Eating was serious business. Libby could choke. He dipped the spoon into the bowl of mashed sweet potatoes. Not too much. But enough food for her to taste.

"I'm not that inexperienced." He touched the spoon to Libby's lip.

His daughter's hands flailed and her lips remained pursed, refusing the food. Tate straightened. Okay, so this daddy thing might take a little practice.

"They're really yummy." He pretended to eat the orange goo. "Mmm."

"Just nudge her bottom lip, like this, and sneak the spoon in before she changes her mind." Val closed her hand around his, sending an unexpected jolt down his arm. "She doesn't quite get the hang of eating yet."

Perfect. Because he didn't get the hang of feeding her yet, not to mention the shock of contact with Val. Time for him to shake out of it. He was a daddy, and this tiny little human needed him to be on his game, not pondering why his body hadn't ditched the Val train fourteen months ago.

Tate mimicked Val's actions, slipping the spoon into Libby's mouth. Out popped the food followed by a cute little tongue and a funny face.

"Way to go, Button." He laughed and used the edge of the spoon to scoop the mess from her chin. "Now all we have to do is rinse and repeat. There's one. Yes! Now two..."

Crash!

Val recovered from her trashcan wreck, but Libby's eyes widened and then her face crumpled.

"Whoa!" Tate mimicked some guy's voice he'd heard on a kid's program. "It's okay. Mommy just kicked the can." He scooted his chair over to make more room for Val to pass. "It's a little tight in here."

The loud sound forgotten, Libby opened her mouth, looking like a baby bird. Smiling, he slipped in another bite.

"I'm sure you've already checked out the best highchairs." He executed another perfect move into Libby's mouth. "Give me a list and I'll buy the same brand for my house. Daddy will buy another one just like this one," he said, slipping into his Libby voice. "Her fingers are so tiny. They're like pinky-sized guitar strings. And those fingernails."

The clatter of bottles broke him out of his dialogue with Libby. He turned toward Val and sobered. She had abandoned her chair opposite him and was now at the sink, jabbing a brush into a baby bottle like a lethal animal lived in the bottom.

"I can help you with those after she finishes eating." He turned back to Libby. "Hold that thought, Button."

He tapped her nose with his index finger and she gave him the cutest grin. He'd have to take photos. Wait until Mom and Uncle Rob saw them. With that little grin, even Senior would be a sucker for her. Her mother, however, didn't share their amusement.

Val turned on him. "You can't waltz into my life like nothing has happened and take over."

"Take over?" He was feeding his daughter—and getting a major hit of cutitis. "I'm trying to be the father my daughter needs. This isn't a one-time visit. I'm in her life to stay. Look at that little face." He blew a kiss toward Libby. What a grin —even with her orange-smeared face. And more cheerful than her resistant mother. "There's no way I could walk away from her."

"That wasn't your attitude in Glen Falls."

She was never going to let him live that down, but he'd lived with worse.

"You blindsided me. You walked out of my life without a word and then turn up ten months later warning me I have a genetic condition. You knew I wanted a family because we had many discussions about our future. The same future you trashed. So don't put this on me. I'm here now."

He scraped the sides of the bowl. "I had no idea I would feel like this about her. There's no going back for me. I will always be a part of her life." He dabbed at Libby's face with the washcloth on the table. "I'll regret missing her arrival and the first months of her life. So pardon me if I have to make up for lost time."

"I wasn't trying to hide her." Val turned the water off and then on. "I was going to tell you about her."

Despite the questions burning in his gut, Tate waited. She had more to say. He could feel it. Val looked older, more exhausted, but she hadn't changed that much. She'd always needed a few minutes to process a situation. A fella just needed to exercise some patience. But he'd get the story. Libby changed the landscape. He needed to know everything —even the parts Val wanted to hide from him.

"When I found out about the MCADD..." Val's voice softened, barely audible above the running water. "I panicked."

"You had nine months to tell me before she was diagnosed." Tate cringed. That had come out sharper than he intended. But he was the injured party. He'd missed out on Libby's first months. Those were gone—forever.

Libby slapped the tray, sending her bowl careening onto the floor.

"Yes, ma'am." He suppressed a grin. "Who says my little girl doesn't have an opinion—even at five months?" He leaned closer. "Mommy rounds up. Daddy is more precise."

He returned the bowl to the tray and his angel showed her demon side. Like lightning, she latched onto the bowl again. His baby girl had some muscle. Careful not to hurt her, he peeled away her fingers. The minute she was loose, she slapped the bowl again.

"And she scores!" A laugh bubbled from him. "You know what? Forget about the past. I don't want to know why you walked out on me. I can't retrieve the time I missed with her. But that's on you. I'm starting fresh as of right now."

"I'm good with that," Val said.

Tate dabbed at Libby's potato-smeared face again and she waved her hands in the air.

"How can such a little person have so much attitude this early?" But he couldn't be angry. He couldn't even be annoyed. She was too cute.

While he cleaned one tiny hand, he glanced at Val. "I didn't come here to argue. I came to spend time with my daughter."

And life would be better for Libby if he and Val kept an amicable relationship. Without Libby's love spell over him, he might have given in to his anger. But some of the emotion stemmed from something deeper.

"I feel guilty that you handled the early months alone," he said. "But that wasn't my choice. So can we focus on finding common ground? For Libby?"

"That's great—really."

But she didn't sound great. She sounded ticked.

"I hoped you'd come to love her like I do." Her gaze narrowed. "But you won't need a highchair in Glen Falls. Libby stays with me."

"Joint custody, Val." Although irritation bubbled inside

him, Tate kept his smile in place—for Libby. A task well within his wheelhouse—until today. The sudden flare of anger surprised him. His daughter had awakened his protective instincts. And he would guard her—even if it meant fighting Val.

"You can see her as much as you want—in Sunberry," Val said, as casual as you please. Like he was some stranger. But he'd stay calm and win because time with his daughter was not an option.

"Our daughter needs special care, a home, healthcare, and an education. I can fill her needs." Tate cleaned potatoes from Libby's curls, which irritated his daughter as much as the conversation irritated him. "I can't do that from a thousand miles away."

"Mmmm," Libby said, waving her arms.

She was still sticky but good enough for now. Maybe he could bathe her and tuck her in for the night. Tate stood, fidgeting with the stupid highchair tray. Val slid in front of him and released the latch. When Libby raised her arms, Val lifted her from the chair, leaving him with an orange-stained cloth. He followed them to the living area.

"Then move to North Carolina," Val said. "Because you aren't taking my daughter out of town, let alone out of the state."

"You don't have a legal leg to stand on, and you know it." Tate stuffed his hands in his pockets to keep from pointing at her. He'd kept his voice down. But if Val continued an unreasonable stance, he didn't know if he could sustain it. "Any judge will support visitation rights for me."

"What do you know about taking care of her?" Val turned away from him and sat Libby on the colorful mat. "You haven't rushed her to the ER during a crisis and waited for the doctor to come. You haven't set an alarm every thirty minutes through the day and night to make sure her sugar was stable."

She shook her finger at his face. "You come waltzing into my home unannounced acting like everything is sunshine and rainbows. Well, it isn't, Tate Carver. Caring for Libby is hard. Right now, she's stable.

But wait until you stare at the ceiling, listening for her every breath, knowing one mistake, one slip, could have devastating consequences. Live with that fear for just a moment and then talk to me about custody."

Tate sucked in a breath. She had a point. But he hadn't lived her fear because she'd kept his daughter a secret. Still—

"You're right. I haven't—because you didn't inform me you were pregnant." He held her gaze for a tense moment, twitching with the tension hanging in the air like a guillotine.

Think, Carver. This is the most important negotiation of your life.

"I'll learn just like you did," he said, keeping his tone neutral, nonthreatening, just like he used in every court case. "I'm inexperienced, not stupid."

Val looked him up and down, but the tremble in her bottom lip softened her glare. "Then you better start educating yourself. Because you've got a lot to learn before you'll even get an unsupervised visit."

"Waaah!" Libby's cheery features dissolved into a meltdown.

"Button." Tate scrambled to the floor and snuggled her into his arms. "It's okay. Daddy will learn."

Val lifted Libby from his lap and her wails stopped. Tate opened his hands, shocked at how empty they felt. Although Val turned away, Libby stared at him from over Val's shoulder. Her long lashes held a tear.

"You wanted to meet your daughter." Val turned to face

him, cradling Libby's head against her shoulder. "Box checked."

The casual dismissal hit harder than he'd expected. His chest ached, the words lodging like a splinter he couldn't pull free.

"Wrong, Val. Libby's not an overdue debt I came to pay. She's a piece of me—the best piece. I'll never let her out of my life. So buckle up and prepare to compromise because I'm not going anywhere."

Val walked to the front door and opened it. "I'd like you to leave now."

No way rushed to his lips. He gritted his teeth. "I'll be back tomorrow," he said. "What time?"

"I'm working tomorrow."

"Excellent." He held her gaze and the door steady. "I'll take care of her while you're away."

She pushed harder against the door. "I'm not leaving you alone with her until you move from inexperienced to knowledgeable."

He hardened his gaze. She didn't waiver. He forced his gaze to Libby. He wouldn't fight Val on this—tonight. If his baby girl needed special care, he'd find a qualified nanny. But he intended to parent her.

"Be prepared to teach me everything I need to know tomorrow." He leaned toward Libby and Val's eyes widened. "See you tomorrow, baby girl."

When he kissed Libby's curls, the faint scent of baby lotion lingered, her soft cheek warm against his lips. Val stepped back, and emptiness engulfed him. But he'd lock the smell and feel of his daughter away to get him through the hours he'd be away.

The door clicked shut behind him and he released a breath. He had a lot to learn, but one thing was certain—he wasn't giving up on his daughter.

CHAPTER FIVE

V AL SURVIVED HER SECOND DAY BACK FROM WORK— because Tate had shifted her focus from being separated from Libby for eight hours as compared to multiple days. Despite Val's aching muscles, a tiny spark of accomplishment unfurled inside her. Two shifts down. No spills, no slips, no relying on her notepad for orders. Small victories, but victories, none-theless. If Tate challenged her custody, she could show she was supporting her child.

Setting her work shoes aside, she crept to Libby's room on socked feet and eased open the nursery door. Soft snores punctuated with a tiny grunt replaced the niggle of fear that had followed her throughout the day.

Val pressed her knuckles against her lips, resisting the urge to kiss Libby's brow and inhale her daughter's soft baby scent. Everything in their lives felt so unstable.

She turned away, hurrying to the living room, its chaos magnifying her life. A soiled burp towel dangled from the armrest of the couch, a soft rattle sat near the window, and Libby's velvety giraffe lay on the floor.

Val gathered each item, her movements sharp. A busy day

in the restaurant had dulled her anger about Tate's intrusion to a quiet ache. She'd run. She'd built a new life. But she hadn't escaped him. Like it or not, he would be part of her life forever. At one time, he'd been her forever, and a part of her still illuminated around him. But she wasn't the young woman who had left Glen Falls and Tate. Although she hated to admit it, he still attracted her. But her daughter's needs outweighed her physical desires. She was the mother of a child—his child. She'd respect the importance of the father-daughter bond, but she'd never submit to him again.

Libby deserved a loving father like she'd had. An empty ache tugged at her heart. She missed Papa's steady guidance and the rare smile that softened his rough edges. How could she deny Libby the connection she'd been forced to sacrifice?

But to let Libby leave her home—the state—churned Val's stomach. That wasn't going to happen. Libby was too fragile, her baby daddy too inexperienced. She couldn't let Tate take her—even for a visit. She also couldn't stop it.

The complicated instructions and care parameters spun in Val's mind. Could she teach Tate how to care for Libby? She was a welder by trade and a server by consequences, not a teacher. One wrong number, one missed detail could result in catastrophic effects for Libby.

Her fingers tightened around the plush giraffe, her breath catching. And what if she could train Tate? What if he was a star pupil? Could she just hand her daughter over to him? Let him take her to Glen Falls?

Not in this lifetime.

A gentle knock announced her dilemma in the flesh: Tate. At least he had the decency to soften his knock so he didn't disturb Libby's nap.

Val opened the door and regretted the sharp intake of breath that followed. Why couldn't she shake her attraction to him? She'd made the right decision. They were from two different worlds. A life with him had been doomed from the start. It still was. While her heartbeat surged a betraying rhythm, she smothered her personal desires and forced a calm demeanor.

"Tate," she said, waving him in.

Awareness was the last thing she needed. But it was hard to resist the way his blond waves caught the light of the setting sun, his ever-present confidence clear in the easy grin he shot her.

"Can you hold the door open? I did a little shopping."

She'd known the boy and then the man since she wore pigtails. He was smart, considerate, passionate. Never had he been a shopper. Her gaze dropped to the pile of baby supplies at his feet: three large boxes of diapers, a case of formula, and —of course —a ridiculous stuffed elephant bigger than Libby.

"Tate." She shook her head at the sheer volume of items. "Where am I supposed to put all of this?"

He grinned "I wanted to help out. I figured you'd appreciate not having to run out for diapers anytime soon. And the elephant? Well, Libby's dishes have elephants on them so I knew you two liked them."

Val caught the inside of her lip between her teeth, but she couldn't stop the twitch at the corners of her mouth. A lifetime ago, she'd stand on her toes and kiss him to show her appreciation. But today was not that life.

Instead, she held up a bag of brightly colored ribbon. "You bought hair bows?"

Tate snatched it from her hands and tossed it onto the sofa. "I thought women were into this kind of stuff. What was I supposed to buy? A catcher's mask?"

"You were supposed to research MCADD and blood sugars," Val said, her tone sharper than she intended. But having him back in her life with that heart-stopping smile made her dream of things she couldn't have—wouldn't have.

"I did," Tate said, lifting his laptop bag. "I've been in touch with my old roommate—he's a doctor now. He said Libby's care would be customized to her needs. Hold on!" He raised his hand before she could speak. "Before you start scolding me, he also pointed me to reading material. I'm catching up, Val. I promise."

She shook her head. He was not going to charm her with that boyish grin. Meanwhile, back at her tiny apartment, what was she supposed to do with all of this...stuff? Annoyed more with her reaction than the purchases and her small living quarters, she hefted the oversized elephant into the living room.

This was not going to work. His presence would always be a reminder—

"Oof!" A soft squishy surface surrounded her face. She batted at a huge plush ear and pedaled her legs to stand. "Did you buy a garage for this thing, too?"

Tate's deep chuckle sounded near her ear and his warm breath fanned her cheek. Strong muscled arms steadied her physical balance but crushed her emotional equilibrium. She stepped away, refusing to acknowledge the sudden warmth that left her stomach in knots.

"You're donating this thing," she said, brushing off her jeans and the feelings his touch triggered.

"Not a chance." His grin widened. "Libby's going to love it."

The baby monitor crackled, followed by Libby's wail cutting through the stillness. Val turned toward the nursery, but Tate was already opening the door.

"I'll get her," he said, disappearing inside.

Moments later, the telltale smell hit her nose.

"What is that horrible odor?" Tate's voice carried into the living room. "Oh... man. What did you eat, Button? If sweet potatoes caused this, they are off your menu."

Val pressed her hand to her mouth to smother her laugh but couldn't stop her shoulders from shaking. Once she could keep a straight face, she hurried to the nursery. She couldn't wait to see this.

"Welcome to parenthood." She leaned against the door frame. "Enjoy."

"Wait!" An expression of determination and horror distorted Tate's handsome features. "You're not serious."

"You wanted to help," she said, unable to hide her amusement. "Here's your chance."

She'd give twenty dollars to video Tate and post it. Yeah, and that might be pushing it. But it would be so funny. The video images flashed in her head: baby daddy squares off with daughter, his look of horror, Libby's grin. Who will win the poopy diaper battle?

When she turned back to the nursery, Tate's shoulders pulsed, first a slight motion and then shaking with his laughter.

"You little stinker." He lifted Libby from her crib, arms outstretched like she might explode again. Which could happen. He glanced her way.

"Very funny," he groused. "So where do I start, Knowledge Ninja?"

"The changing table." Val pointed. "And use plenty of wipes."

"What if we just... hose her off?" Tate suggested, only half-joking.

Val stifled a laugh, her exasperation tempered by the earnest panic on his face—a dad out of his depth but unwilling to back down. "Good luck with that."

Fifteen minutes later, Tate joined her at the kitchen sink, his shirt damp and his patience frayed.

"Our kid is a master escape artist," he muttered, adjusting Libby's towel while she squirmed in his arms. "The nursery looks like a war zone and smells like an outhouse. And her diaper, what's left of it..." He raised a brow solemn as a preacher. "Reclassify it as toxic waste. If you put that thing in the dumpster, you'll probably earn a fine."

"Double bagging helps." She barely managed to deadpan —barely!

"Tomorrow, I'll buy two more boxes of wipes." He turned Libby to face him and poked her bare tummy. She grinned. "As for you, little girl. No more sweet potatoes—ever."

"Hey," Val infused her voice with cheer. "At least you survived."

"Mommy's right," he said. "If I can slog through your latest mess, the sky's the limit."

He turned back to Val. "I admit it. Childcare is harder than it looks." He cradled Libby in the crook of his arm. "But Daddy's figuring it out."

His determination tugged at something in Val, even as her stomach churned at the thought of him learning too quickly.

"The way she was twisting and turning away from her diaper, she'll love the swing set at Mom's house," Tate said. "It's been there forever, but it's still sturdy. I can already see her climbing to the top, fearless and giggling like crazy."

Val straightened, her breath frozen in her chest.

"She's ready for a bath," she said, brushing past him. "And keep her monitor dry. If it comes off, it'll need to be replaced immediately."

"Got it," Tate said, but his brow furrowed in confusion. "What happens if the monitor's off for too long?"

Val's stomach clenched. "We'd lose track of her blood sugar levels. If it drops too low without us noticing..." She swallowed hard, unable to finish.

Tate's expression sobered. "Okay. No shortcuts. I promise."

Five minutes later Val lowered Libby into the baby tub.

While Tate knelt beside her, his large hands hovering uncertainly, Libby squealed and splashed.

"Support her back," Val instructed. "She can sit up, but she's still wobbly."

"I'm supporting her," Tate said, though his movements were stiff.

"Not enough." Val adjusted his grip. "Don't let her lean forward. She could inhale the water."

Tate exhaled a frustrated snort. "She's not as fragile as you think."

"She's not as resilient as you think," Val shot back. "One slip could—"

"I know!" Tate's voice raised before lowering again. "You think I don't get it, but I do. She's not a regular baby. I'm trying, Val."

The tension hung between them like a heavy fog, broken only by Libby's happy babbling.

"You've got to give me a chance," he said.

Val turned away. He was too close, too earnest, too Tate. When he was near, her thoughts raced back in time to the touch of his skin against hers, the way she fit safe and warm in his arms, the way his lips felt against hers.

Tate brushed a wet curl from Libby's forehead. "Wait until Mom and Uncle Rob meet you," he said. "They're going to fall in love."

A cold fist of dread tightened in Val's chest, pulling harder with every glance at Tate.

"Once we're back in Glen Falls, I'll introduce them," he said. "Mom's been asking about her granddaughter nonstop."

Val froze, gripping the edge of the tub. The thought of Libby strapped into a car seat headed to Missouri sent a chill down her spine.

"You're not taking her to Missouri," she said, fear turning her voice low and lethal.

Tate's gaze held steady, unyielding. "I'm her father, Val. My family has a right to know her, just like she has a right to know them."

With her heart thundering in her ears, Val wrapped Libby in a soft bath towel. The urge to clutch her baby to her chest and seek shelter surrounded her, made it impossible to think, to assess. She was making it on her own. She had a job, a home, friends. But she didn't have Tate's resources.

Libby squirmed and babbled. Val pressed Libby's silky head to her cheek and then forced her arms toward Tate. "Put on her clean jammies. I'll get her dinner ready."

She ignored his big grin, obviously delighted with his task.

The knot in Val's chest tightened. Tate was not just a doting dad. She turned to pick up the bathroom, her gaze lingering on her baby daddy and Libby for a fraction too long, the ache in her chest sharper than the fear of what she might lose.

Tate wasn't just buying diapers and stuffed animals—he was laying claim to their daughter. And legally, he had every right.

But what about her? How could she protect Libby? More importantly, how was she going to stop him?

CHAPTER SIX

TATE PACED THE CRAMPED LIVING ROOM, HIS SHOES brushing the frayed edge of the floral rug. Lavender cleaner and baby powder clung to the air—Val's way of making even a shoebox feel like home.

But it wasn't enough. Not for Libby. Not for what she needed.

Restlessness burned through him, his fingers tingling with the need to *do* something. He flexed his hands, the muscle memory of a guitar settling over him like a ghost. A melody curled at the edges of his mind—something that hadn't happened in years.

Tate shook it off. Music didn't fit his life anymore. Libby did.

He stopped pacing, rolling his shoulders, trying to shake the claustrophobia of Val's apartment. The refrigerator hummed. The floor creaked. Silence wrapped around him, thick and heavy.

But for Libby, he'd get through it.

The baby monitor crackled, the soft rhythm of Libby's

breathing settling into the quiet. Then came Val's sharp footsteps.

She stepped into the room, arms folded, eyes locked and loaded.

"How long are you staying?" Her voice was clipped, like she already knew the answer and didn't like it.

Tate followed her into the kitchen. "Long enough to assess Libby's needs and develop a long-term plan."

She brushed past him, yanking open a cabinet. The clang of the kettle hitting the stovetop scraped at his nerves. The cabinet door banged shut. A mug—chipped on one side—landed on the counter with a sharp crack.

"You surprised me," she said, still facing the kettle. "I didn't anticipate your... commitment."

Tate stifled a snort. "You think I flew a thousand miles to dabble in fatherhood?"

She turned, eyes narrowing. "If you're serious about being in her life, you need a job here. Sunberry has opportunities. A hospital. A college. A conference center. You'd find something."

Just like that? Drop his life in Glen Falls like it was disposable?

Tate rubbed the back of his neck. "Our daughter needs resources now. I have excellent healthcare with the firm. Adding Libby won't be an issue. Moving firms? That's a setback we can't afford. Babies are expensive. Yesterday's shopping trip confirmed that."

Her sharp inhale told him he'd struck a nerve.

"I bought those things because I wanted to," he said, softening his tone. "I want to provide for her, Val. I want to give her as much as I had."

"I can provide for her just fine." Val's arms stayed locked across her chest, her stance solid like she'd welded herself to the floor. "I did more than decorate a nursery, Tate. I built a home here. Libby has a pediatrician who knows her condition. She has stability, a routine. She's thriving."

"And she can have all that in Glen Falls." Tate's voice sharpened. "It's not some foreign country. It's our home. Your family's there. My family's there. And so is Libby's."

Val's bitter laugh rang through the kitchen. "Libby's doctors are here. MCADD isn't something you can just throw money at. She's gone almost a month without a metabolic flare. A move could stress her, trigger one."

He held her gaze, frustration mounting. "Doctors make referrals all the time. St. Louis and Memphis have specialists. You act like Glen Falls is some backwater town with no medical care."

"Your doctor friend doesn't know Libby's case."

"Neither did her current doctors until they met her."

Her lips parted, eyes flashing. "You don't get it. You weren't here."

That hit like a sucker punch. He ran a hand over his jaw, forcing himself to stay calm. "That's why I'm here now. To make things right. To be in her life, every day."

Her gaze flicked to the baby monitor on the counter, where the soft rhythm of Libby's breathing filled the silence.

"I won't uproot her just because it's inconvenient for you," she said.

"Inconvenient?" The word snapped out of him, sharp and bitter. "You think this is about *convenience*? You didn't tell me about her. You made that decision alone, and now you want to dictate the terms? That's not how this works."

Val pushed away from the counter, her hands gripping the edge like she needed something to hold onto. "You've been here two days, Tate. Two. You don't get to waltz in and start calling the shots."

His pulse thundered in his ears, but he forced his voice to

stay even. "I'm not a visitor, Val. I'm her father." He let that settle before adding, "And I have rights."

Her face paled. "What are you saying?"

Although the words tasted bitter, he forced them out. "If you won't work with me, I'll have no choice but to petition for joint custody."

Outside, an owl hooted, the soft, haunting sound in stark contrast to the storm building between them. Val's fingers dug into the counter, her knuckles white.

"You wouldn't," she whispered.

"I don't *want* to," he admitted, his voice softer now, but firm. "But I will. Libby deserves two parents who love her. This isn't about our past, Val. It's about her future."

Her laughter came sharp and bitter, a sound that had nothing of the bell-like quality he used to love. "You think a court will side with you? You don't even know what it takes to care for her. MCADD isn't a weekend project, Tate. It's *every single day. Every single moment.* I'm the one who's been here. I'm the one who knows her doctors, her needs—"

"And I'm the one who can give her stability," he cut in. "Financial security. A future. This isn't just about today, Val. It's about what happens *ten years from now.*"

Her eyes burned with something fierce—anger, hurt, maybe something deeper. "You think money fixes everything."

"That's not what I said."

"It's what you meant." Her voice shook. "You got your fancy law degree, sure. But that wasn't *our* plan, was it? It was *your father's.*"

His stomach clenched. "Don't turn this into something else."

"Isn't it?" She let out a hollow laugh. "That 'fancy degree' sure didn't work for *me*. And it won't work for Libby."

"That 'fancy degree' will give her more than a cramped

apartment over a diner," he shot back before he could stop himself.

Her mouth snapped shut, but not before he caught the flicker of something vulnerable in her expression.

He scrubbed a hand over his face, forcing down the heat rising in his chest. "I don't want to fight with you."

"Could've fooled me."

"I'm trying to give her the best chance, Val." His voice was raw, tired. "And you think that's *here*? That I should uproot my life, move to Sunberry, and pretend Glen Falls never existed?"

Val's arms dropped to her sides. "I can't go back."

Tate hesitated, something in her tone lifting the hair at the nape of his neck. Her voice had lost its cutting edge. No longer defiant, but flat, almost hollow.

His stomach tightened. "Why not?"

Something flickered in her eyes—something raw and untouchable.

She lifted her chin, meeting his gaze dead-on.

"Because Papa told me I wasn't his daughter anymore."

Tate stilled.

For a moment, he wasn't in Val's cramped apartment. He was back in Glen Falls, in the Reeser family's garage, the smell of motor oil and warm metal in the air. Paul Reeser, sleeves rolled up, wiping grease from his hands, saying with quiet pride, *"That girl's got more grit than any boy I've ever raised."*

Now, that same man had *disowned* her?

Val's chin lifted, but the fight was gone. "I broke their hearts when I left," she said, voice steady but thin, like she was holding herself together by sheer will. "And when I came back to warn them about MCADD, they couldn't get past what I'd done." A shaky breath. "They haven't met Libby. They haven't called. As far as they're concerned, We don't exist."

Tate's pulse thudded in his ears. He searched her face, looking for the lie. But it wasn't there.

Paul Reeser had built an entire business with his own hands, raised four kids with a stubborn kind of loyalty Tate had always envied. He *wasn't* the type of man to turn his back on family.

And yet, he had.

"Ruger and Brett?" Tate asked, already knowing the answer.

"Didn't even have to say anything." She dropped her gaze to the floor and then returned it to his. "I saw it in their faces."

Tate swore under his breath, massaging his neck. Her own brothers? The ones who used to chase off boys who looked at her too long? The ones who taught her how to throw a punch?

"Your mother?

Val hesitated a fraction of a second. Just long enough to alert him.

"She wasn't there."

Unbelievable. Tate swallowed, the weight of her response pressing against his ribs. Paul might be stubborn, but Deb? She was the heart of that family.

"She still has my number," Val said, her voice whisper-soft. "I called her, but it went to voicemail. She hasn't called back."

He shoved a hank of hair away from his forehead. "That's harsh."

Her lips pressed together. A flicker of something in her eyes—like she was waiting for him to challenge her, to tell her she was exaggerating. Like she'd had to defend this before.

"You could've called me," he said. The words came out rough, not an accusation but close.

Val let out a dry laugh, shaking her head. "And say what, Tate? That I was pregnant? That your parents would rather pretend I didn't exist than admit their son knocked up a mechanic's daughter? That I had to pack my whole life into the trunk of my car and drive until I found somewhere I could breathe again?"

Her voice cracked on the last word. Just a little.

Tate's jaw clenched. He'd always known his parents weren't Val's biggest fans, but *this*?

"I could've done *something*," he said, voice low.

Her eyes flashed. "Like what?"

"I don't know." And that killed him.

Val turned away. "I didn't have a choice, Tate."

"You did." His voice came softer now. "You could've told me."

She let out a slow breath. "I *did*."

Tate frowned. "What?"

She turned back around, and he saw it then—the exhaustion, the deep, bone-level hurt that had been hiding behind all the sharp words.

"I *did* tell you," she said. "Over and over. The longer you were in Virginia, the worse it got. Your texts slowed down. The emails got shorter. You stopped playing, Tate. Because you didn't have time."

His stomach knotted. "Law school was—"

"Tough? I know," she cut in, shaking her head. "I knew how much you loved music, and I watched you let it go because your father told you to. I *couldn't* do that. I couldn't stand there, waiting, while you became someone else."

"So you ran."

"I *had* to," she whispered.

The air between them thickened, sucking out all the oxygen.

Tate took a slow step closer. "You didn't have to do it alone."

Her lips parted, but no sound came.

And for the first time since this fight began, he saw it—beneath all the fire and steel, *she was tired*. She'd been carrying this weight too long.

A muscle ticked in his jaw with the thought to fix this, her. But how?

Val sucked in a breath, squaring her shoulders like she was closing the door—on him.

"You're welcome to be part of her life," she said, voice steady now. "But you don't get to disrupt it."

His hands curled into fists. *Part of her life*. Like a distant uncle who showed up for birthdays but never for the hard stuff.

He forced his voice to steady. "I'm not a visitor. I'm her *father*," he said. "And that means I'm not walking away. Not again."

She stared at him, something unreadable flickering across her face.

"I mean it," he said, his voice quieter now, but firm as steel. "I'm *not* going anywhere."

Silence settled between them, thick and charged. The kind that held too many words unsaid.

Tate ran a hand through his hair. *Dial it down.* "I get why you're mad, Val. I understand why you think I don't have a right to walk in and change everything." He paused, leveling his gaze on her. "But you don't get to rewrite history."

Val's chin lifted, eyes challenging. "Oh, I *don't*?"

"No." His voice was calm, steady, but his chest burned. "You say I stopped playing music. That I let law school take over. Maybe I did." He stepped closer. "But you never gave me a chance to choose."

Val's mouth pressed into a tight line.

"I wasn't *done* fighting for you," he said, voice rougher now. "You left before I even knew I had to."

Her hands curled into fists. "Fighting for me?" A hollow laugh escaped. "Tate, you were already halfway gone."

"That's not fair."

"No?" She took a step forward, close enough that he could see the tightness in her jaw, the way she was holding herself together by sheer will. "You talk about choices like they were still on the table. But you made yours long before I ever packed my bags."

Tate shook his head. "That's not—"

"You think I wanted to leave?" Her voice sharpened, but there was something else beneath it. Something frayed. "You think I *wanted* to drive away from everything I'd ever known? That it didn't kill me to start over in a place where I had no one?"

Tate swallowed hard. "Then why?"

Val's breath hitched. "Because *I was already losing you.*"

The words landed like a blow to his midsection.

"You stopped playing, Tate. You stopped *dreaming*. And I watched you bury yourself in law school, doing everything your father wanted—while I became nothing but the girl who didn't fit into that world."

His stomach knotted. "That's not true."

"Yes, it *is*." Her voice softened, but not in a way that meant she was backing down. If anything, it made the words cut deeper. "I loved you. But I couldn't stand there, waiting, while you turned into a man who only existed to please his father."

Tate's jaw tightened to stop the words burning in his mind. She was wrong. Only one problem stopped him—she *wasn't*.

Because the truth was, there *was* a moment, years ago, when he realized the music had faded. When he sat in a quiet apartment, staring at his guitar in the corner, and realized he hadn't touched it in months.

He'd told himself he was too busy. That law school was just temporary, that once he graduated, *then* he'd have time to pick it up again.

But the months turned to years.

And Val had left.

His throat felt tight. "You never even said goodbye."

She flinched. Just slightly. But it was enough.

Her arms dropped to her sides, the fight bleeding out of her. "I couldn't," she said in a hoarse voice.

"That's not good enough." He took another step closer, something hot and desperate burning his gut. "You should've told me. *You should've told me, Val.*"

She let out a shaky breath, gaze flickering to the baby monitor. The soft sound of Libby's breathing filled the silence.

When Val looked back at him, her expression was raw. "Would it have changed anything?"

Tate's pulse pounded. "I don't know."

"Exactly." Her voice barely rose above a whisper. "And I couldn't take that chance."

The air between them felt fragile, like one wrong move could break everything.

"I would've followed you," Tate said.

Val let out a breath that was almost a laugh, but there was no humor in it. "No, you wouldn't have."

Tate opened his mouth to argue, but she shook her head. "You wouldn't have, Tate. You were too deep in it. You had your father's expectations, your career lined up, your life planned down to the minute. You weren't *mine* anymore."

His chest ached. "I still loved you."

"I know," she said quietly. "But you *wouldn't have chosen me*."

She didn't say it to hurt him. She said it because it was the truth.

Tate rubbed at his breastbone. "And now?"

Val straightened. "Now, it's not about us."

"Maybe not." He held her gaze. "But that doesn't mean we don't have unfinished business." Tate made himself step back, breathe. "I don't want to fight with you."

"Then stop."

"I can't." His voice was quiet but firm. "Not when it comes to Libby. But you're right about one thing."

Her brows furrowed. "What's that?"

His voice came steady, even as his gut twisted. "I let you go once." He paused, letting that settle before adding, "I'm not making that mistake again."

Silence stretched between them, heavy with everything unsaid.

"So where does that leave us?" he said.

Val leaned against the counter, arms still crossed. "We figure out how to do this without tearing each other apart."

"I can work with that."

"Libby's asleep. I'm exhausted. We're not getting anywhere tonight."

Tate wanted to push, but it would only lead them back into the same battle. "Fine. But this isn't over."

"It never is."

Tate grabbed his jacket, heading for the door. His hand was on the knob when she spoke.

"Tate."

He turned.

Her arms had dropped, and for the first time, she didn't look like she was preparing for another fight. "Libby's world is small right now," she said. "But it won't always be."

He nodded. "I know."

"We have to get this right."

"We will."

She held his gaze a moment longer, then turned back to the counter.

Tate hesitated, his grip tightening on the doorknob. Walking out was easy. Proving he'd stay—that was the part neither of them believed yet.

He let go of the knob.

"See you in the morning, Val."

This time, she didn't tell him not to come back.

CHAPTER SEVEN

ALONE AT LAST.

Val sank onto her small living room couch, the dim light from a single lamp casting long shadows across the space. The silence surrounding her pressed in, broken only by the soft hum of Libby's baby monitor. Inside, Tate's argument buzzed through her head, every word replaying like a broken record.

She'd created this mess because she'd lacked the discipline to deny his love, lacked the courage to admit their worlds were too different for a happy union. Running had solved nothing. But she couldn't undo the past or escape the consequences of her decisions—not with Libby's needs tethering her. Lawyers like the one she needed to fight Tate didn't come cheap.

Frustrated with her weakness, she surged to her feet and kicked the over-sized stuffed elephant. "Get yourself together!"

Independence had been her armor for years. When her friends teased her about grease-stained nails and her knack with a welding torch, she'd made new friends. Papa's garage had been her refuge, even with her brothers constant teasing.

They'd been a unit and with them behind her, she'd stood tall. So how had she gone from forging her own path to fighting tooth and nail to keep her daughter safe?

The shrill ring of her phone startled her. Val sank onto the edge of the couch, her legs suddenly too weak to hold her upright. She clutched the phone, grounding herself in the image of her sister's flawless makeup and flirty brown curls.

"I'm so glad you called," Val whispered, voice trembling. "You always know when I need you most."

"Talk to me." Hannah's melodic voice drifted through the line, wrapping around her like a comforting hug. "Is Libby okay?"

Val swiped at her cheek, annoyed to find it damp. "Not if Tate has anything to do with it."

A sob caught in her throat, and she pressed the back of her hand to her mouth to keep it from spilling out too fast. "We argued," she said, breathless between choked sobs and sniffs. "And he just—he doesn't get it. None of it."

She curled into the corner of the couch, knees drawn tight against her chest while the words poured out. She told Hannah everything—how Tate had questioned her judgment, how he'd made light of Libby's condition, how he'd forgotten to be careful with the monitor. All of it tumbled out, her voice breaking again and again.

Hannah stayed quiet on the other end, just like she always did when Val unraveled. No interruptions. No judgment. Just listening.

"He's not taking her out of my home," Val said at last, her voice hoarse. "I'll hide her before I let him do that."

"Easy Mama Bear," Hannah said. "He's a guy. They're clueless. Remember Jeremiah during Covid? He was a splash-and-go guy until I made him sing the happy birthday song while washing his hands."

"Exactly!" Val's voice rose. "Bathing Libby isn't rocket science. It's basic parenting."

"Okay. He's got some work to do." Hannah's tone shifted to something steadier—softer but serious. "But he is her father. So... what's your plan?"

Val exhaled, her shoulders drooping under the weight of the question. She stared at the dark screen of the baby monitor, the faint static hum a distant comfort.

"I'll figure something out. I always do." Her voice dipped to a whisper. "But this time... I'm scared, Hannah."

There was a pause. Not silence, exactly—just the space between two hearts across the miles, one bracing the other.

"I've always admired your strength," Hannah said, her calm cadence smoothing the edges of Val's panic. "But even the strongest woman needs help."

Val blinked hard, the burn of tears forcing her to pause. She reached for a tissue and dabbed at her eyes, then whispered, "I didn't get where I am in Sunberry without help. I trusted the Murphy family. They've stood behind me when my own family wasn't around."

"Your family *was* available." Despite the gentleness in her sister's tone, the truth rang out harsh and accusing. "You shut us out. That's why Momma and Papa were so hurt. It took them days to talk to me after they found out I kept your secret."

Val covered her face with her hand. "I'm so sorry. I never should've asked you to keep that from them. I didn't think about what it would cost you."

"You always had my back, Val." Hannah's voice grew quieter, tinged with the pain she rarely revealed. "That's why I couldn't betray you—no matter what."

Tears blurred Val's vision. "I never meant to hurt you or anyone."

"I know," Hannah murmured. "You made a mistake, but you don't have to let it define the rest of your life."

Val sucked in a steadying breath. The pity party was over. She had a daughter to raise. "I can't make impulsive choices anymore. Libby depends on me."

"So let me help." Hannah's voice carried an unwavering strength. "You're not alone. You never have been."

"Thank you," Val whispered.

"And you know I'll always tell you the truth, even if it's not what you want to hear."

"I'll listen," Val said, her voice breaking into a half-laugh, half-sob.

"I'm holding you to that."

When a sound resembling a strangled cat erupted from Val, some of the pressure pressing her thoughts eased.

"Here goes," Hannah said. "Number one: Tate's a respected lawyer. A judge is going to grant him visiting rights."

"I know," Val said. "But he minimizes Libby's condition. She could go into a crisis and he wouldn't know what to do."

"And he can afford the best medical care, including trained staff."

Val clenched her phone. "Why do you have to be so practical?"

"To help you, big sis." This time a hint of humor tinged Hannah's words. "Two: he'll learn to care for Libby just like you did and just like I will if you ever bring her home," Hannah continued. "That's me, telling you I want you to come home. Friendly reminder here: remember how terrified you were?"

"I still am." Val choked on her words. "But he acts like MCADD is no big deal. He doesn't understand how fragile she is. How one mistake could mean—"

"Breathe," Hannah said, her voice soft but firm. "Did you tell him about your fears?"

"In agonizing detail." Val rubbed at the ache developing behind her right eye. "I'm embarrassed to think about that discussion."

"He also bought diapers and clothes. I'd say that was considerate, especially for a guy," Hannah said. "I may have even used him as an example for Jeremiah. I hate to admit it, but—"

"Oh no!" Val thumped her fist against her throbbing head. Why didn't she think of that before?

"What now?" Hannah said. "Did he buy her a pony or something?"

"No, but what if he uses my fears in court? Could he use that to question my competence? Look at me. I'm an unwed mother. We receive financial aid. Could he take her away?"

"Val!" Hannah's firm tone echoed through the phone. "No one is taking Libby away. You're a great mom under a lot of stress."

"I'm so tired I can't think straight."

"I'm coming to Sunberry," Hannah said. "I'll borrow Mom's car."

"No!" Val stood, spine stiffening. "You don't have to do that. I'm okay. Really." She paced in front of the sofa. "It's just been a week—work, leaving Libby, then Tate..." Her forced laugh sounded weak. "I didn't mean to dump on you. But I'm done. Rant's over. Tomorrow's a new day."

"I miss you," Hannah said, her sincere sentiment almost crushing Val's surge of strength.

"I'm sorry," Val said. "I'm being such a downer."

"Don't you dare apologize for sharing your troubles with me," Hannah said, her voice sharp with warning. "It shows me you care. Shows me you trust me and value my opinion."

"I've always trusted you. And you've been my voice of reason."

"You're in a difficult situation," Hannah said. "I'll never minimize my wonderful friends. But friends don't always share our history like family. They didn't witness the episodes that shaped us. I lived those stories with you. Please come home," Hannah said, her words choked with emotion. "We can work this out just like we have since we were kids. So don't make me beg—If I thought it would help, I'd get on the floor."

Val dabbed her eyes. "You're making me cry. I treasure our life episodes just like I treasure you."

"I hate the distance between us. But if you need me in Sunberry, I'll get there, even if I have to hitchhike the entire way."

Val checked the baby monitor. "I'm just a call away. Thanks for talking me off the ledge."

"You're okay?"

"I've got some serious soul searching in front of me. But I'm fine."

"Kiss my niece for me. Love you two."

Val hit the End Call button, her fingers still curled around the phone, her heart a tangle of guilt and unease. Hannah had begged her to come home. Begged.

But home wasn't hers anymore.

She opened Libby's app, needing her routine—something she could control.

Her stomach sunk. Libby's glucose had dipped. Not dangerously low, but lower than it should be.

Stay calm. What had Hannah called her? Momma Bear. It's nothing. Libby was fine. Her sugar had fluctuated in the past. She'd checked before bedtime, and everything had been normal.

Val rubbed her breastbone, her heartbeat accelerating. Better to check.

She crept into the bedroom, keeping her steps light on the old wood floors. In the nightlight's soft glow, Libby lay on her tummy, her tiny hand resting near her cheek.

The sour scent in the air froze Val's steps before she reached the crib.

No. No, no, no!

Spit-up pooled on the sheet beneath Libby's face. Not just a little. Enough to soak through her sleeper.

Ignoring her racing heart, she scooped Libby into her arms, feeling the damp chill against her skin. Libby stirred but didn't fuss. Her eyelids fluttered but didn't open fully.

Too quiet.

"Hey, baby girl. Momma's got you." She pressed a kiss to Libby's clammy forehead and then lay her down on the changing table. With quick, smooth movements, she stripped off the soiled sleeper, wiped her clean, and grabbed a fresh one.

Libby wretched. The small, shuddering movement sent a stream of vomit onto the fresh fabric. From the other room, the glucose app alarm shrilled. Despite her shaky hands, Val pressed Libby's arms and legs into a clean sleeper and hurried to the counter for her phone.

Critical dip detected.

The next few minutes blurred together—Val dialing the on-call doctor, balancing Libby against her chest, rubbing slow circles on her back while she waited for the line to connect.

"Bring her in. She's likely dropping too fast to process nutrients," her doctor instructed. "We'll start an IV as soon as you get here."

Val was already grabbing Libby's diaper bag. "I'm on my way."

. . .

THE STEADY DRIP, drip, drip of the IV was the only sound in the quiet hospital room.

Val sat on the plastic chair beside the bed, Libby's tiny fingers curled around hers. The nurse had finished the IV placement. Now, they waited.

She ran her thumb over Libby's soft skin, her heart breaking at her daughter's perfect little face—so peaceful now.

It hadn't been a full-blown MCADD crisis. Nothing like the horror she'd lived through in July. They'd caught it early because she hadn't waited. But she almost had.

The evening's events raced through her mind, over and over, each repetition racing her heart faster. What if she hadn't checked? What if she'd been asleep or in the shower?

Fighting down the panic, she reached for her phone with her free hand and dialed a number she'd never been able to delete.

He answered before the first ring ended.

"Tate," she whispered, the strength she'd held together all night finally slipping. "We're at the emergency room."

"I'm on my way."

CHAPTER EIGHT

TATE TOOK THE CORNER TOO FAST, TIRES SCREECHING against the pavement, his gaze roving the hospital signs for the emergency entrance. He gunned the engine into the designated lot and stepped to the pavement before his rental had come to a complete stop.

Beneath the entrance sign, he curbed the urge to bang on the glass as the electronic doors opened.

"Libby Reeser?" he said before the desk clerk could speak. "I'm her father."

When she pointed out the hallway to Libby's exam room, he bolted into a run. He probably looked like a crazy man, but he didn't care. His little girl was in emergency. Emergency!

At the end of the hall, he slid to a stop and entered. Val sat on a chair beside a tiny crib, her head bent, her hands cradling one of Libby's.

The air left his lungs and only a fast fist to his mouth stopped an agonized groan. Libby's tiny body lay curled beneath a hospital blanket, a line of tubing taped to her hand, leading to an IV bag hanging above her.

Tate struggled to draw a breath. This wasn't some abstract medical condition anymore. It wasn't words on a screen or numbers in an app. It was his daughter. Hooked up to an IV.

A slow, twisting fear coiled in his gut, his pulse hammering in his ears. When Val looked up, the fear haunting her gaze curled inside him. In three strides he reached her side, stopping at Libby's bedside.

"She's so small," he whispered, brushing her tiny foot. "She's too little to be here."

"They caught it early." Val's steady voice grounded him.

Libby had to be okay or Val would be losing her mind—like he was. Still, exhaustion had cut deep grooves around her mouth and her eyes seemed to have sunken into her skull.

"She's stable," Val said. "They're just giving her fluids."

Tate's breath shuddered through him and he pressed his hand to his face, struggling to regain control.

She's okay. She's okay.

He turned to Val and the fog from the blinding fear lifted. She sat so still—like if she let go, even for a second, she'd fall apart.

He reached down and—without a word—took her hand.

Warm. Steady. Unshakable.

She didn't pull away.

Was that a sign? Was she finally going to let him in?

If that were true, he'd never let go.

Tate clenched Val's hand reassuring himself as much as her that he was here, would be here—for Libby.

A soft grunt sounded from the crib. Libby's chest lifted and fell in even fragile breaths. She was going to be okay. Soon, they'd take her home and this nightmare would end—for now.

The steady drip, drip, drip of the fluids, the hum of hospital machinery, and the muffled voices of nurses in the hallway seemed to pulse in his ears. He was here. He should have been here sooner, but he was here now.

His breath hitched in his chest. He lived almost nine hundred miles from his daughter. What if he had been in Glen Falls when Val called? What if Libby had taken a turn for the worse? Instead of by her side, he'd be halfway across the country, pacing an airport, useless.

That was not going to happen. Not in his lifetime!

Val shifted beside him and he eased his death grip on her hand and stroked her fingers, trying to smooth away any pain he might have caused.

"I can't..." He cleared his throat. "I can't do this from a thousand miles away."

She stilled beside him, then slowly lifted her gaze. "What?"

"I can't be in Glen Falls while my little girl is here," he said, voice low but firm. "It's not possible. Not going to happen."

Val studied him for a long moment, like she was trying to work out whether she could trust what he was saying. "Tate, I—"

"I'm not promising anything right now." He lifted his hands. "I haven't done the legwork. But I can promise this— we are going to live in the same town so..." A shudder shook his shoulders at the risk of another call. "So if you call, I can be there."

Tamping down the panic, he focused on her. He hated springing this on her. Fear still lined the downward pull of her mouth. But this couldn't wait.

"I just need some time to figure out how," he added. "But this?" He gestured at the hospital crib. "This isn't an option. I can't be a flight away when she needs me."

Something flickered across Val's face—relief, maybe. Or fear. Maybe both.

"Tate..."

"I mean it, Val. We'll work this out."

She exhaled, then gave a small nod.

She wasn't ready to believe it yet. That was okay.

His actions would prove his commitment to her.

THE FOLLOWING WEEK, Tate leaned against the rough-hewn railing of his uncle's cabin, his gaze tracing the winding path that disappeared into the Mark Twain National Forest. Maybe here, he could find answers. Or at least enough clarity to take the next step.

Beside him, Uncle Rob rummaged through a tackle box that had seen better days. The jangles and heavy frustrated sighs told Tate the lantern on the porch table wasn't throwing enough light for the job. But at least its flickering glow pushed back the darkness from the dense trees.

"You ready to hit the creek?" Rob held up a small lure. The cherry scent of his pipe hung in the damp air, mingling with the earthy aroma of pine and decaying vegetation.

Tate huffed out a breath. "I suppose."

With Rob's headlamp flickering ahead of them, they picked their way along the narrow trail, the night sounds pressing around them. In the distance, the creek whispered over smooth stones, a rhythm Tate had always found calming. But tonight, his mind was anything but quiet.

A melody had taken root in his head, one he couldn't shake. The notes played through his fingers, moving across invisible frets. He barely realized he was miming chords in the air until Rob stopped at the water's edge, and the tune ended.

"It's been years since I've done this," Tate admitted.

"All the more reason to get back to it." Rob held a match to his pipe, the brief flare of light illuminating his lined face before fading into the dark. "Night fishing clears the head like nothing else. You could use it, from the sound of things."

Tate let out a dry chuckle. "I wish. Nothing could clear my mind of last week's royal mess."

"I've seen my share of those," Rob said. "The worst one happened when I told your grandfather I wasn't joining the firm. But after hearing your story with Val, you may have me beat."

Tate cast his line into the water. "I didn't visit Val to threaten her," he said. "But after the scare at the hospital, things got clear—real quick."

"Fear has a way of cutting through the nonsense," Rob muttered.

Tate waved at an insect buzzing near his ear. "I thought my job had taught me to be objective. To remain calm in complicated situations." He paused, letting the ripple of the water quiet his thoughts. "I've worked through most of the details. I need someone to cut through the noise."

Rob chuckled. "Objectivity is easy when you're dealing with strangers. It's a whole different ballgame when it's your kid."

Tate swallowed hard. "That's what threw me. The first time I held Libby, this flood of..." He hesitated, struggling to name it. "Something I wasn't prepared for. Like pure sunlight filling me up. I can't explain it."

Rob didn't look up as he baited a hook with practiced ease. "I'd bet my next song lyric you were feeling love."

"I knew I'd love her. But that strong, that fast..." Tate shook his head. "I haven't felt like that for a long time."

Rob motioned for him to sit on a fallen log. "So what's your plan?"

Tate leaned forward, elbows on his knees. "Grandmother's cottage." Saying it out loud made it feel real—like a tangible path forward. "I hired a moving company to pick up Val's car and her things. I bought airfare for Val and Libby to fly to Memphis. No way was I letting her drive here alone."

Rob nodded. "You've been busy."

"The move was the easy part. Val is complicated," Tate admitted. "I've had to take the bits and pieces she shared and draw my own conclusions. I think she's been running on empty trying to support Libby and keep her healthy."

Rob exhaled through his pipe, the ember glowing in the dark. "Sounds like she needs a solid partner."

Tate cast his line again, following the lure until it disappeared into the dark water. "Needing a partner and wanting one aren't the same thing. But at least she's coming home and accepting my offer to stay in Grandmother's cottage."

Rob reeled in a line to check the bait. "So she's not totally onboard with your solution?"

"Not even close," Tate muttered. "We're coparenting, but that's it. We've got to get past our history. And I guess I'm not helping things by being grumpy myself."

Rob smirked. "Sounds like you've got some fences to mend. What's holding you back?"

Tate picked up another pole. "Fear." The word felt heavy on his tongue. "I love Libby, but what if I can't be the father she needs? What if I miss something critical and unintentionally hurt her?"

When a shudder traveled through him, he pricked his finger with the hook.

Rob gave him a level look. "I don't see that happening."

Tate rubbed his thumb over the small bead of blood welling at the tip of his finger.

Rob took another drag of his pipe. "I'm no expert, but I remember you and Marshall. It took me forever to talk you into taking off your bike's training wheels. Marshall never wanted them—he refused because his big brother didn't have them. We went through half a dozen Band-Aid boxes, but he learned to ride." Rob's eyes softened. "You were the cautious one. That's not going to change."

Tate swallowed hard. "I hope you're right."

"Val's probably worried about the same thing," Rob added. "Fear often comes out sideways. That could be why she's acting different."

"It's more than fear for her," Tate said. "She's carrying guilt, too. I wasn't the only one she left without a word. She didn't tell her family either."

Rob whistled low. "Heavy load to carry."

"I thought we were close before, but there was so much she was hiding. She told me she never thought she'd fit into my life—or my family's." Unlike the obstacles in his life, the stream rushed forward, mindless of the debris and stones blocking its path. "That was news to me. I mean, I know we live better than most, but I never treated her differently."

Rob sighed. "Sounds like she's been battling her own demons."

"When I stepped back from my own hurt, I started to understand. But that doesn't erase everything else between us." He exhaled, trying to make his mind slow. "And I still have to deal with Gabby."

Rob turned, the lantern illuminating his curious stare. "What about her?"

Tate hesitated. Gabby had been everything steady and familiar. But now?

"She's been there for me through everything," Tate admitted, guilt twisting in his gut. "She's smart, patient, good with my family—and she loves me. I should... feel the same way."

Rob studied him. "But you don't."

Tate shook his head. "I mean, I love her. But not how a man should love the woman he plans to marry."

"Well." Rob clicked his tongue. "I'd say you just answered your own question."

The second baited pole lay at his side, but Tate had lost interest. Before him the water twisted around the rocks like the tangled threads of his life. He'd made his decision about Libby and Val. Now he had to face Gabby.

And he wasn't sure which conversation was going to be harder.

CHAPTER NINE

Why hadn't Tate come home?

Gabby stood at the window of Tate's house, her fingers worrying the pearls at her neck like they could give the answers. But just like the dozens of times she'd checked the drive before, Tate's green Rover didn't appear.

Hank, Tate's black lab, whined near her feet.

"I don't know where he is," she said, stroking the dog's sleek head.

That was the problem. The same problem that had robbed her of sleep last night. According to the firm's admin, Tate had returned from North Carolina two days ago. But he hadn't come home—to her. Which was out of character for him. While she tended to hide her concerns, Tate and Val had been more open. But three days? That was too long. Was his absence a symptom of deeper trouble?

Of course it was! She shook her head, her anger building. *Stop denying it!*

She didn't *want* to understand, but she did. He was turning back to Val, the same way he'd done before. They'd started off as three friends. Then, they'd gone to one couple plus her. They'd left her behind, tossing out crumbs of friend-ship when they weren't on a date.

Gabby tapped her clenched fist against her chin. When would she stop repeating her actions, expecting a different outcome? Stand up, or stand by and let him drift away like she'd let her mother's chaos define her. Always the enabler. This had to stop!

The threat was real. Fifteen years of cleaning up behind her mother's addiction should have prepared her for this situation.

As if on cue, Tate's dark green Range Rover turned into the drive, the morning sun reflecting off its chrome grille.

With adrenaline pulsing through her veins, Gabby ushered Hank to the backyard and then hurried to the front. Eager to greet her absent lover, she stepped onto the wrap-around porch with its simple framed columns.

Though her heart raced with every passing moment, she fixed her expression into calm neutrality—the one he said he admired.

Tate parked at the base of the sidewalk but didn't wave or acknowledge her presence. He retrieved his travel bag and slammed the rear door. Not even a glance her way.

He was probably tired. She swallowed hard. Or he was ignoring her.

Head down, gait slow, he moved up the walk, ignoring Hank's excited bark from the side yard.

Gabby swallowed a sob. What had happened to the man who had left upset but determined, his posture proud and erect?

"Tate?" she said.

He looked up, his features grave like he'd just attended a funeral "Hey, Gabby." He gave her a one-armed hug.

Her chin trembled. Had the baby died? She managed a

weak smile, almost afraid of the discussion before them. "Rough trip?"

"My flights were on time."

From the fenced backyard Hank barked again.

"You could have taken him to Uncle Rob's." Tate walked toward the door but didn't place a hand at her back. He deposited his bag in the foyer.

"He gave me a reason to be here." She tried to brighten her smile. "Everyone in Glen Falls knows we're engaged, but I still like to keep up appearances."

"I better say hello." Tate turned toward the rear entrance. "He's already scratched up the back door."

Gabby halted, trying to steady herself. What was that? Her fiancé returns after a week's absence and leaves her for the dog?

Breathe, Gabby.

She was thinking like the hysterical women Father always derided.

Gabby flexed her fingers and drew in a calming breath. Voice calm? Check. Posture erect but somewhat relaxed? Check.

This was Tate. Her fiancé. The man she wanted to spend the rest of her life with. This wasn't Father. Tate recognized her efforts, saw her. Until today. He'd had a challenging week. No different than after a difficult case. He needed time to defuse.

While Tate threw the ball for Hank in the back yard, she prepared coffee like a dutiful fiancé. Or was it more like an experienced wait staff?

Stop, Gabby!

Anger bubbled deep in her mind. She'd had a challenging week too!

The two plain white mugs she grabbed from the cabinet

clattered together. She'd write a reminder to add everyday china to her wedding registry. If they still *had* a wedding.

By the time the coffee finished, the scrabble of Hank's nails on the polished hardwood floors sounded behind her.

She squared her shoulders and rearranged her expression. "Breakfast?"

"I ate at Uncle Rob's before I left."

How nice for him. She handed him a cup of steaming black coffee, his favorite blend.

Nothing.

He wrapped his long fingers around the mug but didn't drink.

"I canceled our weekend trip," she said, keeping her voice calm. "In the future, I'd appreciate a notice if you change travel plans."

His gaze shifted to the window, the lines around his mouth deepening. "I've been a lousy partner, lousy everything. Pretty much a lousy man."

Gabby sucked in a breath, the fine hairs along her forearms lifting in response to the weariness in his voice. She knew that bone-weary sound, had heard it often from Father. It always preceded trouble.

"Hey." She cupped his jaw, infusing her voice with the love in her heart. "You're beating yourself up. We're navigating a difficult situation. I'm glad you're home. I missed you."

She ran her thumbs beneath his jaw to soothe herself as much as him. Especially since he kept staring at his coffee. Wasn't he going to look at her, hug her, something?

Put the coffee down, darling, and put your arms around me—like you care.

"Talk to me, Tate." She brushed hair from his forehead with her fingertips. "I've been running awful scenarios in my head for five days. Tell me what's going on."

Tate stared at the mug in his hands.

Hank wiggled between them and Tate exhaled, almost a laugh but not quite.

"Outside, boy," he murmured, turning toward the door.

Gabby stiffened. This wasn't Tate. Whatever clouded his mind was very bad.

She blinked—and breathed. Finally, he turned toward her. His gaze flickered with—guilt, exhaustion, and something else she couldn't name. But it wasn't love. It wasn't *I missed you*. It felt more like a peck on the cheek when she was expecting a passionate kiss.

"It's a nice day," he said, his tone flat like all the life had been drained from him. "Let's talk outside."

Gabby was probably ruining thousands of dollars of orthodontic work to stay calm, but she followed Tate, *followed him*, to the patio.

Stay calm. He's processing. And so was she! How many times had she listened to Father's same excuse? But not Tate, never the man she'd chosen to marry. That's why she'd fallen in love with him.

The cloudless sky promised another hot, humid day. But at present the tall pines shaded the patio. While Gabby settled into the solid wooden chair, Tate dropped to his seat with a heavy sigh.

"Did you see your daughter?" She forced a smile, hoping her tone would follow the action. It didn't.

His weariness gave way to a wide smile. "She's beautiful."

"I didn't doubt it." Gabby tamped down her growing resentment. "You're her father. Val's doing okay?"

Tate threw a ball and Hank raced after it.

"She's struggling," he said. "Libby's condition is a lot worse than I expected."

Gabby swallowed, almost afraid to ask. "Is the baby going to be okay?"

"I think so. But she needs constant monitoring, lots of

specialist visits, professional care." He took the slobbery ball from Tate and threw it again, the force causing the chair to scoot across the concrete. "I'm moving them here."

Gabby froze. Here? To Glen Falls? To his home?

No wonder he was walking like a man twice his age. But Val and his little girl, here? This changed everything. This was going to threaten her life with Tate. She had to stand up, speak up.

"As the baby's father," she started, forcing a calm tone to mask the fear clutching her heart. "I understand your financial responsibility..." For once, Gabby welcomed Hank's intrusion. The dog's wagging tail and insistent nudges broke the tension crackling between them, giving her a moment to collect herself. Unexpected disasters were common in the Stanford household. She could do this.

"I'll support you anyway I can," she said, finally able to speak. "But this is a small town and our neighbors may talk. What about...I mean where will we live—after the wedding?"

For the first time, Tate turned to her, his forehead lined in confusion. "I'm moving them into Grandmother's cottage, not my house."

Relief melted Gabby's spine and she sank against the chair back. This was salvageable. Val and her daughter hadn't taken Gabby's place—not yet. But ownership was nine-tenths of the law. She was living in Tate's house. She was engaged to marry him.

Tate signaled Hank to lay down and the lab dropped to the ground with a sigh, much like her own relief. She loved his house. While Tate was away, she'd scrolled through paint samples and furnishings. But it wasn't just his home that she loved. Her move and marriage meant she'd finally shed the burden of her mother's care—if Mother continued to maintain her sobriety.

"The cottage needs an update," Tate said, jerking her

thoughts to the present. "I've already contracted out the work. I'm surprised you haven't heard. Senior and I had a major blow up at the office. He lost his mind when I told him I was using Grandmother's trust to renovate the cottage."

Gabby's nails bit into the armrests. Too bad Senior couldn't stop Val from moving to Glen Falls. Now she'd have to tidy up this mess.

She inhaled a deep, steadying breath. Although disconcerted that she hadn't shed Father's decrees like she'd thought, she bolstered her resolve.

Yearning for his touch, she placed her hand over his warm flesh. "I'm sorry your father isn't more understanding. Meeting parental expectations can get tiresome. But he'll come along after he acclimates to the idea."

Tate's laugh sounded hollow in the silence. "Family expectations?"

Hank whined.

When Tate took her hand, Gabby's heart filled with love and hope. "You and I have been dealing with family issues our entire lives."

She squeezed his fingers, showing him how much she appreciated his acknowledgement of their common bond.

"The scourge of being the offspring of the Carver and Stanford Law Firm," he continued, but the warmth he'd shown her in the past year had faded. "Val could never understand that."

A hint of success shivered across Gabby's shoulders. The threesome was returning. But this time Val, not Gabby, would be the third wheel.

"How was it, seeing her again?" she said, pushing past her fear.

"Okay, I guess," Tate said.

However, his fixed distant gaze didn't inspire confidence.

"I was so blown away by Libby and MCADD, I didn't think much about what had happened between us."

"You aren't still angry about the way she left?" Because she was.

"A bruised ego seemed childish after I learned the care Libby needs."

"She broke your heart," Gabby said, unable to let it go.

"More like pulverized it."

"I can't forgive her," Gabby said. The minute the words were out, she wanted to cheer. After years of hovering beneath Father's orders, she'd spoken her mind, admitted her feelings. Being with Tate had given her that confidence and she wasn't going back. When Tate remained silent, she moved forward.

"After she came to the house..." The memory sent a chill along Gabby's shoulders. She and Tate had just enjoyed a lovely breakfast and quiet conversation. Just two people in love starting their day. And then Val showed up on their doorstep. Val, the best friend who had abandoned her friendship for no reason.

Gabby shook off the painful memories. She and Tate had built a new life. One with a bright future. Now, Val was returning to destroy it. But she would not stand aside without protest.

"Anyway," she started, choosing her words. "I guess she knows we're together. Did she say anything?"

"It didn't come up."

Never came up! Like she and their proposed marriage didn't matter.

When Hank sighed and repositioned, Gabby glanced at Tate. His chin had dropped toward his chest, emphasizing the fatigue lines around his mouth and eyes. This horrible situation had taken a toll on him. He hadn't slept well. But neither had she.

While she wanted to comfort him, wanted to hold him, tell him life would work out fine for him, she also needed comfort. He couldn't even look at her. Just sat mute, making her poke and prod for information.

"She abandoned both of us." Gabby's voice shook, threatening to break through her control. But she was tired of being strong. Tired of being the clean-up person. Tired of ending up the loser.

"Val and I have been best friends since elementary school." Gabby smoothed the fabric of her simple black skirt. "She knew all my secrets—even about my mother."

"When she moves back, give her a call," Tate said. "She's going to need a friend."

"She betrayed me!" Gabby cringed at the volume of her voice, but at least her outburst had dissolved Tate's glazed expression. "Yet I feel guilty."

His gaze narrowed on her, like he was actually seeing her, seeing her pain too. "Guilty about what?"

Since she couldn't trust her voice, she motioned between the two of them.

"I fell in love with my best friend's boyfriend."

"I don't think that's a concern," Tate said. "She made a new life in Sunberry. If Libby was normal, Val would never have contacted us."

An unusual flare of anger surprised her. "That's not the point. My best friend doesn't care about my feelings. Didn't even give me the benefit of a phone call. Yet, I envy her."

His silence wrapped around her, threatened to steal her breath as quickly as Val was stealing her life. When would he pay attention to her needs? Reading emotional cues wasn't that hard.

"Have you ever thought about just leaving? About starting over somewhere else? Away from everyone's expectations?"

The words escaped before she could stop them, sharper

than she intended. Father would have scolded her for such impulsiveness. Mother would have poured another drink. Gabby didn't care anymore. She needed Tate to react, show he cared. She'd had enough of her fiancé's hangdog look. Had enough of doing the right thing. Had enough of doing what was expected of her.

Tate couldn't even verbalize a response, and she wanted, needed, more than a blank look and a shake of his head.

"After we're married, I want to travel," Gabby said. "The honeymoon to Tahiti will be great, but I want to take a fun vacation at least twice a year. Father was too busy and Mother? She was probably worried about her access to her favorite drink!"

Silence.

Gabby tightened her grip on the chair's worn wood. This wasn't like her. Gabby Stanford didn't give in to outbursts. She didn't even recognize her own words. Maybe she should make an excuse to leave, run an errand. Tate probably had clothes at the cleaners. The drive would clear her head.

Don't let go, whispered in her mind. The tether holding her to Tate felt too fragile.

He placed his mug near his feet and stood. "Gabby?"

She pushed to her feet and clung to his solid body until hers stopped shaking.

"I'm sorry," she murmured against his Oxford shirt. "I'm tired and scared. I know how much you loved her. It's just that I've tried so hard to show you we're the perfect match."

The subtle change in his posture rang through her like a shot. She clutched at his shoulders, but his hold didn't have the same intensity. Something was wrong. Terribly wrong.

"Tate? You're scaring me."

He stepped back, leaving his hands on her shoulders, his blue gaze intense and...sad.

"I love you," he said, his voice low and quiet. "But not the way you deserve. I have a special-needs daughter and my focus has to be on her. I can't be the husband you deserve."

No! The word clawed at her throat, but she refused to speak it. She shook her head, grasping for some invisible anchor to keep her world intact. Yet, even as Tate cupped her cheeks, she felt the cracks widening.

His decision was final, but it didn't have to be hers. Not anymore. Her breath steadied with the sag of her shoulders. A thought emerged in her mind, raw and frightening at the same time. Who could she be—if not the dutiful fiancée?

His gentleness only made it worse, and her breath caught. She shook her head, resisting his warmth. When he pressed his forehead to hers, her knees wobbled.

"I've spent my entire life trying to prevent my mother from being the talk of the town. Now, I'm going to be."

CHAPTER TEN

When Val stepped from the plane into the busy Memphis terminal, tears blurred her vision.

"We made it, baby girl," she whispered inhaling the baby shampoo fragrance of Libby's silky curls.

Around her, travelers rushed to their gates, the beep beep of shuttles sounded, and the aroma of airport food scented the air. Wheeling the small bag complete with Libby's special diet, diapers, and changes of clothing behind her, Val followed the overhead signs to the baggage claim. At first she wondered how she was going to manage Libby, her small roller bag, and the huge duffel she'd checked, but the airport rented carts. After the twelve-minute wait for her duffel to slide onto the carousel, a kind gentleman loaded it onto her cart and she and Libby wheeled most of what they owned outside.

"One more road trip with your Aunt Hannah and we'll be at our new home."

Libby's velvety soft palm patted Val's chin. "Ma, ma, ma, ma."

"You're a genius talking at barely six months," Val cooed, weaving around two teens on their phones and stepping through the exit into bright sunshine. "Wait until Aunt Hannah hears you."

"Val!"

A wave pulled her attention to the rear bumper of the weathered two-toned Focus. Relief released the tension in Val's stiff muscles. There couldn't be two vehicles waiting in the pickup line with a mismatched primer gray hood and the rest of the car a muted silver. Val broke into a trot, pushing the cart before her and causing Libby, bouncing in her baby sling, to giggle.

Standing near the dented bumper of her 2008 Ford, Hannah waved, her smile as bright as Libby's eyes. Her sister paused, held up a perfectly manicured index finger to the airport cop, and then broke into a run.

Within seconds her sister's arms locked Val and Libby in a vice-like embrace.

"You're home!" Hannah kissed first Libby's cheek and then hers.

When Libby fussed, Hannah dropped to her knees and touched Libby's button nose with her finger.

"You're beautiful!" Hannah whispered.

Libby's long spiked lashes fluttered, her rosebud mouth formed a pursed-lip pout, and her tiny forehead wrinkled like she wasn't sure what to make of her boisterous aunt.

Hannah laughed. "What's with that face?"

"She's concerned about her crazy aunt." Val lowered her voice. "But you better be more concerned with the cop. He's coming this way and he's not smiling."

Hannah grabbed the cart and wheeled it to her car parked along the curb. A memory of the day Papa had replaced the car's hood rushed to the surface, tugging Val's heart. She had been teaching Hannah to drive when a deer had crashed into them. Now, like her hair after an early flight, the car wasn't much to look at, but it ran well, dependable as her sister. Papa might not clear time to paint Hannah's car, but he'd always kept the family vehicles in top running condition. Something her Honda had missed. Like her car, she also needed a touch of Papa's love.

"Leaving now, officer." Hannah gave the cop a finger wave and opened the door for Val. "Baby seat installed according to your instructions. Tate put it in, but I had Jeramiah make sure it was extra tight."

In record time, Val secured Libby in the car seat and scooted into the passenger seat.

Hannah shot her a watery smile and then shifted into drive. "I'm so glad you're home."

"I've missed you too," Val said, reaching for her bag to prepare Libby's next meal.

Dread and hope churned her stomach. Part of her lamented the loss of her Sunberry life and friends. But they'd never been able to fill the void left by her family.

At least she had her sister back.

Twenty minutes later, Hannah navigated the multiple lanes crossing the mighty Mississippi into Arkansas.

"The cottage is supposed to be ready by the time we get there," Hannah said.

Val removed Libby's empty bottle and checked her blood sugar. Still stable—unlike her crazy life at present.

A warm palm squeezed Val's arm.

"Is she okay? I know the trip worried you." Hannah glanced in the rearview mirror. "She's so perfect in every way. I can't wrap my head around the fact that she has ... anything wrong."

Heeding the overwhelming urge to touch Libby, Val reached through the bucket seats and arranged Libby's elephant blanket.

"I'll teach you everything about her care." Val waited for the constriction in her throat to ease. "You're our backup. If anything happens to me—"

Hannah's grip tightened. "Nothing is going to happen to you or Libby. You're home now. And our family is going to show you their love even if I have to beat it into them with my wiffle ball bat."

Val grasped the memory to avoid a family discussion. "It worked for Jeremiah's brother. I couldn't believe my diva little sister had so much bottled-up passion. I've never seen you so mad. Good thing it was a plastic bat."

"Axel didn't think my bat was lightweight," Hannah said. "He was black and blue for weeks. Teach him to badmouth my sister."

"I can't believe he agreed to be the best man at your wedding after that beating."

Hannah grinned. "I might have threatened him."

Val laughed and quickly covered her mouth to keep from disturbing Libby. "Why doesn't that surprise me?"

"Because I'm your sister." Hannah paused. When she glanced away from the road, worry shadowed her gaze. "Are you sure you want to live in the Carver cottage?"

"No." The sound of her denial was as raw as her feelings. "But your trailer is too small, and you and Jeremiah need your space. Besides, one of us needs to have a successful relationship.

Sorry, I'm a grouch. I'm still questioning my sanity on the move. I mean a rent-free home with a yard where Libby can play? That's amazing. Part of me is so grateful for Tate's generosity. The other part? I feel like I'm being bought. I'll always be in his debt. How do I blend the two and come out with my self-respect intact?"

"I don't have the answers," Hannah said.

Val huffed out a calming breath, which failed to soothe her jittery hands. "Tell me about the cottage."

"I only saw it before the renovations started. It's kind of retro, but neat and clean. And not a hint of mold." Hannah passed a slow-moving vehicle. "Trust me, I searched every corner for a hint of the creepy stuff."

"I have no doubts. You could always sniff out a problem better than one of Papa's hunting dogs." Val swallowed at the sudden pang of longing. "Does Papa still keep dogs? I don't know any more about our family than I know of Tate's."

Hannah's long fingers warmed hers. "Nothing's changed—except you weren't there."

"I'm scared," Val whispered, the words eking through her closed throat.

Although her gaze remained on the highway, Hannah's fingers tightened. "Tate's still on my watch list. Just because he took care of your move and gave you a house doesn't mean he's cleared in my book." Her gaze narrowed. "Not after leaving you for Gabby."

The memory of Tate's graduation with Gabby and his parents by his side roared to a hot burn, licking at Val's confidence. "He didn't leave me. I left him because I didn't fit in his glitzy world. Nothing has changed except now I need his generosity—for Libby."

She replaced the hurtful memory with Libby's gummy grin. "I'm moving for Libby. Tate's always wanted a family. He'll be a good father, and Libby deserves his love."

"I get it," Hannah said. "You and Papa were always close."

Tears stung Val's eyes. How had she ruined such a loving relationship with Papa? More importantly, how did she repair it?

"If Tate even looks sideways at you, call me," Hannah said. "I ruined a perfectly good bat on Axel. But I can buy another one."

"You're on quick dial in my contacts," Val said, grateful that her sister didn't pressure her. "I hate depending on Tate. I mean, Libby needs a safe environment, but—"

"He's not living there with you, is he?"

Val stiffened. "Absolutely not! He's engaged to Gabby." Like she could forget it.

While Val leaned against the headrest, Hannah drove in silence, and a soft snore sounded from the backseat. Outside, vast stretches of farmland streamed by her window. Rice paddies, glistening with standing water, lined the road.

"Are you sure you're making the right decision?" Hannah's whispered words magnified Val's doubts. "Jeremiah could stay with his parents for a while."

"We've already had this discussion."

Hannah glanced at her. "You're nervous about Tate's cottage. I get it. What if he messes up and kicks you out? I'm just saying, Momma and Papa have an extra room and Brett and Ruger—"

"No!" A half-sob leaked from Val. She wished she could count on her own brothers. But they'd made their position clear—against her, just like her parents.

"Once we're settled, I'll find work. I was good in the restaurant—even got a promotion." But what she wanted to do, loved to do, was weld at Reeser's Garage—with her family. She blinked back more tears. "Libby's condition should improve with age. I can find something part-time when you can watch her."

"Tate should help out too."

Terror lifted the hair on her arms. Could she ever leave Libby in Tate's care?

"You know that watch list you were talking about?"

Hannah nodded, a smirk lifting her ruby lips.

Val pointed at her eyes. "He's under my microscope with pins in his toes!"

"Toes?" Hannah's painted nails tapped the rhinestone steering wheel. "I had a more intense area."

Instead of laughing, doubt shivered along her spine.

One hour later, Hannah turned into the parking lot for Glen Falls Rest Home. Squatting beneath six large pecan trees, the structure seemed smaller than she remembered.

Hannah lifted Libby from the car seat, balancing her on her hip. "Ready to meet your great-grandma, sweet pea?"

Libby kicked her legs, making a soft, pleased sound. Hannah grinned. "Guess that's a yes."

Val's frozen smile wobbled. Time to face the piper. She just hoped Granny was in a forgiving mood.

When the glass double doors opened, a sharp antiseptic aroma greeted them. Hannah led the way, addressing nurses by name down the long hallway, her sneakers silent on the tile floors. When they reached the small room at the end of the hall, Val stopped at the threshold.

Seated in a high-backed chair, Granny Eller stared out the window, a knitted shawl draped over her shoulders. The afternoon light caught the silver in her hair, but her sharp eyes captured Val's the second she stepped inside.

"Well, I'll be," Granny said, her voice raspier but still edged with steel. "About time."

The lump in Val's throat made it hard to speak. "Hi, Granny."

Her grandmother's gaze flicked to Hannah, then to the bundle in her arms. "And this must be my great-grand-daughter."

Hannah crouched down, bringing Libby closer. "Meet Libby."

The creases in Granny's face doubled in a wide smile. "Now we have four generations of Reeser women. Maybe once you and your mother come to terms, we can get a photo. I'll hang it on the wall over my chest. Give this place a feeling of time and love." She brushed a trembling finger over Libby's tiny fist. "She's something special."

Libby gurgled in response, grasping onto her great-grandmother's hand.

When a satisfied smile spread across Granny's features, Val's shoulders relaxed. Things would be okay—at least between her and Granny.

"She's got a strong grip," Granny said. "Just like her mama."

Val swallowed hard. "She's stubborn, too."

"Runs in the family." Granny's gaze sharpened, pinning Val in place. "So. Is Glen Falls your backdoor or are you looking for another place to run to after this?"

Val followed a stain on the floor. "No, ma'am. Me and Libby want to come home—to stay."

Granny patted the mattress. "I'll give you a few weeks to make up with the family. But if you haven't finished the job by that time, I'm stepping in. Now, sit down and tell me what's been happening."

Val dropped to the edge of the bed. "I messed up."

Granny shook her head and kindness shone even through her thick glasses. "Most of us have. Once you learn that and keep it right here." Granny tapped her temple. "It's easy to forgive. Now tell me the short and long of it so I can help you feel better. Can't have you down in the mouth when you need to raise my great granddaughter."

Granny didn't comment, didn't interrupt, just listened and nodded while Val told her about the months away from her home.

"So Tate wants to be a real daddy?" Granny nodded, her gaze focused on a distant memory. After a pause, she dipped her chin like she'd finalized a decision. "See that you hold him to that decision. This is your home. You and Libby need to stay here."

Val's breath whistled by her lips, Granny's words melting her fear that she'd never be able to come home.

Granny's smile softened. "One thing's for sure—there's a whole lot of love waiting for her here. For you too."

"I hope so, Granny." Val kissed her wrinkled cheek. "If not, I'll come up with a backdoor just like you taught me."

CHAPTER ELEVEN

TATE SCANNED THE COTTAGE'S NEW NURSERY, TAKING IN every cotton-candy pink ruffle and frill with an unsettling truth—he'd lost control of his own daughter's space before she'd even set foot in it. The words *not her world* rotated in his mind. This was supposed to be a fresh start—a place to make new memories with Libby, and hopefully, with Val too.

Val would not be impressed. Ha! Val would be madder than the wasp hive he'd knocked off the front eaves. An image of her eyes wide, taking in the room, her hand over her mouth to hide whatever polite but horrified expression she'd let slip.

How was he supposed to convince her that moving to Glen Falls was a good idea, that he was serious about coparenting, when he couldn't even keep Mom from bulldozing his intentions?

Walking into Libby's new bedroom felt like a hike through a Pepto Bismol fun house. Except he wasn't having a good time. He was nauseous. Unlike Gabby and Mom, Val preferred simple décor in earthy tones. The elephant theme in her Sunberry apartment might have surprised him, but she sure hadn't chosen pink pachyderms.

He flicked at a gauzy ruffle. Geez, the stuff covered the windows and the crib. Even the rocker's comfy cushion had a ruffle out of the stuff. And he really liked the chair, had envisioned hours snuggling Libby, just the two of them.

He checked the time. Too late to change the nursery now. Val would arrive at any minute. Sweat beaded at his temples and trickled along his hairline. He hadn't been this nervous the first time he asked Val to go to prom. However, a trip to the Bluff for dinner followed by the high school dance didn't compare to the high stakes of Libby's homecoming.

"Isn't the nursery spectacular? Perfect for our little princess." Mom stepped up behind him. "The minute I saw the photo I knew I had to create it for my granddaughter. I can't wait to meet her."

Unsteady, he leaned against the doorframe, pressing his palm to his forehead to quell the urge to rip down every pink ribbon and ruffle.

"Mom, I thought we agreed we'd keep it simple. Just the basics. This is too much."

His mother, oblivious in her excitement, simply smiled. "You said you wanted her room ready. I know Val might have her... tastes, but this is my granddaughter's first real homecoming to us. She deserves a space that's—well, fit for a Carver."

He winced. Fit for a Carver?

Aw man, that was just the kind of statement that would set Val off like a rocket. Although he loved his parents and wanted the best for them, especially after Marshall's accident, this was not going to fly with his baby momma. To be honest, he also wasn't a fan.

Libby was a part of him, the best part. She wasn't a status symbol or something that needed to be polished to perfection. Best stop this now before his parents went too far and destroyed the tentative bond he'd rebuilt with Val.

"It's not about that, Mom. I want Val to feel comfortable here, and now—" He gestured around the room, the walls blurring in his frustration. "This doesn't feel like us, or like something Val would want."

His mother's smile wavered, and a flicker of hurt creased her sophisticated demeanor. "I don't understand. Libby has family here, and we're part of that family. I loved you boys, but I always wanted a little girl to spoil. Now, I have a grand-daughter. There's no shame in loving her and wanting to give her nice things."

He bit the inside of his lip. He hadn't meant to hurt her feelings. He also didn't want a lecture on loyalty and family legacy. He could almost feel the argument bubbling up, just waiting for Val's reaction to tip it over the edge.

"I know you're excited," he said, calling on his courtroom training. "But we need to take this slow. Give Val time to adjust to the changes so she wants to stay in Glen Falls."

"Of course she'll want to stay here." She kissed his cheek. "I'm just thrilled to be a grandmother. But I'll honor my promise to back off today. You two take all the time you need. But—"

Tate raised his hand, feeling like a condemned man. "I'll bring her by tomorrow. But this is important. I want this to work. If Val isn't comfortable, I could lose my chance."

"You have as much right to be with her as Val." Mom's eyes narrowed. "She's not keeping us from our grand-daughter."

Tate pressed his palm against Mom's back, guiding her toward the door. "So let's make sure this is an amiable transi-tion. Life will be better for all of us, especially Libby."

His mother paused on the stoop, her expensive yellow suit matching the pot of purple and yellow flowers near the steps. "Please talk to her about that nickname. They're fine for children. But she'll soon want a sophisticated name. Elizabeth is much better."

"Her name is Liberty," Tate said.

Mom's eyes widened. "I see."

Which she did not. 'I see' was code for 'that's unfortunate,' which used to be her favorite response.

"Mom." He guided her toward her gleaming SUV, trying to phrase his words so she'd understand without squashing her enthusiasm. Although she didn't fit the typical grandmother image, she'd embraced the role, stocking up on every baby item imaginable.

"No more shopping sprees for a while, okay? The drawers are full of clothes and sheets."

She slid behind the wheel, and he closed her door. Within seconds, the buzz of a power window had him turning back to her.

"Val doesn't have to worry about unpacking boxes. We had a space problem so I took care of them. Our church was thrilled with the donation. There's a big need for baby items."

Tate's stomach plunged like the time he tried to cliff dive at the river and did a belly flop. He rubbed his abdomen. This time it was more painful.

The luxury sedan backed from the drive and Mom waved like she was the guest of honor in the Thanksgiving parade. However, he'd been relegated to the goat. Val was going to ban him from the premises.

Ten short minutes later, Val stepped from Hannah's car, sending Tate's heart into a strange double thump against his ribcage. Was he imagining things? It almost looked like— Nah, it couldn't be. She'd been giving him the cold shoulder since she'd walked out. Still, he could swear he saw a flicker of hope on her expressive features.

Just keep lying to yourself, Carver. Even if he'd had a prayer, Mom had doused it for him.

Val paused on the sidewalk and took in the cottage. Since he'd hired the painter before Mom got involved, he'd selected a sunny yellow tint.

Gran had always called yellow a cheerful color. Except the smile he'd grown to love and missed didn't appear on his baby momma. When she turned to get Libby, guilt and sadness closed his throat. He'd seen the same expression on a client's face at sentencing: trapped and resigned.

It was his job to change her impression. Squaring his shoulders, he moved to the rear passenger door. "How was your flight?"

His mood launched upward at the sight of Libby waving her tiny hands in his direction. His pull on the door handle failed. Locked.

He tapped at the glass. "Hey, sweetheart. Daddy missed you," he murmured, his voice thick with emotion he hadn't planned to show.

Her smile was instant, all drool and delight. In that moment, his nervousness faded. She was his daughter, his reason for trying to build a bridge, even if it meant fighting battles on two fronts—with his family and with Val.

At Val's nudge, he stepped aside, and the door clicked.

"I'll get her," Val said in a clipped, no-nonsense tone.

Undaunted, he peered over Val's shoulder at Libby. "That sweet little face has occupied my mind since the day I left her." Although part of him acknowledged his near boy-like enthusiasm, he couldn't stem it. Didn't want to.

"She might need a moment." Val unbuckled the harness. "She hasn't been around you for over two weeks."

"It was like waiting for Christmas morning when I was five." What the heck? Now, he couldn't control his motor mouth. "I swear she's grown, and prettier than ever."

Val scooped his daughter into her arms, but Libby's bright look found his.

"You remember Daddy, don't you?" Like a lonesome puppy, he trailed them to the house. But he couldn't force his focus away from Libby's cheerful face from over Val's shoulder.

When Val stopped at the door, he grabbed the opportunity and cupped Libby's head, giving her a loud smooch on the forehead.

She grinned.

"Daddy missed you so much."

Val didn't care. She moved forward, making him feel like he had entered some crazy basketball game with his daughter. He moved forward and Val swung to the right, leaving him face-to-face with Hannah. The smirk on her face dissolved his sappy grin. He hardened his gaze to match hers.

"Next time you go all gaga dad..." Hannah lifted one eyebrow. "Remember, I'm recording it and posting it to Instagram."

"You'll have lots of opportunities because I'm not stopping." Tate squared his shoulders. "She's my daughter. If I want to make a fool of myself, deal with it."

Hannah didn't laugh. Instead, her eyes narrowed. "If you're not serious, Carver... if you're playing around with my sister's heart again, or hurting my niece, you'll regret it." Her tone had turned icy, the kind you felt down to your bones, and for a moment he could only stare at her, thrown off balance by the sudden weight of her words.

He swallowed, straightening up, feeling the shift within himself. "I was never that kind of guy. Val dumped me, remember. As for Libby? I'll do whatever it takes to be with her."

She eyed him like she was measuring the truth in his words.

"You better be for real, Carver." Hannah moved forward, her nose two inches from his, letting the silence stretch. "If you screw this up, I've got a bat with your name on it."

"Idle threat." He stepped back. "Everybody in Glen Falls knows what you did to Axel. And if you hadn't, I would have."

Hannah's eyes widened. Truth was, he'd surprised himself. Most of the time he went with the flow, an effective defense mechanism for growing up in the Carver household. But Libby, the responsibility of being a dad, or just negotiating with Val, had changed him.

He turned toward the entrance where Val and Libby had disappeared. He liked the new Tate, but he didn't think he was going to like dealing with Val when she learned what had happened to her stuff.

Inside, Val rotated in the small living area, her eyes flat with disappointment. He should have stayed with Grandma's vintage charm. Like Val's apartment in Sunberry, it gave off a welcoming vibe that made you want to sit down and stay a while.

But Mom had once again highjacked his vision, leaving a stainless steel, wood and iron industrial look that would chill a polar bear.

He let out a breath that felt heavy—like the guarded expression in Val's dark eyes.

"I hope you kept the nursery simple," she said, her voice low, but edged with something sharp.

He swallowed, feeling like a man condemned for crimes he hadn't committed—or hadn't meant to. "We might... need to make a few adjustments," he admitted, steeling himself for her reaction.

"Libby's bag is in the backseat and our duffel is in the trunk," Val said. "Please bring it in."

CHAPTER TWELVE

WHEN VAL OPENED THE NURSERY DOOR, HER EARS RANG. No elephants. No jungle animals. No soothing gray and yellow theme. Instead, the tiny room looked like the aftermath of a cotton candy explosion—walls washed in sugary pink, ruffles spilling over the crib, and a rocking chair draped in fabric that screamed fragile, do not touch.

She counted to ten, inhaling a steady breath.

Stay calm. It's room décor, not a terminal diagnosis.

Except her self-talk didn't relax her curled fingers. Whoever had exchanged her elephants with the insides of a boudoir—

Easy momma bear. It wasn't a complete disaster. Her things were probably in the chest. She moved to the dresser, pulling open one drawer after another. Expensive designer baby clothes, rows of tiny shoes, a miniature purse glittering with rhinestones filled the space, but not one item, the ones that held pieces of her life and the friends who'd supported her, were visible.

Her gaze bounced from each ridiculous piece, searching

for even a trace of her things. The blanket from Mrs. Carter, gone. The handmade baby booties her friend Sarina had sent, gone. Every piece of the life she'd carefully built for Libby in Sunberry had vanished, swallowed by the Carver version of baby luxury.

When she completed her scan, she stopped on Hannah, leaning against the doorframe, arms crossed. "Want me and Libby to go to the park while you knock him on his butt?"

Although her tone remained light, her sister's gaze held a warning. "I think she's a little young to witness Dad's humiliation on her first day."

"Excellent idea. She'll be okay for forty-five minutes." Although Val managed to keep a pleasant tone, she couldn't suppress the twitch in her lips. "This won't take long."

She crouched to check Libby's blood sugar, her fingers working automatically as the monitor beeped softly in her hands. When the numbers flashed green, relief softened the tension straining her neck.

Hannah tilted her head, her smirk deepening. "I can still send Jeremiah to his parents' house for a while. You and Libby are welcome at my place. Just say the word."

"Hold that thought until you get back." Val adjusted Libby's blanket, brushing her tiny hand with her thumb.

"Back?" Tate's heavy steps approached. "It's been almost two whole weeks." He reached for the rocking chair, his large hands fighting a pink ruffle that refused to stay in place. "At least give me five minutes to snuggle her?"

"Forty-five minutes, starting now," Val said.

Hannah snorted, clearly enjoying his struggle. "That rocker's got more frill than sense, Daddy."

When Libby cooed, her tiny fist grabbing at Tate's finger, Val's frustration ebbed. Seeing them together—a father so completely enchanted by his daughter—made everything harder.

"I'll be back in forty-five." Hannah scooped Libby into her arms and raised a brow at Tate. "So much for not messing up."

Val counted to ten again and then waited for the front door to click closed. Tamping down her temper, she crossed her arms. "Where are her things?"

He flinched, rubbing the back of his neck like a teenager caught sneaking in past curfew. "We'll go shopping. I wanted to do that anyway. Thought we could pick something out together—just the two of us." His voice softened. "We've got to be back by four, though. Libby's nurse is stopping by."

"Nurse?"

Tate raised his hands in submission, a pathetic cross between a wry smile and a grimace distorting his features. "I looked into daycare, just like you asked. Got her a spot in the best one in town. But Senior...? He hired a nurse."

Her jaw tightened, the anger bubbling up before she could stop it. "Your dad hired a nurse for my baby? Does he think I'm incapable of managing my own child?"

"No." Tate's voice grew earnest. "He hasn't even met her yet, but you know how they are. My mom is so excited about her. And Senior..." He hesitated, his shoulders sagging. "Libby's got him wrapped, and he's only seen photos."

Val's anger faltered. Tate's parents already felt close to Libby. But hers? Although she'd moved back to Glen Falls, the distance between her and her family remained. Momma and Papa hadn't even met their granddaughter yet. A pang of sorrow cut through her frustration, followed by a pang of guilt.

"I'm glad they've shown an interest in their granddaughter. But that doesn't mean I'll let them steamroll over my decisions," she said, her voice firm. "I won't let Libby become part of some... Carver Show."

Tate nodded, his expression serious. "I get it. They're

excited about being grandparents and they don't know how to rein it in. But they love her already. A kid can't have too many people in their love circle, right?"

Val turned away, her throat tightening. She wanted to believe him, wanted to trust her life coparenting with Tate could work. Wanted Libby to be surrounded by love from her grandparents—both sets of grandparents. But the idea of his family making important decisions about Libby? No way. She would not be a background character in her own daughter's life.

"I'm losing everything," she whispered, her voice breaking despite her best efforts to hold it together.

"No, you aren't," Tate said, stepping closer. "We'll figure this out. Together."

She shook her head, the dresser edge biting into her fingers. "I won't let go of everything we had. Libby and I— we've built a life, Tate. I'm not giving that up."

"You don't have to," he said, his voice steady. "But you also don't have to shoulder all of the responsibility anymore. She has two parents now. I'm here."

Val swallowed hard, the truth of his words cutting through her anger. But that didn't erase the pressure building in her chest, the feeling she had to fight harder, work faster, prove to herself—and to Libby—they weren't pawns in someone else's game.

"Forty-five minutes," she said, her voice quieter with the slowing of her heart. "When Hannah brings her back, this... this room will be... normal."

Tate watched her for a moment, his eyes searching hers before he nodded. "Mom and Senior want to meet her. I figured you'd both be tired from traveling but tomorrow..."

"Right now, all I want is a garbage bag—a big one."

He straightened, and she half expected him to salute. "Got it."

Val wadded an impossible ruffle from the crib's bottom into a ball and tossed it in the corner. Next, she yanked a soft pink sculpture of a tiara from the shelf.

Tate returned and held open a large black plastic bag. "Here's how I see it—this is your call. You tell me what stays, what goes, and what we're returning to the store."

"Tempting," Val said. "But I don't think the baby boutique has a return policy on a grandmother's overzealous decorating.'"

"Then we'll donate it and get your stuff back in here."

She hesitated, glancing around the overly decorated space. "You mean that?"

"Yeah. I do."

"Okay. The ruffles go first."

Tate grabbed a handful of fabric. "Gladly."

Val ran her fingers over the ridiculous ruffled canopy that loomed over Libby's crib. "I can't believe your mother thought this was a good idea."

"Believe it." Tate yanked down a handful of pink chiffon, tossing it into the bag. "She once made my aunt a wedding cake that was bigger than the bride. Mom doesn't do subtle."

"Rhinestones, Tate! She's six months old." The absurdity of the situation fueled her irritation.

Tate added the balled ruffle to the bag but remained quiet.

"They want to meet their granddaughter? Fine." Val pushed a pink fuzzy throw rug into the bag, punching it with her fist for good measure. "I'll explain the rules to them tomorrow."

Tate's glance flicked toward the ceiling, his lips pressing into a thin line. Val froze, recognizing the movement.

She'd seen his subtle tell so many times before. Like the night she'd insisted they sneak out to a dance in Poplar Bluff, Gabby adamantly against the idea while Tate stayed quiet, letting his barely there eye roll speak for him. He had that same look now—a mix of resignation and resistance.

"Don't," she said, straightening. "Don't give me that look. This isn't optional."

He sighed, turning back to the closet and pulling out a giant teddy bear that nearly swallowed him whole. "I heard you. But I'm not promising they'll like it." He tossed the bear onto the pile by the garbage bag, its fluffy arms sprawled in surrender.

"They don't have to like it. They have to follow it," Val said, her tone clipped. "And speaking of rules, call your dad and tell him to email me the nurse's résumé."

Tate froze, glancing at her over his shoulder. "I'm sure he checked her out. You should see the requirement list he goes through before he considers a new associate at the firm."

"This isn't an associate, Tate. This person will be responsible for Libby." She crossed her arms, narrowing her gaze on him until he twitched. "I'm not handing her over to someone I haven't vetted."

"Got it," he said with a curt nod, turning back to the closet.

Val let out a slow breath, her frustration ebbing. She hated playing the bad guy, but Libby's care wasn't something she could compromise on—not with anyone. Sunlight reflected from a crystal bedside lamp, and for a fleeting moment, her fingers itched to smash it against the stone fireplace in the living room.

"What happened to my stuff?" she asked, her words coming out in staccato pants. "The things I packed for her?"

Tate paused, pulling a stack of folded blankets from the top shelf. "Church donation."

"Donation?" she repeated, the word tasting bitter on her tongue.

He set the blankets on the dresser, his expression cautious. "Mom said there wasn't enough room—"

"So she gave away the things I selected. The things my friends bought. The things Libby is attached to?"

Val bit back the angry retort rising to her lips. The thought of strangers sifting through Libby's belongings made her chest ache.

She gestured toward the pile of baby goods they'd just removed. "You'll be making another trip to the church. Exchange this"—she swept her hand forward, her voice cold—"for any of my remaining things. Expect to buy anything you can't retrieve."

"Not a problem," Tate said, his tone neutral but his shoulders stiffening.

Of course, it wasn't a problem. Heaven help him if he even hinted of a problem.

"If you want me to stay here..."

Tate lifted his palms. "I got it. Church. Exchange. Shop till I drop. I promise I will restore Libby's nursery exactly as before."

Ragged pants crackled around her and it took a moment for her to realize they were hers. The fight was over. Tate understood. She forced her clenched fists to relax and waited until her breathing returned to normal.

"I'll make sure your parents understand that too." She softened her voice but couldn't summon a pleasant expression. "I'm not trying to keep them from Libby, but she's not their project. She's my...our daughter."

Tate's gaze met hers, and for a moment, the tension in his face shifted. "I know," he said, his voice low but steady. "I'll make sure they understand."

Val nodded, and the vice around her torso loosened—a fraction. She bent down to tie up the garbage bag, the scent of lavender from the baby blankets reminding her of quieter days, simpler times.

"Call your dad." She met Tate's gaze. "And make sure he knows this isn't negotiable. It's better coming from you. I don't want to fight with your parents."

"I will," he said, his tone firmer now. "They'll get it. Promise."

The resolve in his voice convinced her of his commitment. For the first time since stepping into the overdone nursery, they were on the same page. She pressed her hand against her heart, trying to quiet its rapid beat.

"I'm not sure if this is possible?" she whispered. "I don't want to fight about every detail."

"We won't," Tate said.

To avoid looking at him, she surveyed the now-bare room, ending on the chandelier, the last vestige of the Carver family's overreach.

"I hope so," she said. "Because this"—she gestured to the stripped room—"is just the beginning."

Tate grabbed the bear, his features showing an emotion she couldn't read. "Understood. But Val?" He hesitated. "You don't have to fight me, too."

A suitable response died on her tongue. She turned away, unable to meet his look of...longing? Her vision blurred and her chest ached with the weight of everything she couldn't say.

By the time they'd loaded the nursery disaster into the Rover, Hannah returned with a sleeping baby. "The nursery looks normal. What about the rest of your things?"

"Senior dropped them off at the Glen Falls Baptist Church," Tate said. "There's some confusion about the exchange. I told them I'd be there in five minutes to straighten it out."

"Check that app and go," Hannah said, pointing toward Val's phone. "We'll be fine."

Ten minutes later, Tate held open the heavy carved door to the Glen Falls Baptist Church, but Val chose to follow him down the hall to the church secretary's office. Although her family frequented another denomination, she remembered Mrs. Thurman, who brought her old SUV to the Reeser Garage for repairs.

When Tate approached, Mrs. Thurman adjusted her reading glasses and peered at them over the rim.

Tate rested his hands on the desk and offered his most diplomatic smile. "I think there's been a misunderstanding about some donated items."

"Mr. Carver," Mrs. Thurman said with a polite but firm expression. "The donation was made in good faith. The items were given for charity. Reclaiming them now... it's highly unusual."

Tate leaned in, resting his palms on the desk. "I understand that. But this wasn't a donation—it was a mistake."

"Mistake or not, we don't typically return items once they've been received."

"My entire kitchen set is in that donation pile," Val said. "Appliances. Dishes. I need those back."

Mrs. Thurman gave her a sympathetic look. "I understand, dear, but—"

Tate straightened. "Look. I'm sorry about the confusion. My family overstepped." He softened his voice. "I'll make a donation in return, something fair. We already have some brand-new baby items in the car. But I want her things back. She and Libby just moved here. This isn't about money. It's about what's hers."

Silence stretched between them. Mrs. Thurman looked at Val, back at Tate, and then sighed.

"Give me an hour to sort through everything. We'll make an exchange."

Tate nodded. "Thank you."

Mrs. Thurman hesitated, then gave Val a small smile. "I hope you and your little one settle in nicely, dear."

Val nodded, still too stunned to speak. She followed Tate out of the office and into the hallway before she could relax.

Tate turned to her. "That good enough?"

She turned toward him, the weight of the moment pressing against her ribs. "Thank you," she said, the words thick but honest. "For the cottage. For helping me get my things. I—I couldn't afford a house for Libby, not on my own. And I know that."

Tate's expression softened, the hard lines of his jaw easing. "It's not charity, Val."

"I know," she said. And she did. But it didn't feel that way. Not entirely. "I came back so Libby could have her father. Not... a benefactor." The last word stuck, like it didn't belong in her mouth.

Tate stuffed his hands in his back jean pockets. "I'm not trying to make you feel—"

"I know," she cut in. "And that's what makes this hard." She forced herself to look at him. "I was raised in a family where we took care of our own. We worked for what we had, even when it wasn't much. I walked away from all that. My choices put me here. So if I let you fix everything, if I lean on you too much... what does that say about me?"

Tate frowned. "That you're smart enough to take help when it's offered?"

"That I'm someone who's still trying to figure out how to stand on my own," she countered, voice quieter now. "I appreciate what you've done, Tate. I do. But I need to build something for myself here. Not just step into the space you're making for me."

Silence stretched between them before Tate finally nodded. "Alright." He glanced at her car. "But Val—letting people have your back doesn't mean you're weak. You know that, right?"

Her throat tightened, and she swallowed hard. She did know that. But knowing and feeling weren't always the same thing.

CHAPTER THIRTEEN

THE NEXT MORNING WHILE TATE WAITED AT THE ROVER'S rear passenger door, his heart thumping in his ears, Val adjusted Libby's dress. The frilly thing looked like it belonged on a creepy porcelain doll instead of a squirming baby.

"Mom strikes again," he muttered, reaching for Libby. "Come here, sugar. Let Daddy take you to the royal carriage."

"She hates this dress," Val said, handing her over. "The color is nice, but it's so slippery I can barely hold on to her."

Tate balanced Libby on his hip, leaning in to nuzzle her neck. Her giggles bubbled up, light and joyful.

"I love you," he murmured against her powdery-soft skin, his throat thickening with emotion. When the moment overwhelmed him, he switched gears, making silly noises and nibbling her cheeks until she squealed.

"Does it ever normalize?"

Val slung the diaper bag over her shoulder. "Her blood sugar? As long as she eats consistent meals and stays healthy—"

"No." Tate buckled Libby into her car seat. "I mean my

reaction. Every time I look at her, it's like someone's squeezing my chest. I even tear up when I hold her."

Something softened in Val's gaze, causing his heart to beat a little harder.

She slipped into the passenger seat and then turned to him with an arched brow. "I think that's called love."

Tate closed the door and climbed behind the wheel. "Well, I loved you, and I didn't start tearing up every time I picked you up for a date."

"What time are the royals expecting us?" Val said.

He fiddled with the rearview mirror, which was already positioned to keep Libby's car seat in view. Was it his imagination or had that comment about dating her hit a nerve?

"Royals?" Since Val was busy with her bag, he studied her features. She was nervous about visiting his parents, but that wasn't all. "That's perfect. Mommy can always make us laugh. Then again, Grandma had that covered with her choice in baby clothes. I've never seen a parachute baby dress."

"I only kept two of your mother's selections. This was the tamest of the bunch," Val deadpanned while her fingers drummed her thigh. "But I figured she should wear one your mom purchased for her visit."

"Thanks for doing that." He started the car, which was easier and safer than admitting how her kindness got to him. "Mom can go overboard but her heart's in the right place."

When Val didn't respond, he drove in silence, the bright autumn day fighting his stormy thoughts.

Loving Libby came easily. Coparenting with Val? He huffed out a breath. Too weird for words, especially his feelings. He'd fallen in love with Val in fourth grade—as much as a ten-year-old could muster. But he thought she'd drained every feeling from him when she left. She hadn't. Now, he didn't know what to do with it.

All he knew was that the picture in his head—a real family, messy and unlikely—wouldn't leave him alone.

Tension coiled in his gut, dark and restless, like a storm refusing to break. The clear skies didn't fool him. One bad moment with his parents could unravel everything he'd just begun to rebuild with Val and their daughter.

By the time he turned onto the circular drive to his parents' estate, he was patting his pockets for an antacid. He already knew how Val viewed the property, with its towering columns and perfectly manicured lawn. The place looked and felt less like home and more like a monument to his father's success.

Although the estate included a weight room, a media room, and a huge room off the pool, he and his friends had never hung out there. Instead, the three-bedroom Reeser home had been their favorite place. And they weren't the only Glen Falls kids to gravitate to the Reeser table, which always had enough food for an extra mouth.

Guilt and determination battled inside him, tightening his grip on the steering wheel. He'd better sharpen his negotiating skills. Because Val and Libby needed to feel welcome in his parents' home no matter what it took.

Mom must have been on guard at the front window because the minute he guided Val up the front steps the double entry doors opened. Mom and Senior waited in the reception area like the day they'd welcomed the state senator Senior had supported.

Inside the marble foyer his mother, Constance Carver opened her arms. "There she is! My precious girl."

While Val and Libby stared at his mother's wide smile, Tate held his breath. Then, Libby gurgled a welcome sound and leaned for his mother and wonder of wonders, Val released her daughter.

"Oh, those curls!" Connie tucked Libby into her elbow so

the dress flowed around her. "Just like Tate's when he was this age."

When Val hesitated, her fingers lingering near Libby's back, Tate placed a reassuring hand on her arm. "She's a sweetheart," he murmured.

Standing at Mom's elbow, Senior looked as out of place as a circuit judge in a jail cell. He tried a pitiful cross between a snort and a playful noise to capture Libby's attention. Although she didn't cry, Libby wrinkled her forehead, causing the dumb flowered headband to slip over her brows.

Tate bit back a laugh. His little girl wasn't easily impressed.

Undeterred, Mom gestured toward the living room. "Let's sit. Senior, be a dear and ask Juanita to bring refreshments to the living room."

Tate cleared his throat to cover a chuckle. Go Mom. He hadn't seen her take charge in some time.

"You forgot the cardigan that matches the dress." Mom sat in her favorite armchair near the fireplace. "Carvers can't go on visits half-dressed. No, they can't," Mom said in a silly high-pitched voice. Then she turned to Val, her smile gone.

"I need to apologize." Mom smoothed a careful hand over Libby's back, her voice quieter than Tate had ever heard it. "I —I didn't realize I was giving away things from your friends, Val. I thought I was just clearing out extra baby items. If I'd known... I would never have—" She shook her head, pressing her lips together. "I'm so sorry."

Tate felt the tension ripple through Val before she exhaled, her arms tightening around herself. She didn't look away, though. Didn't shut down like she used to. Instead, she nodded once, waiting.

Mom hesitated, then her hand grazed Libby's tiny foot peeking from beneath the dress. "I remember the booties my mother knitted for Marshall," she murmured. "I still have them. All these years, they've brought me comfort. I should have known better." She released a shaky breath. "I won't make that mistake again."

Tate held his breath waiting for the silence to end. Then Val moved, uncrossing her arms, stepping just close enough that she could reach out, resting a hand on Libby's back—right next to Mom's.

"It's okay," Val said, her voice soft but steady. "I get it now, and we were able to retrieve our things." Her fingers traced a slow, absentminded circle over Libby's dress. "You held on to those booties because they were a piece of Marshall. And I... I still have my memories." She swallowed, glancing at Libby, her eyes shining with something that looked a lot like acceptance. Then she looked back at Connie. "And now, Libby has you."

Mom's chin trembled before she let out a watery laugh. "Oh, honey."

Val smiled, a small, real smile, the kind Tate hadn't seen in a long time. "I'm glad she has a grandmother like you."

Mom pressed a kiss to Libby's forehead. "Me too."

Libby let out a tiny grunt, grabbed the headband off her head, and chucked it to the floor with all the enthusiasm of a championship pitcher.

Val pressed a hand to her mouth, shoulders shaking—then she lost it, laughter tumbling out in breathless waves.

Tate bent down, retrieving the headband, shaking his head. "Guess she's got opinions."

Val swiped at her damp eyes, lips twitching. "Like her momma."

"Oh, sunshine." Mom adjusted Libby in her arms. "You're just like your daddy. Not a fan of anything too fussy."

Tate smirked. "Hey. I wear suits every day."

Mom gave him a knowing look. "You complained about your christening outfit for years."

Val laughed again, the sound pulling something tight in his chest—something dangerously close to hope.

And then his father cleared his throat.

Tate didn't have to look to know the laughter was dead on arrival.

Val must have felt it too because her shoulders stiffened, her fingers curling into fists at her sides.

Slowly, Tate turned.

Senior sat ramrod straight, his expression unreadable. But his gaze? It was locked on Val, like she'd done something to his mother instead of giving him a granddaughter. Tate's fingers tightened around the discarded headband in his palm.

It wasn't over.

Not even close.

Tate guided Val toward the loveseat, positioning her so she was within reach of Libby. Which was the wrong move because Val's sharp elbow was digging a small hole in his ribs.

"We'd like to talk about Val and Libby's transition," Tate started, hoping he'd interpreted her cue and blowing the tone. He sounded more like he was making a deposition than a heartfelt appeal. "Libby has special needs, and Val is the expert in her care."

Val pulled a folder from Libby's bag and handed it to his mother. "These are detailed instructions from her doctor. I'll also need you to attend a training session at the cottage, where you can learn how to prepare her meals and use her monitor."

Looking more like he was holding a poopy diaper than educational material, Senior flipped through the folder. "That won't be necessary. Although I appreciate your efforts, we've hired a nurse—"

"She'll need training too," Val said, her tone firm. "Libby won't leave my care until I'm confident you can keep her safe."

While Tate's stomach swan-dived to his toes, Senior bristled.

"Of course, dear," Mom said. "We'll do whatever it takes, won't we, Earl? But the cottage must feel cramped. You can host the training sessions here. We'll cater lunch and make it a proper family affair. Will your mother be coming?"

Tate's palm hit his forehead before he could stop it, and his quick handrub through his hair didn't fool anyone.

Val stiffened beside him, her back straight like she'd been slapped. Tate touched her, hoping to calm her pride and independence before she went off.

"We can always have it at my house," he said, offering Val a compromise. "It's smaller, and it would be easier to keep an eye on Libby while we talk."

Val exhaled. "That does sound easier. Mixing her formula can be messy."

"That's what I pay Juanita for," Mom said, brushing an imaginary speck of dust from her trousers.

"We'll do it at my place," Tate said, hoping he didn't sound rude, but he had to end this before it went sideways. "Find a day that works for the two of you and let us know."

"What about Gabby?" Senior said.

Tate cursed under his breath. Leave it to Senior to raise a major issue with all the subtlety of a courtroom cross-examination. Still, secrets had already gotten them into this mess. Transparency led them forward.

"Gabby moved out." Tate met Senior's surprised expression and held it. "I explained Libby was my focus. The engagement is off."

The heat pump's gentle hum emphasized the suffocating silence. For once, Mom couldn't fill the pause with conversation. Senior leaned back in his chair, his expression unreadable.

Tate tightened his hand on Val's waist, willing her to

acknowledge he'd prioritized Libby—and Val. As for Senior? He could deal with it.

Beneath his fingers, Val's muscles tensed and then softened. From her set features, he doubted she'd forgiven him, but something had shifted. At this stage in the mess, he'd take any morsel Val threw his way.

"Juanita, please bring me the baby activity mat I bought. It's in the nursery closet." Mom kissed Libby's cheek, leaving a smear of lipstick. "And a tissue, please."

"She's spunky," Senior said.

Tate's shoulders drooped like he'd crossed an invisible gauntlet and survived.

"That means she's smart." Mom smoothed Libby's dress, hesitating on her chubby thigh. "Is this the monitor?"

"Yes," Val removed her phone from her purse and held it out so they could see the screen. "This is the app I use."

Although confusion wrinkled their brows, they listened to Val's explanation. His parents had to learn the ropes like he had. Tate rubbed his neck, remembering how overwhelmed he'd felt.

His daughter seemed too little to have such a big problem. Worse, he'd felt inadequate to protect her. Although he'd handled the rigors of law school without a stumble, MCADD knocked him to his knees. Especially with his girl's life in the balance. But repetition helped, and Val was an excellent teacher—if Senior didn't get too pushy.

When Mom set Libby on the colorful play mat, she cooed and waved her arms. While he grinned like the goofy mouse dangling from a trapeze, Val slid to the floor to supervise Libby's play. Taking Val's cue, Tate scooted to the floor and created a small, protective layer at Libby's back.

While Libby squealed and reached for one bright station to another, Tate tried to read the room. Unbelievable. Senior had actually grinned—and hadn't cracked his face.

Libby was reeling him in just like she did everyone in her orbit.

And Mom? She'd always brightened around people. But today was different. Libby's presence created an inner glow in Mom. She looked...happy. Not the superficial kind, but truly happy.

Since the death of his brother, his parents had inhabited an emotional desert. Now, in less than ten minutes, Libby offered them a tiny island of paradise.

Wearing a silent frown of confusion at the casual atmosphere, Juanita rolled in a food cart with a spread of mini-quiches, golden pastries, and colorful fruit kabobs.

Tate shook the unicorn rattle near Libby, who cooed and grabbed for the toy. More wonders at the Carver estate. They were having a carpet picnic on Mom's handwoven Persian rug. Libby had transformed Constance Carver, a firm disciplinarian, into a doting grandmother in less than five minutes.

Mom picked up a serving tong. "She'll like the puff pastry," she said, her tone indulgent. "Pierre only uses the finest ingredients."

Val blocked the offered pastry. "If you look at the instructions I brought, you'll note her dietary limitations. Her little body can't metabolize high-fat foods."

"She sure looks like she'd like them," Senior said.

Val added a fruit kabob to her plate and pinched off a piece of banana. "I've introduced her to rice, oatmeal and barley cereal, and the orange vegetables."

When Libby lunged at the banana and gummed the morsel, Tate's chest expanded with pride. "Nothing wrong with my girl's appetite. She's gumming it like it's baby caviar."

"We just started bananas last week." Val pushed a gooey piece of gummed fruit back into Libby's mouth. "Tomorrow is unsweetened applesauce."

Tate waited, tense. However, instead of oppositional, his

parents seemed mesmerized by Libby's interest in the snack her mother held. Relief as sweet as his daughter's pursed lips slumped his shoulders.

He popped a tart into his mouth, savoring its buttery filling. Libby grinned, her little tongue pushing more goo onto her lips. The unappetizing drool dripped onto the stupid dress, which seemed only fitting. The slippery fabric would make a better napkin than baby apparel.

Senior leaned forward in his chair. "Looks to me like she's happy with the banana."

Tate would bet his new Rover Senior wanted to pick up Libby. He just hadn't gotten up the courage.

Yesterday, he'd envisioned a knock-down drag-out, but his little Libby had paved the way to harmony—at least for now. Man, he was hungry. When he added two more tarts to his plate, he noted Val's. Focused on Libby, Val hadn't touched her food. How many meals had she missed while she met Libby's every demand?

Not anymore. She might not believe him, but she'd soon learn he was in this for the long haul.

He lifted his napkin, but Val was already blotting Libby's mouth. However, Libby had a different agenda. She shook her head so instead of cleaning the banana goo from her chin, the napkin spread it over her cheeks.

"You little stinker." Val's giggle seemed to energize Libby's movements. She babbled louder and batted at the napkin with a miniature hand, her tiny mouth scrunched into a fierce frown.

"There's that sass!" Tate said. "I'm sure the flaw comes from the Carver gene."

Senior guffawed, his laugh so loud Libby froze her wide blue eyes wide in surprise. Val glanced at Tate and a flicker of uncertainty passed between them. Yeah, his parents' reactions surprised him too.

Twenty minutes later, Libby's head bobbed against Mom's linen suit, leaving small stains from her mouth and nose. Tate grinned. Mom, who dressed for the simplest of occasions, seemed unfazed by her soiled clothes.

He stepped in front of Val. "Here, Mom. I'll take our little munchkin. She's had a big day."

Tears moistened his mother's eyes, causing a hitch in his breath. She brushed Libby's curl-covered head with a kiss and then mouthed *thank you*. He swallowed hard to overcome the sting in his eyes. The meeting had challenged his family, but it had also opened their hearts.

Ten minutes later, he slipped behind the wheel. "Thanks for agreeing to do this. It means a lot to them."

"It's for Libby," Val said, but her tone had lost its sharp edge. "It went better than I anticipated."

"I think my parents learned more than how to care for Libby." The steady hum of the Rover's engine drained the last feelings of restlessness from him.

"So did I," Val said. "Despite their fancy estate and airs of importance, they care about their granddaughter."

"I think they forgot how new love feels." Tate shifted into drive. "Thank you for making them—and me—a part of her life."

"You keep saying we're a team," Val said. "I need you to explain it."

He stopped before turning onto the main road and turned to her. "It means I'm not giving up on us, Val. Not yet."

Her eyes widened, but she didn't respond. The silence stretched between them, thick with unspoken words and fragile hope.

CHAPTER FOURTEEN

Us!

How could a two-letter word turn her world on its head? Groggy from her restless night, Val tapped her phone. At least Tate's reveal hadn't triggered Libby.

The morning sun streamed through her bedroom window, warming the small room and casting a golden glow over the brass bed left over from Tate's grandmother. Although Val yearned to nestle deep in the covers for another ten minutes of solitude before Libby awakened, she pushed to her feet. True to his "us" commitment, Tate would arrive at 7:00AM to help with Libby's morning routine.

The man had yet to be late, which annoyed the fire out of her. One day. Just one day, she'd like to check off a mistake. She still broke out in a cold sweat analyzing every potential hazard awaiting Libby. But Tate? Rock solid as his grandmother's cedar chest resting at the foot of her bed. Which was the precise reason his word *us* continued to give her heartburn.

In record time Val rushed through her morning routine and trotted to the kitchen to start Libby's oatmeal. Within minutes Tate's light tap sounded at the front door. Val swiped a strand of hair that had worked free from her quickie ponytail.

"Morning." Tate let himself in and set a white bag with the Bluebird Café logo on the side. "Muffins fresh from the oven. I had extra time so I stopped on the way here. Libby still asleep?"

On cue, babbling sounds emerged from the monitor.

"Awe." Tate's warm hand squeezed her shoulder. "She knows Daddy's here. Special outfit or am I free to pick?"

Annoyed by the riot of sensations in her belly, Val waved him off. "Free choice."

She'd welcome five minutes escape from her crazy thoughts. How could he think about an us with so much turmoil in their lives? Val switched on the burner and set down the pot of oatmeal. The smack of her heavy-handed clatter vibrated up her arm.

"Well gee, Val," she muttered. "Let me count the ways. One: Tate is speaking to his parents while I'm estranged from mine. Two: he didn't betray his best friend or me like I did. Three: he isn't trying to reboot his disastrous life, which I am!"

She slopped the oatmeal onto the burner with a hiss. None of that changed the truth. Tate and his family were fancy law firms, polished shoes and prestige. Her family owned Reeser's Garage, the same small-town shop they'd owned for two generations. The variance was too great— wasn't it?

Val switched on the coffeemaker. Even if they could figure out their differences, she wasn't sure she could handle his parents wanting to give Libby too much, too soon, and on their terms. Plus, she wanted Libby to learn and value hard work and people were more important than things.

"Someone's dressed and ready for a yummy breakfast."

Tate seated Libby in her highchair. "Mom sent me three dates for their training session."

Val spooned oatmeal on a saucer to cool.

"She's trying her best to make this work," he added, his tone casual, but his intent gaze gave away the weight. He pulled his phone from his pocket and read off three dates. "Pick one that works best for you. I'll tell Mom and your family."

Val's hand froze on the spoon, her chest tightening. "My family?"

Tate nodded, his expression calm but unwavering. "Yeah. This is a good chance for everyone to meet Libby—and to start moving forward."

She turned on the faucet and filled the pot, scrubbing at the crusted debris on the sides with unnecessary force. "I don't think they'll come."

"They might," he said, his voice calm but persistent. "Libby changes things. Don't you, sweet girl?"

Libby squealed and smacked her hand against the tray. "She's already started with my family. You might not see it, but I do. I think she can do the same for yours if you'll give it a chance."

A dry laugh erupted from Val's throat, but it didn't mask the ache from the image of her mother holding Libby, cooing like she had with Connie the day before.

"Hannah and I stopped at my grandmother's on the way here. She'll come if she's feeling up to it. But Momma?" Val shook her head, fighting the tears. "I tried calling her. She still hasn't answered. And Hannah's tried too."

"That's the past," Tate said, stepping closer. "This is a chance to try again. For Libby's sake."

The sincerity in his voice filtered through her, causing her eyes to mist with unspoken emotion. No! She couldn't afford to lose focus. Libby had just suffered a crisis, not a full-blown one, but they'd still been forced to the ER. Her daughter stayed her priority. She couldn't let anything distract her.

"So, do I need to help get things ready at your house?" Soon Libby would be ready for her fruit, but Val didn't leave the sink, unwilling to meet the truth she'd see in his steady gaze.

While she gripped the counter, Tate talked to Libby, encouraging every bite. Val had reached out once to Momma and she wasn't giving up. But for now, that was all she could do. With Tate and his *us* bomb, his parents, Gabby, her family —it was a recipe for disaster, risking her precious daughter. Squaring her shoulders, she blinked back her tears. She would not risk another mistake.

Too much hurt. Too much time had deepened the rift between her family. She'd inflicted too much damage to repair, but she was grateful that he'd tried. Had thought about Libby and her parents—even when she couldn't.

She poured two cups of coffee and grabbed the muffin bag and the jar of pears. Avoiding the way sitting at the small dinette with Tate and Libby felt like a real family, she placed a muffin and his cup in front of him.

"It's not easy standing against your parents." Her flat chuckle sounded hollow in the small kitchen. "I'm kind of an expert on that one. But thanks for offering to host the sessions in your home. I really didn't want to worry about making a mess in your mother's kitchen. I mean..." She waved a hand toward the oatmeal pot on the stove and the splatters on the burner glaring at her. "Look at the way I cook."

Tate chuckled, the rich sound filling the cozy kitchen like it belonged there. "I meant it when I said we're a team," he said. "Team Libby. Whatever she needs, we'll figure it out."

His words struck something in her, making her chest tighten in a way she didn't want to name. A team. The idea comforted and at the same time terrified her.

She swallowed past the lump forming in her throat. "Team Libby," she echoed, her voice quieter than she intended. "I like that."

"Speaking of which." He opened the pears with a pop. "I should probably mention I have a dog."

Surprised and relieved at the change in topic, she met his gaze. "A dog?"

"Hank," he said, his lips curling into an easy smile. "He's a seventy-pound black lab. But he's terrific with kids. Thought you'd want to know before you come over."

"That's... actually great," she said, the tightness in her throat easing. "I've been thinking about getting one for Libby. I mean, dogs are great for kids, right? They're good companions, teach kids responsibility, kindness."

Tate's grin grew, the kind of smile that made it hard to look away. "You'll like Hank. He's loyal, laid-back, and..." He shrugged, the motion casual. "Probably more spoiled than he should be, but don't hold that against him."

A laugh bubbled out of her, unexpected but welcome. For a moment, the image of Libby chasing a dog around the yard filled her mind.

"I'd love to meet him," she said, her words coming easier now, the knot in her chest loosening.

"He's at my place. We can introduce Libby to him before your training." Tate spooned pears into Libby's mouth. "One warning: he's obsessed with his ball. If you throw it once, he'll pester the tar out of you."

She nodded, imagining the scene, a new life for her and Libby. Was Tate right about softening her parents? Hope, an almost forgotten feeling, flickered in her chest—not just for Libby, but for her too.

"Hank sounds sweet."

"He is." Tate paused, his voice dropping. "He got me through a lot. I wasn't in a great place after you left."

She broke off a piece of muffin like she'd broken both of their hearts. "I'm sorry."

"I accept your apology. But it would make it easier for me if I understood your rationale," he said, his tone low but insistent. "I know you think I let Senior's expectations control me. But what happened to force you to make the break then?"

How did she begin to explain something she still didn't understand—at least not all of it. She pushed the muffin, now in a crumbled mess, aside. "Why does it matter now?"

"Because it does." His gaze held hers. "If we're going to do this—really coparent Libby—we have to be honest with each other. No more secrets."

The weight of his words made it hard to draw a breath. Memories of that dreadful time where confusion clouded her thoughts shamed her.

"When—when I look back—" She sipped her coffee, holding it with trembling hands. "I don't recognize the girl who packed up her things and left."

Shame heated her cheeks. Tate would despise her. Think she was unfit. But she was a good mother. She inched her gaze upward, determined to show him she'd changed.

"I felt bad because I made up an excuse to miss your law school graduation."

She could almost imagine the realization dawning in his sharp mind.

"Is that why you came up the weekend before and…" Something flickered in his gaze. Did he still think of that night too? Wonder, like she did?

"Created Libby," she murmured, shaking off the tug inside her. "The Libby part was unplanned. I felt like I was losing you, but I needed to see you, talk to you before I made a decision."

She looked away, hoping he'd say something. But he only

watched her, his emotions unreadable. "You showed me you loved me, but you were still slipping away," she pressed on. "Slipping into what your parents wanted for you.

I didn't regret our night together, but... I felt guilty. One night couldn't make up for your graduation." She shook her head, unable to witness the disappointment in his face. "Glen Falls is a small town. I mean, UVA, Tate. If they didn't have a top sports team, most of us hadn't heard of it."

She glanced up to see if her pitiful attempt at humor had lightened his mood. Nope. But she couldn't read his intensity. She drew in a steadying breath. Just spit it out!

"I know how it feels to want to make your parents proud. The day I earned my welder's certification and Papa hugged me—" Tears blurred her eyes with the image of Papa's smile. "That was pretty great. You deserved that moment. With the way your parents felt about me? I would've ruined it."

"My parents don't get to pick who I love," Tate said, his voice low, encouraging. "I do."

"You tried. But around your parents I felt like I was wearing the wrong clothes at a party I wasn't invited to." A half-sob, half-laugh escaped her. "In the end, my love for you won out over consideration for your parents. At the last minute, I drove to Charlottesville. I was just going to attend the ceremony, congratulate you, and head back. That way your parents had you alone for a day of celebration."

Tate's sudden inhale lifted the hairs on her forearms. "You saw us with Gabby?"

"You and Gabby make the perfect couple. She's everything I'll never be. But more important, don't want to be."

His expression darkened, his jaw tightening. "That was Mom and Senior's doing. They were always trying to push us together. But you knew that. The three of us used to laugh at their efforts."

Although her throat tightened with emotion, she forced

out her words. "I'm a good welder, and I loved working in the family business. I'm also a good mother. Libby's your daughter, but I want her to know the value of a dollar and the pride that comes with earning it."

"So you left," Tate said, his voice flat. "You decided what was best for me without asking?"

"It wasn't like that! I loved you! I could never be the person you needed. Gabby was perfect. I knew she'd make you happy. She's always loved you."

"Wow." Tate shook his head. "That doesn't sound like love to me. You're doing the same thing Senior is—pushing me toward his vision of how my life should be."

Val blinked. No way was she behaving like Earl Carver. Control wasn't love. Then, what? A sickening realization knifed into her and twisted.

She pressed her palms over her face, suppressing the wave of nausea. "You're right," came out on a sob. "I was afraid—afraid in time you'd stop loving me."

She didn't move. Couldn't look at him. Couldn't believe how she'd caused the very thing she'd feared.

And now she had to own her mistake.

She swiped the tears from her cheeks. "Mystery solved. I shut everyone out and kept Libby from the people who would've loved her to protect my childish self."

"We used to talk about everything," he said, his tone soft and filled with...sadness? "What did I do to make you afraid to talk to me?"

"It's not you. I've just always felt our differences, especially around your parents."

"People can change," Tate said. "It doesn't mean it's too late."

"Will you ever be able to forgive me?"

"I didn't think so at first." He worked his jaw, displaying his discomfort.

His words *at first* circled her mind. What did that mean? He despised her but was overlooking his feelings because of Libby? Or...there was still a chance. And if Tate could forgive her..., maybe her parents could too.

"It still hurts." He tapped his fist against his chest. "You didn't trust me. But with Libby, I don't have the luxury of hurt feelings. I will do anything to ensure her happiness."

Although grateful for his love and commitment to Libby, her heart twisted. She'd thrown away what they'd once shared. She'd never be able to reclaim it. But at least they could be friends.

"Thank you for your honesty." She swallowed past the constriction in her throat. "Maybe my family will feel the same way."

"I can't speak for your parents, but I know how I feel about Libby," he said. "There is nothing she could do to make me stop loving her. Would you?"

"Never," Val said. "But she—"

He raised a brow. "Libby can help remind them of that love. We'll start small. The training session at my house is a good excuse to bring everyone together. Hannah can help convince them to come."

Val shook her head, tears spilling over. "I don't know if I can face them. Not after everything that's happened."

He reached out, his hand steady over hers. "You won't have to do it alone. You've got me. And you've got Libby. We'll do this together."

The memory of her last conversation with Papa sent an icy chill through her. She'd dared to believe in second chances that day too. The heartache from that experience hit hard with Papa's remembered word, unwelcome.

CHAPTER FIFTEEN

IT WOULD NEVER WORK!

Tate turned the Rover onto the winding road toward Uncle Rob's cabin, his thoughts turning like Hank circling to make his bed in the cramped passenger seat. He hadn't planned to tell Val he was considering...what? Getting back together? Building a family? He didn't know. Hadn't thought about it enough to even work it out. Yet, the words came spilling out to her.

The craziness had to stop. But combined with his over-crowded schedule to help with Libby, work, and his insomnia, resolution seemed doubtful.

A gurgling sound from his gut drowned out the hum of the engine. Hank blinked at him, and Tate ruffled his ears.

"I got it bad, buddy. This last-minute cabin trip better rescue me. I feel like I'm underwater and going down for the last time."

Hank's tail thumped the seat like he agreed with Tate's assessment. More likely, Hank knew a car ride often ended at Uncle Rob's cabin, and Hank loved running free in the woods.

Located near the boundary to the Mark Twain National

Forest, Tate could reach the cabin in twenty-seven minutes. Perfect for a desperate last-minute getaway. Tate turned onto the dirt road just as the final rays of sunshine cast shades of amber and lavender across the evening sky. Despite the early fall chill, Tate lowered the window, taking in the towering pines that flanked the narrow road, their needles reaching toward the sky.

When the Rover bumped around the final bend in the road, the cabin's silhouette glowed at the forest's edge, the wooden exterior blending seamlessly with the natural surroundings. Uncle Rob, lighting a lantern outside the cabin's entrance, raised his hand.

When Rob opened the passenger door, Hank launched like a rocket, his four paws landing full stride to run zoomies between the cabin and the creek.

"Hank's a tad housebound," Rob said.

"Ya' think?" Tate embraced his uncle, soaking in his steady demeanor.

"Did you get a chance to stop for supper?" Rob turned toward the cabin. "If not, there's chili on the stove."

Tate shouldered his guitar case and closed the door. "Maybe later. Right now, I just want to breathe."

"Life a little complicated in Glen Falls?"

Tate followed Rob up the plank steps leading to the porch, his boots thudding to his slowing heartrate.

"Complicated? A new daughter, a former girlfriend, a broken engagement, and family drama. Why would that complicate a guy's life?"

"Then it's a good thing you stopped by." The entrance door creaked from Rob's push. "You can always hide out here for a while."

Inside, the cabin wrapped around Tate, as comforting as his uncle's booming laugh. Far from his parents' expensive estate and his modern home, the rustic cabin fit him more like his favorite sweatshirt. Every time he crossed the threshold, it whispered welcome home.

A simple building, the log cabin included an open front area, complete with a kitchen, and large sitting area, a single bedroom, a bath, and a tiny loft. However, the most impressive feature, other than the wraparound porch, was the natural stone fireplace, which encompassed an entire wall. This evening a fire blazed in the hearth, filling the room with the scent of pine and wood smoke.

Rob handed Tate a mug of chocolate and waved him toward one of two worn armchairs facing the hearth. "Except for a few frayed edges, you look good. Fatherhood agrees with you."

Too bad, he didn't feel good. "Libby's awesome. The rest of the family?" The fire crackled and hissed much like his new extended family. "Needs serious work."

Rob picked up his cup. "Families usually do. Thus, the reason my brother lives in a fancy estate in town and I live here. The forest suits me. Of course, the Carver drama is old news. So let's hear what's going on in your life."

Tate leaned against the worn upholstery, letting the familiar chair settle his thoughts. "I can't wrap my hands around the changes in life."

"One step at a time works for me." Rob stood and added another log to the fire. Sparks flared and refreshed the pine and smoke scent. "Just start talking. Once you hear the problems, solutions start to surface—most of the time," he added with a wry smile.

Tate raked his hand through his hair, meeting a tangle far less complex than his problems. "I always thought information made decisions easier." Tate shook his head. "Man, did I get that wrong."

While Rob filled his pipe, sending the aroma of cherry pipe tobacco into the cozy room, Tate ran through the events since Val had moved to Glen Falls through the latest issues with Val's parents.

Twenty minutes later, Tate stood and took the now empty mugs to the kitchen. "That just about covers it. Good thing. That's enough for any man."

"Sounds like your life is looping on a repeat playlist with no breaks between tracks."

"Tell that to my earworm that keeps me up all night," Tate said. "That's the real reason I'm here. I came up with a plan, but it's shaky."

"Well, I've made worse decision out of desperation."

Tate paced in front of the hearth. "I have enough problems with our family. But Libby deserves all the love she can get. It's my job to make sure that happens."

Rob leaned forward, a thoughtful expression on his features. "Families are tricky, but I admire you for trying. I wish someone had tried that with our family—before me and your dad got too set in our ways."

"Exactly. Val's convinced her family won't forgive her. I have doubts, so I figured I could use Val's training sessions to bring her family together."

"Val's got backbone and heart in equal measure. That's a rare mix." Rob opened the door for Hank. The big lab lapped water from his bowl and then plopped down at Tate's feet with a groan.

"You made a good pick with him." Rob motioned toward the dog. "The two of you match. People are the same way. You see them together and know they're a pair. I always thought that about you and Val. She adds spice to your life."

"Right now, she's adding spice to everyone in the family. You should've seen Senior bristle when she told him he'd have to learn how to care for Libby. He'd planned to throw money at the problem, same as always. But that didn't fly."

"Sorry I missed it," Rob said. "I love watching someone

take my brother down a notch. It's payback for the way he constantly harassed me growing up. Earl was always right and always the last one to shut up."

A memory of Senior's angry features flashed in Tate's mind, creating a tug at his lips. "It was pretty funny. Senior didn't think so, but he's coming to Val's training. I'll bet Mom had a hand in his decision."

"Connie has more backbone than she lets on."

"Marrying Senior forced her to adapt," Tate said. "I was prepared for the Carver family obstacles. Val's family problems threw me."

Rob rested his elbows on his thighs and stared at the flames like they had the keys to life's problems. "That's surprising. Paul and Deb Reeser seemed pretty laid-back to me, salt of the earth kind of folks. And Paul's the best mechanic around. He's kept my old pickup running for a decade."

"He's also the one keeping the distance between Val and her family—everyone except Hannah. With a little finesse, I think she'll help me convince them to meet Libby."

"Can't imagine that being too hard with Deb," Rob said. "Every woman has a thing for babies, especially grandbabies. Who knew?"

"I never understood the baby attraction until I held Libby. I can't explain it, just like I can't explain why I have to get the Reeser family to the house. But it's going to happen."

Tate laid out the plan details to Rob, who listened without interruption.

"This made perfect sense at two a.m.," Tate said. "Now, it sounds thin. The last time I tried a *thin* case, I lost."

"I'm no expert on family matters," Rob said, humor in his tone. "But if Hannah's willing to work with you, and you get Deb and Paul to the house with Libby? You probably have a shot.

"Deb will take one look at her grandbaby and the feud will be over. Paul's not stupid. An unhappy wife makes a husband's life miserable." He held up his pipe. "Which could be the reason I never married. Anyway, if the old man breaks, the sons will follow. And you'll have a big, happy family."

Tate groaned so loud Hank scrambled to his feet. "I wish. Hannah's been working on Val's mom for months without a breakthrough."

"And you plan to change that?"

Tate nodded. "That's the plan. At least I'm going to talk to Deb and Paul."

Rob relit his pipe, sucking to make the embers glow in the bowl. "Use those courtroom negotiation skills on them."

"I'm giving it my best. There's something else I wanted to run by you." Tate reached for his guitar case resting by his chair. "With all this...drama, my survival instincts kicked in."

He opened the case and removed the acoustic guitar. The smooth surface beneath his palm calmed his galloping nerves.

"When I graduated, I quit playing to focus on my job. But what if a man could do both?"

A slow smile spread on Rob's face.

"I've started writing music again," Tate said. "Care to join me—like old times?"

"Nothing I'd like better." Rob disappeared in the bedroom and returned with his Lowden. "Making music soothes the soul."

Tate plucked the low E string, adjusted the peg, and then strummed a warm chord progression. "Someday I might be good enough for a Lowden, but for now my used Alvarez works just fine. This melody came to me the first time I rocked Libby."

Memories of holding Libby—her warmth, the soft grunts and squeaks she made—took over, guided his fingers over the frets with ease. When the last note lingered in the air, he found his uncle's smile.

"I hear every beat of your heart in the music." Rob mimicked the opening chords, the rich warm tones from the Lowden F-50 filling the room. "Have you started on the lyrics?"

Tate hesitated, not quite ready to leave the wonderful tone or reveal the poignant words he'd attached to his feelings. "They're coming."

Rob nodded, his unruly hair falling over a heavy brow. "Still raw?"

"It's Libby's song."

"I like it," Rob said. "I think it could launch a music career—if you wanted one."

"I've got people depending on me now, so I'm not ready to make the leap. But it's good to know I'm not just blowing smoke."

"Have you got room for me at one of Val's training sessions?" Rob asked. "I need to meet the reason you picked up your guitar again."

"You're welcome any time. Just give me the time and place. I'd also like to bring Val and Libby out here."

"I need to go to Memphis soon," Rob said. "If you're ready by that time, I could run your song by a few folks. As for the cabin, you are welcome to bring Val and the baby here while I'm gone."

Tate's hand dropped to his lap. "Ah, maybe for a day visit. I don't think I'm ready to consider a weekend alone with Val —like a couple."

He strummed another chord, but it sounded offkey.

Rob adjusted his seat to rest one foot on a stool. "Something else on your mind?"

Tate played three chords in a minor key. "I told Val I wasn't sure I could forgive her."

The fire crackled and hissed.

"Problem is...I keep seeing us together—like a family." Tate's thumb stilled on the strings. The words hung, raw and dangerous like they might crack if he repeated them.

He strummed three more chords then looked up. The melody faltered, then found its footing again, steadier this time, like the music said the part he couldn't.

The fire enveloped the log, sending blue, yellow, and red flames around the bark. Heat pressed against him, but it didn't come close to the fire burning the knot in his gut.

"Love's kind of like music," Rob said copying Tate's earlier chords. "A sour note doesn't ruin the song. It just means you need more practice. Libby's a solid reason for renewing efforts with Val."

Although Rob's voice stayed easy, his gaze didn't waver. Tate shifted, sifting through his words again and what his uncle wasn't saying. *Try again?*

"I think it's more than just being Libby's mother," he admitted, pushing his doubts aside and forcing his feelings into words. "Despite everything, I still care about her."

Rob looked up from his guitar. "Has she given you any signs that she feels the same way?" Tate got the feeling his uncle already knew the answer.

"With all of our family drama and Libby's condition, it's hard to tell."

"Helping her reconnect with her family is big." Rob played two more chords. "Shows everyone, especially Val, family's important to you."

Tate's fingers skimmed over the frets in a surge of hope. "I just want Libby to know both sides of her family love and support her. And maybe...," Tate huffed out a breath. "Maybe Val and I can find our way back to each other too."

"You were always the glue in the family," Rob said, his dark eyes shiny with moisture. "Without your love and support, I don't think your mom and dad would have made it after Marshall."

"My golden boy brother," Tate said, relieved for an easier topic. "I wish he was here. He'd probably have some good advice. Things always came easy to him."

"Don't sell yourself short. Marshall knew what he wanted and went after it," Rob said. "You were more methodical. When I first took you fishing, you stood back watching for a long time. Then, you picked up your rod and made a perfect cast. Marshall never waited for instructions. He grabbed the rod, got his line tangled up, figured it out, and cast—just like his dad."

"Marshall liked everything I hated. That's why I was never jealous of him. I was glad Senior spent more time with him. He took the pressure off me." Tate gripped Rob's forearm. "Plus, I had you. Thanks for being there for me."

Rob placed his calloused hand over Tate's. "Nothing has given me more pleasure than teaching you to fish and hunt."

"And the guitar."

"Life can get interesting," Rob said, picking a familiar melody. "But I believe things work out for the best. Me and Senior are more like fire and oil than brothers. Senior was all about the firm and the money and power it brought. I couldn't live that way. But you've done okay."

"It doesn't have to be all or nothing."

"You may be right." Rob stared into the fire. "I worried about you after Marshall passed. You've always been tuned in to other folks—especially your mom and dad. I figured you'd shelve your own dreams, try to stand in where your brother left off."

"I just wanted us to be a family again." Every time Tate thought about how things used to be, sadness followed. "Marshall's accident sucked all the life out of us."

"Marshall was a good kid, but he wasn't you," Rob said.

"I'm working that out."

Rob laughed. "Oh, trust me, I see it. Hear it every time you take on your dad."

"Val had a lot to do with that," Tate said, recognizing the truth in the words. "I thought if she could weld in her dad's shop, I could do something different too."

"Looks like you're making headway."

The fire licked at the logs, making the shadows dance in the cozy room. Hank rolled to his side, stretched, and resettled near the hearth.

An ember of love flickered to a glow in Tate's heart. "Thanks. I'm getting there."

When Hank stood and shook forty minutes later, Tate pushed to his feet. "Looks like the judge just smacked the gavel."

"Sure you don't want to spend the night?"

"No rest for the wicked." Tate embraced his uncle, enjoying the strength in his hug and their bond. "I still need to talk with Hannah. I've just got enough time to get home. She's out with friends and supposed to call in about an hour to go over our big coup."

"Including folks is the key." Rob walked toward the door. "Everyone wants to feel like they belong, like they're needed."

Tate nodded, taking in the advice. "I'll keep that in mind."

"You've got this." Rob gave Tate's shoulder a firm squeeze. "You've always had a good head."

Tate opened the Rover's door and Hank leaped inside.

"Nothing worthwhile is easy," Rob said.

"I think Hannah and I can pull off the family thing, but me and Val...?" Tate slipped into the driver seat, the chilled leather resistant like Val.

Rob leaned against the car door. "Healing and rebuilding trust don't happen overnight."

"I know," Tate said, suppressing the groan that went along

with the knowledge. "It's just hard wondering if she feels the same and if there's a way to fix what went wrong."

Rob reached out, taking Tate's hand in his own. "You're on the right path, son. Just keep following your heart, and everything else will fall into place. Remember, I'm always here to help you navigate through this."

"I appreciate that more than you know," Tate said. "It means a lot to have your support."

He switched on the engine, hoping someday he'd regain the love he'd lost.

Two days later Tate parked behind the Reeser Garage. Although he and Hannah had devised a good plan, Mr. Reeser didn't follow it. Instead of a casual meeting at the Bluebird Café, Paul Reeser insisted the meeting had to take place at the Reeser Garage—with Val's brothers.

"Nothing like meeting on neutral ground," Tate muttered, slamming the Rover's door harder than necessary.

The scent of motor oil and the tang of old rubber filled the building. Overhead, fluorescent lights buzzed and cast a stark glow over the concrete floor, stained with years of oil spills and the stubborn marks of heavy machinery. A stack of tires leaned against the far wall, and an old radio, its speaker crackling with static, played country music low in the background.

Tate turned and hesitated. They were waiting for him.

Hannah stood near the workbench, arms crossed over her chest, offering him a tight smile—forced, but at least an effort. She was the only friendly face. Paul, standing by the hydraulic lift where a rusted-out truck loomed overhead, folded his arms, his posture as unyielding as the steel beams supporting the ceiling.

Tate rolled his shoulders. This place had always felt

foreign to him, with its rows of wrenches and grease-covered rags, a world where hands got dirty and work boots left prints on the shop floor. A world that had once been Val's.

Now, it felt more like enemy territory.

"Papa, I know you're mad." Hannah's voice was softer than usual, but steady. "And I get it. You feel like Val abandoned us. Like she didn't trust you. But that's not the whole story."

Paul didn't answer. Her brothers, Brett and Ruger, stood stiff beside him, their expressions unreadable.

"Val was scared." Hannah leaned forward, urgency pressing into her tone. "She was pregnant, alone, and she thought coming back meant—"

"She thought what?" Paul's gaze narrowed, his glare sharp enough to cut metal. "That I'd throw her out? That her mother and I wouldn't love our own grandchild?"

Hannah flinched and glanced at Tate.

He nodded. Time for him to take over. He turned to Paul, his jaw tight but his voice calm. "Mr. Reeser, if you're looking for someone to blame, blame me."

Paul's eyes snapped to him, cold and unyielding. "I already do."

Tate nodded once. He'd expected that.

"You're right to be angry," Tate said, voice steady. "But you're angry at the wrong person."

Brett scoffed. Ruger muttered something under his breath, but Paul's silence was the loudest thing in the room.

Tate pressed forward. "You raised Val to be strong. To take responsibility. And that's exactly what she did."

Paul's mouth pressed into a hard line.

"She left because she thought she had to." Tate exhaled. The gloves had to come off. He'd either make an enemy or an ally out of Val's dad. "She thought coming home pregnant with a Carver's kid would bring nothing but disappointment and shame. That she'd see it in your eyes, and in the way this town talked about her. She thought she'd lose you."

Something flickered in Paul's expression—a crack in the armor?

"She was wrong." Paul's voice was rough, laced with emotion he wasn't ready to show.

Tate held his gaze. "She knows that now. But she didn't then."

Silence stretched between them. Then, Paul dropped his arms. "Where is she?"

Hannah squeezed Tate's arm, relief flashing in her eyes. Tate didn't smile—not yet. But for the first time, he saw it.

Paul Reeser was ready to open his heart to Val and Libby.

CHAPTER SIXTEEN

GABBY ADJUSTED THE STACK OF CASE FILES ON HER DESK until the edges aligned perfectly, then smoothed her hands over the leather blotter. Order brought focus. Control. Something she needed these days. Growing up in the Standford home had honed her patience, a trait that had always served her well—until this week with the strained relationship with Tate.

Although cordial, he'd maintained a cool distance between them, which was embarrassing. She'd never thrown herself at him and wouldn't start now. Did he believe she'd lost every sense of propriety?

The knock on her door was brisk, confident. Her pulse hitched.

She already knew who it was before she said, "Come in."

Tate stepped inside, his presence filling the room in a way that had nothing to do with his size. He looked like he belonged anywhere he went—like he could walk into a boardroom or a dive bar and command attention. She forced herself to sit back, spine straight, hands folded in front of her.

"Tate," she said in a modulated tone.

"Gabby."

He didn't sit, which meant he wasn't staying long. She held her breath, anticipation curling the edges of her control. It had only been a week since he'd broken off their engagement. A week of waiting, hoping, telling herself that maybe he'd made a mistake. That maybe things weren't working out with Val, and he'd come to his senses.

"Val's giving a training session at my place. It's mainly family—just a casual get-together to introduce our little girl and talk about her condition. We'd like for you to come." He said it gently, his voice laced with something softer than she expected. "I thought... maybe this would be a good chance for you two to talk."

What? Gabby swallowed, pressing her nails into her palm beneath the desk. He wasn't here to reconcile. He felt bad, sure—he was a decent man—but not enough to undo what he'd done. He didn't love her. He never had.

No! She wasn't giving up.

"It's a generous offer," she said, working to keep her voice smooth, practiced. "But I don't think we can undo the time and distance between us."

"Not undo. Review the good things in your relationship and restart." His brows pulled together, concern flickering in his eyes. "You two were best friends since middle school. That kind of history doesn't just disappear."

"I appreciate the invitation." Gabby forced a smile, but it felt like a business transaction—polished, controlled. "I'll think about it."

"I'm sorry about how things ended between us." Tate hesitated. "And I know this isn't what you wanted. But I still want us to be in each other's lives. Not like before, but as friends. Like we all used to be."

Friends? Like a consolation prize? "I'll think about it," she said, forcing down the anger surging through her veins.

He studied her for so long she worried he had sensed her feelings. But Val had been better at that task than Tate. Still, his slow nod wasn't reassuring.

"Alright," he said, his blue gaze still intense, still massaging her heart. "Just wanted to put it out there."

She nodded, a silent dismissal.

When the door clicked shut, she released the breath she'd been holding. She'd hidden her disappointment well. Just like she always had. But disappointment didn't mean defeat. There were still ways to tip the scales back in her favor. And Senior? He had more influence than Tate realized. Perhaps it was time to remind him what was at stake.

CHAPTER SEVENTEEN

AT THE STOP SIGN, VAL CHECKED THE BACKSEAT BABY mirror and smiled. Without a care in the world, her little darling chewed the stuffed giraffe. Safe. No signs of trouble. Today marked her darling's seventh month birthday. Fifty-nine days, seven hours, and thirty-two minutes since her last crisis.

So why did that countdown continue, popping up at random moments in her day? Why did it hitch her breath and stutter her heart like she had to brace for the moment when everything would change again? Because it still could happen with a cold, or a GI upset. Sixty days had been their longest streak. Then July had stolen her peace, followed by the mini-scare with Tate. Now, they were close again. Too close.

She should be celebrating, not generating a new stomach ulcer. But all she could think was—how much longer?

The Honda crept forward, tires snapping gravel under-foot, and came to a halt beside Tate's sleek Rover. Val cut the motor, willing her heart to slow with the faint pings of the engine. The first time she'd pounded on Tate's door, she'd been unaware of the structure. Today, her curiosity took over.

This was Tate's home, the place where he sought safety and solace.

Unlike the Carver estate, Tate had chosen a modern farmhouse nestled on a few acres outside the Glen Falls city limits on the way to Lake Wappapello. The soft gray exterior with its large windows and wrap-around porch suited him. Understated, but comfortable. Perfect for rocking Libby to sleep in the fresh air and sunshine. Which would not happen today.

Training was training. She'd explained the importance of education and the risks with mistakes. Today, she'd provide more details. Besides, she sucked in a steadying breath, Tate's parents were already attached to Libby. They'd be focused on celebrating, not criticizing her teaching hiccups.

"My head's got it right," she murmured, loading her training file into her diaper bag. "It's my stomach that's lagging behind."

She opened the rear door and soaked in her precious sleeping girl. Was there any baby cuter than her Libby, snug in her car seat, her chubby cheeks flushed with the warmth of the sun? It seemed cruel to interrupt her dreams. However, they were on a mission—an important one.

"Here we are, sweetheart," Val whispered, brushing a stray curl from Libby's forehead. The baby's eyes fluttered open, and then she stretched, tiny arms and legs quivering awake before a toothless grin melted her anxieties. "Mommy's going to be a super instructor—just for you."

Val unfastened Libby's harness and tucked her into a blanket to protect her from the chill in the air. Shouldering the stuffed diaper bag, Val swung Libby to her hip and turned to the house. When the scent of wood smoke tickled her nostrils, she scanned the roofline for a chimney.

"Looks like your daddy started a cozy fire for us."

The front door swung open and Tate emerged, his eyes

lighting up at the sight of them. "Good morning," he said, descending the steps to meet them.

"Here we are. It was a scramble, but we're early as promised." Val adjusted Libby, not sure if her daughter's weight or Tate's welcome had unraveled the tension coiled inside her.

Tate held out his hands to Libby. "I've missed my baby girl. Hi, angel."

When Val handed Libby over, Tate's long fingers brushed hers, sending a tingle along her arms. Would she ever get over the sensual awareness of the man? Pushing the sensation aside, she followed him through the carved oak door.

Inside, the house enveloped her in a comforting embrace. The scent of polished wood mingled with a faint hint of cinnamon. The living room stretched out before her, open and airy, without losing its charm and cozy feel. On her right, sunlight streamed through the large front windows, casting a gentle glow on the hardwood floors. However, the stone fireplace with its rugged charm created the room's focal point.

"I'm not sure where you want to set up," Tate said, unbundling Libby with sure confident hands. "There's plenty of seating at the dining table or in here by the fire. Whatever works best for you."

Instead of sitting on the worn leather couch or deep armchair, Tate selected the thick woven rug in front of the hearth. Libby, happy to be unrestrained, reached toward the diaper bag. While Val placed the handouts on the heavy wooden coffee table, Tate gave Libby her stuffed giraffe, which went to her mouth.

"I'd like to introduce her to Hank while you get ready," Tate said. "Sit Libby on your lap and I'll get him."

Val finished with her educational materials, stored Libby's food in the refrigerator, and then settled on the rug, which softened the hardwoods more than she'd expected. Within moments, the sound of thick nails scrabbling against the floorboards filled the silence. Hank and Tate approached them. Although Tate held Hank's harness, the big lab didn't pull against his hold. Instead, the dog moved forward cautiously, his nose twitching at Libby's tiny feet.

Libby sat up straighter and her constant jabber stopped. Val held her breath. Libby dropped her favorite toy and squealed, not in terror but an excited, joyful sound.

"Easy boy," Tate said, holding the dog's harness.

Hank touched his nose against Libby's cheek and retreated, like he was waiting for her to make the first move. Libby waved her arm, patting at Hank's sturdy leg, and the big dog dropped to his belly beside her.

Val couldn't help the smile spreading across her features. "Have you been training him for this?"

"Remember Kurt Allen? He was a few years behind us. He has a two-year-old." Tate ran his hand over the dog's sleek coat. "Hank was a pup the first time he met Kurt's little boy. Hank did the same thing with him. I've never seen anything like it. It's like the dog knows little humans are to be handled with care. I figured he'd be good, but I still wanted to be sure. He's smart, but he's still a dog."

"I appreciate your caution. Gentle, sweetie." Val grabbed Libby's hands and guided them in a smooth stroke down Hank's back. "I hope my presentation goes as smoothly as their meeting."

Libby leaned forward and toppled toward Hank's flank.

The big dog groaned and rolled to his side.

"Hello!" A familiar voice called out near the front door. "Val, Tate? Favorite aunt ready for support detail!"

"Hannah!"

"I've got her." Tate scooted closer to watch Libby.

Val pushed to her feet and met Hannah, relief washing over her like a gentle wave. "Thank you for coming."

"Are you kidding?" Hannah laughed. "I couldn't miss my niece's coming-out party."

"Training," Val said. "And I'm expecting you and Tate to be my star pupils. Tate's parents may be a little...resistant."

"You've got this." Hannah squeezed her fingers. "Besides, look at that sweet face. How could anyone be cranky around that little ray of sunshine—even dodgy Senior Carver. Is that coffee I smell?"

"Help yourself." Tate waved them toward the kitchen. "I think Hank's in love with his new girl, but I want to stay close just to be sure."

Val led the way to the kitchen, where the sleek stainless-steel appliances gleamed under recessed lighting. The aroma of fresh coffee mingled with the scent of baking bread.

"I see you haven't lost your touch," Val said, eyeing the spread on the long island.

"I might have had some help," he said, just as the doorbell rang.

Val's stomach did a flip. "Tell me your parents aren't coming early too?" She just wanted a moment to breathe, talk with her sister, before having to be on her best behavior.

"Caterer," Tate said.

Val placed a hand against her heated cheek. "I've been so worried about the training and the handouts, I hadn't considered refreshments."

"Relax." Hannah touched her arm. "Tate's got it under control. I checked."

Tate groaned. "That was a check? It felt like an interrogation."

"Hey!" Hannah placed her hands on her hips. "That's what sisters do. Val's been a little stressed so I've got her back."

"Thank you," Val said, her chest expanding. "Both of you."

Tate lifted Libby's hands in the air like a cheer. "Team Libby!"

Libby giggled.

Hannah poured coffee into a sturdy mug. But when Libby giggled again, Val hurried back to the hearth to check on her. Tate blew a raspberry on Libby's tiny belly, which promptly jiggled with her laughter. Hank stood and rooted Tate's face.

"He's not sure you're playing with her," Val said, amazed at the dog's behavior.

Hank let out a soft woof. Val barely registered the sound until he nudged her leg. Following his gaze, she turned toward the creak of the door opening.

Hannah stepped through first, her expression unreadable —until she eased the door wider.

Val's lungs failed to expand. The world tilted.

Momma. Papa. Brett. Ruger.

They were all here.

Her vision blurred, her heart slamming against her ribs. She blinked hard, like the movement would clear the impossible sight before her. She'd imagined this moment too many times, but always as a distant hope, never like this. Never real.

"I thought...." Her voice barely made it past her lips. She swallowed hard and tried again. "How...? Who's running the garage? It's a workday."

Momma stepped forward first, eyes glistening. "We had to come meet our granddaughter," she whispered, her gaze locking onto Libby, now nestled in Tate's arms. Her voice wobbled. "She's beautiful, just like you were."

A lump swelled in Val's throat, thick and unrelenting. "Momma?"

Papa shifted, his broad frame tense, his hands shoved deep in his pockets. His jaw worked like he was fighting himself. Finally, he cleared his throat. "We were wrong," he said, his voice rough as gravel. "I was wrong."

The words filled the space, thick with regret and something else—something breaking open inside of her. Papa, the man who had once told her she wasn't welcome, stood here, staring at her like she was his lost little girl again.

"Not knowing what happened to you..." His voice caught, and that single hesitation shattered her.

Her feet moved before her brain caught up. She rushed to him, arms wrapping tight around his solid frame.

His big hands, rough from years of work, settled on her back, holding her like he'd never let go.

"It was awful," he murmured against her hair. "We thought we'd done something to drive you away. Feared the worst. And then when you came back..."

"No, Papa," she choked, shaking her head. "It was me. I should have talked to you."

His arms tightened. "I'm so sorry," he whispered. "I couldn't stand to see your mother so heartbroken. It made me so... angry—until Tate showed up and made me listen."

Tate.

She turned, still wrapped in her father's embrace, and found him watching her, Libby babbling in his arms. There was something in his gaze—tender, but unsure, like he was waiting to see if he'd done the right thing.

"Libby needs her grandparents," he said.

And she needed her family. He'd done this for her. For them.

A strong clap on Tate's shoulder made her snap back. Brett, her once overprotective older brother, stood beside him, offering a firm but wary grin. "We should've known it was this guy." He huffed a breath, sizing Tate up. "Calls himself a fancy lawyer, but he's got more guts than sense."

Ruger, ever the mischief-maker, folded his arms and smirked. "Only reason we didn't flatten him last Thursday is 'cause he's our niece's daddy. Otherwise, he'd be a grease spot under the new tow truck."

Thursday?

Val's brows furrowed, but before she could ask, Hannah tilted her head, her smile sly. "Tate and I might have conspired to enlighten the rest of the hard-headed Reeser clan." She winked. "It was time. Shoot, past time with this stubborn bunch."

Val pressed her palm to her chest. Her heart pounded. Her throat swelled. They forgave her. Were here. And Hannah and Tate?

They were all smiling at her. Smiling? As in happy. The happy family she remembered.

Tate rubbed the back of his neck, offering her a sheepish smile. "I know it was kind of heavy-handed."

A nudge at her hip made her glance down. Hank had positioned himself like a brick wall between Libby and the newcomers, his thick body blocking their approach. A low whine escaped him.

Papa held up his hands in mock surrender. "Any chance we can hold our granddaughter without her attack dog going after us? Your mom's been nagging me ever since Tate's confession."

Val laughed, the sound light and freeing. She scratched Hank's ears. "It's okay, boy."

"He met her ten minutes ago and has already assigned himself to guard duty." Tate handed Libby off to her grandfather and grabbed Hank's collar. "Come on, buddy, let's give them some space."

While Tate led a reluctant Hank toward the back door, warmth enveloped Val's shoulders and a scent of roses and home filled her senses.

Momma.

"I'm so sorry, honey," she whispered, her voice thick with emotion.

Val squeezed her eyes shut and clung to her. "I missed you so much."

Laughter rippled through the room.

"Look at you, little one." Brett held Libby high in the air, grinning as she kicked her chubby legs and babbled at him. "I think we're gonna have to spoil you rotten, you know that?"

Ruger peeked over his shoulder. "And teach you all the mischief your mom used to get into."

Val rolled her eyes, but she couldn't stop the smile tugging at her lips. The weight she'd carried for months—the doubt, the loneliness, the ache—shifted. It didn't disappear, but it lessened, just enough.

"Give me my adorable grandbaby," Momma demanded, reaching out.

Tears blurred Val's vision. This. This was her dream come true.

She turned to Tate, her heart full to bursting. *Thank you*, she mouthed.

It was just a dip of his chin, a simple movement he'd done countless times. But combined with his tender gaze cleared the path to her heart. This man. This kind, generous man had gone to her family and pushed them the same loving way he'd pushed her home. She could suppress it. Deny it. But the love she'd felt for him remained, full and warm.

Libby clapped and giggled as her grandmother kissed her cheek.

They were home.

And never again would they wander from it.

Her daughter would grow up wrapped in love—playing with cousins at family picnics, celebrating birthdays and holidays, knowing she belonged. Knowing she was cherished.

Just like Val did in this moment.

"Granny?" Val looked from Momma to Hannah.

"I reported the breakthrough to her yesterday," Hannah said. "But she decided to sit this one out. Said she'd seen enough family fireworks in her time. However, she expects us to come over next weekend for her four-generation photo."

Soaking it in, Val clenched her fists like she could hold the moment tight and never let it get away. This moment. This feeling. This love.

Outside, Hank barked, and a sleek pearl-white Mercedes Benz rolled to a stop outside the front window. Her happy bubble popped, leaving her shaky. A solid presence warmed her side. Tate.

"We've got this," he murmured.

Val squared her shoulders. Tate's parents were a far greater challenge, but for the first time in months, strength straightened her spine. She stepped forward, ready to embrace whatever came next, and halted.

Behind the Carver Benz, a BMW Z4 Roadster rolled to a halt, its blue metallic coat glistening in the sun. The door opened and Gabby Standford stood, her long blonde hair reflecting the October sun.

"We're on a roll with mending relationship." Tate squeezed her shoulder. "We can't replace the hurts from the past, but we can restart—for Libby and us."

CHAPTER EIGHTEEN

THE SITUATION WAS SALVAGEABLE.

Squeezing her handbag in a death grip, Gabby followed Senior and Connie Carver up the familiar path to Tate's home. The situation wasn't optimum. Success required checking her emotions at the door, just like dealing with Mother. She'd lived twenty-eight years with fear and resentment. Plus, she had Senior in her corner, and he was a formidable ally and opponent.

But with each forward step, memories flashed in her mind, cutting her resolve. A month ago, she'd parked her car in this garage. She'd been the hostess of this home. She'd been the future Mrs. Tate Carver. Now, she followed his parents to the front door like an uninvited house guest.

But it didn't have to stay that way—not if she stayed vigilant.

Seize every opportunity. She'd often despised Father's words. But not when she stood to lose everything. Not today. Besides, she loved children, and she missed her best friend— even though Val had betrayed her friendship. Convincing this small group of people she'd come to reconnect with Val and support Libby shouldn't be a problem. In the meantime, she'd watch and learn.

Fixing a demure expression on her face, Gabby shifted to the right so Val was in clear view. Senior moved closer, almost crowding Val. Her friend's cheek quivered from the strain of her stiff smile.

And there it is. Gabby resisted the grin tugging at her cheeks. Senior's perspective of Val hadn't warmed, probably never would—just like she shouldn't call Val her friend, not after her betrayal.

The Carvers moved inside and she stepped forward. Now, it was her turn.

Gabby met her former best friend eye-to-eye, toe-to-toe, her hours of preparation paying off. Appearance? Perfect. The bow on her white silk blouse flowed perfectly beneath her navy blazer, and her skirt fell to her knee, showcasing slim hips and toned calves.

"I was so glad to hear you're feeling more stable in your new mother role," Gabby said, keeping her tone soft, with a touch of empathy.

"Thank you for coming," Val said, her wary smile emphasizing the fatigue lines bracketing her eyes and mouth. "I hope we'll have time to talk later."

"I'd like that." Gabby swallowed, battling the old memories, the good ones Tate had referenced. How could she still miss Val's friendship? Miss the nights when Val offered support after a miserable struggle with her mother's alcoholism? Miss the way Val welcomed her when the popular girls had rejected her?

Yearning, sharp and unexpected, twisted Gabby's heart. Val had stood beside her during her mother's episodes. Val had listened to her heartaches. Val had supported her when other friends had disappeared. She missed that friend, the friend she never dreamed would betray her.

No! She missed her life with Tate.

Her vision sharpened. Val was watching her with an odd expression on her haggard face. Had she guessed her feelings?

Scrambling to reaffirm her purpose, Gabby turned to Tate's open but cool gaze. His heart had always belonged to Val. She'd known from the beginning, she'd been the stand in. But their friendship could withstand the time test, and he could learn to love her. Had learned, until Val returned. She must show him she could be a good stepmom, and she was the best choice for his family and his career.

"Thanks for coming," Tate said, his polite smile absent the tenderness she'd known and loved.

"You were right to remind me." Gabby glanced between Val and Tate, relieved her voice had the smooth quality she'd practiced. If she could just get him alone, show him they were the best match... "I need a moment to talk later."

Tate shook his head, his gaze touching Gabby's before pointing at Libby cooing at her grandmothers. "Can't today. Daddy will be needed so Val is free to give her presentation and demonstrate how to mix formula, load apps..." He shrugged. "It's pretty complicated."

Gabby nodded, swallowing the thick lump of disappointment. "That's why I rearranged my schedule to come. I want to learn everything I can so I can help care for her. She's adorable."

Thank goodness, she'd always liked kids. That trait would get her through this awkward phase. Besides, Libby bore a strong resemblance to Tate, making her bond and her chances for success easier. Across the room, the grandmothers, Deb Reeser and Connie Carver, were already fawning over Tate's daughter. They also exhibited a stark contrast to the cool professionalism between Senior and Paul Reeser, who kept a respectful yet distant rapport.

Ignoring the room's undercurrents of envy and competition and her own awkward placement in the group, Gabby moved toward her future stepchild, aligning with her in-laws. If the grandparents' mutual affection could bridge the social gap, Libby could also bridge the gap between her and Tate.

Val walked to the hearth, the warm fire glowing behind her. "Thank you for coming today. I'd like to start with the general MCADD information and how it affects Libby.

MCADD stands for Medium-Chain Acyl-CoA Dehydrogenase Deficiency. It's a rare genetic condition that affects how the body processes fat for energy. Most of us can go for hours without eating, and our bodies will break down stored fat to keep going. But for Libby, her body can't do that. Instead of using fat as fuel, her body gets stuck and can't make the energy she needs. That can lead to a dangerous drop in blood sugar—called hypoglycemia—which can happen quickly and become life-threatening if not treated.

"The biggest danger is fasting. When she goes too long without eating, her blood sugar can drop, and her body can't adjust for it. That can cause weakness, vomiting, seizures, and in severe cases, even coma."

A low gasp sounded in the room and Val paused to let the unsettling news sink in.

"A simple cold or stomach bug that makes her stop eating can turn into an emergency fast. So we have to be careful to make sure she eats regularly and protect her from viruses or infections.

"The good news is we have technology to help. Libby wears a continuous glucose monitor a CGM—that tracks her blood sugar. Momma," Val said. "Push up her dress on her right leg so everyone can see it."

Deb Reeser moistened her lips and then lifted the baby's dress. A shudder raced across Gabby's shoulders. Although she'd seen a lot of disturbing things during her years of dealing with Mother's addiction, empathy tugged at her heart. Why did innocent children have to be afflicted with this condition?

"The monitor connects to an app on my phone," Val continued. "So I can see her levels at any time. If her blood sugar starts dropping too low, I get an alert, and we can act fast to get her what she needs.

You might see me checking my phone a lot—it's not for texts or social media. It's how I make sure she's okay. If you're ever watching her and hear an alarm from my phone or her monitor, it means her blood sugar is dropping, and we need to respond quickly.

"I can set the app up on your phone so if she's staying with you or I'm not available, you can check her sugar levels. That's one of the things I'm going to show you. But even with the app, we still need to pay attention to physical signs—if she's weak, cranky, or sleepy when she shouldn't be, she might need food right away. But this gives us another layer of security so we can all work together to keep her safe.

"The most important thing is preventing long periods without food. She has to eat every few hours, even overnight. If she ever gets sick and can't keep food down, we don't wait it out—we take her to the hospital so she can get IV sugar. We also have an emergency plan and a special letter from her doctor that explains to ER staff exactly what she needs.

Here's what you can do to help:

—Never let her skip meals—even if she doesn't seem hungry, she has to eat on schedule.

—If her monitor or my phone alerts us, we need to check her sugar right away and give her fast-digesting carbs—juice, glucose gel, or a sugary drink can help in an emergency.

—If she's vomiting or refusing to eat for more than a couple of hours, call me. We'll likely need to go to the ER.

—Overnight, she has to have a snack or special formula to prevent fasting.

—She always wears a medical ID bracelet, so if anything ever happens and I'm not there, first responders will know what to do.

"As she grows, she'll start learning how to manage her condition herself, but until then, we have to be extra vigilant. She'll be able to do most things other kids do, but we just have to make sure she's eating regularly and getting the right care if she's ever sick. The monitor and app will help us stay on top of things, but technology isn't perfect, so we'll still need to be aware of any symptoms she shows.

"I know this might seem overwhelming but having you all understand and support us means everything. I just want Libby to have a happy, normal life, and with the right care, she can. If you ever have any questions, please ask—I'd rather you ask than worry or guess. Thank you for loving her and helping us keep her safe."

Val paused to give a loving smile to her daughter, still the center of attention on Deb Reeser's lap. "Now, we'll break into two groups to review Libby's monitor and the accompanying app, prepare her formula, and go over her diet."

The slight tremor in Val's voice sent a bolt of awareness through Gabby. Throughout her planning phase, she'd considered conflicting feelings but not this sharp. Val had betrayed her. Why did she continue to mourn the loss of their friendship?

"MCADD can be a little scary at first." Val's voice elevated in pitch, a sure sign of vulnerability. A shiver arced down Gabby's back. This was something she could use.

"I have no medical training, not even in first aid," Val continued. "I haven't been around a baby in years. But a baby with a serious condition? I was afraid to sleep." Val bit her lip and her chin trembled. "I was terrified Libby's blood sugar would spike and I wouldn't hear the alarm. I'm not telling you this for sympathy. I know many of you share those fears, and I'm here to help us all feel more prepared."

When Tate pressed his hand to Val's side, Gabby's gorge rose in her throat. This was too much! She understood Deb Reeser's nod of reassurance. Of course Val's mother had her back, but Connie Carver's quick kiss to Libby's fingers? Enough already. She was Tate's intended bride. Val was an old lover who had produced an heir. Just because they welcomed Tate's daughter into the family didn't mean they had to accept Val.

"This handout should clarify the information I've given." Val passed out a document. "But feel free to ask questions. If I don't have the answer, I have a physician friend who agreed to be on speed dial."

When Val paused, her gaze scanning the family members, Gabby rearranged her features into her best half-smile. The expression had always defused her mother, even on her worst binges. But Val didn't drink, and her former friend had noticed minor nuances about her everyone else missed.

Val held out a paper to her, a small furrow forming between her dark brows. Gabby nodded, holding her breath, praying her signature demeanor hid the underlying resentment churning her belly.

"Perfect," Val said, moving forward. "Let's break into groups. Grandparents first. Momma, Papa, Mr. and Mrs. Carver, please meet on the sofa. Second generation." Val waved at her siblings and Gabby. "We have a lovely brunch set up in the dining area. Enjoy, until it's your turn."

While Senior and Connie sat on the sofa, Gabby joined Hannah, Brett, and Ruger in the dining room. An array of platters holding appetizers, finger sandwiches, and delicate pastries covered the table, with two pitchers of iced tea and lemonade awaiting the end of the assortment.

A pang of sadness settled inside of Gabby. Did they see

her as the pathetic, abandoned fiancé? Her stomach pitched. This was an opportunity, not a pity party. To be successful, she required information. What had happened since Val left Glen Falls? Val's siblings would know those details, and she needed them to feed to Senior.

Gabby picked up a plate and joined the line behind Val's sister. "Libby looks so healthy. Val is doing a super job. But it must be hard managing her health. Is she planning to go back to work in the garage?

Hannah remained open, displaying no shadows of doubt that Gabby had ever noticed in her sister. "You know Val. She's like the world's greatest supermom. I told her to wait, but she is very determined—now that she can return to the garage." Hannah emphasized her statement, giving her brothers a pointed look. "Val's always been strong, you know?"

Gabby added a miniature quiche to her plate. "Yes, she's really something," she said, dropping her voice to a whisper. "She'll need tenacity with Tate's parents. Mr. Carver still looks resistant."

Hannah glanced toward the kitchen where Mr. Carver stood behind his wife. "Senior Carver has always been a legend in his own mind. Val's doing a great job. Plus, she's got an ally. Connie will do anything for her new grand-daughter."

Gabby followed Hannah's gaze. Constance Carver might love her granddaughter, but that would only get Val so far with Senior. Four years working at the firm had given Gabby an inside view of Earl Tatum Carver II. The man was formidable. To him, Val would always be the mechanic's daughter and never good enough for his son. Soon, he'd learn Gabby was his ally.

"I'm so glad you came," Hannah said. "Val missed your friendship."

Guilt twisted Gabby's already shaky stomach. "I've missed her too."

And she had. In truth, Gabby's plan would benefit Val too. Val and Tate could never be happy together. Val had even shared that sentiment with Gabby during their numerous late-night conversations. Although Gabby didn't agree, Senior and Val did. As long as Val held that belief, she could never be happy with Tate.

Tate's low chuckle cut through the hum of conversation. Gabby glanced at the doorway. The late afternoon sun streamed through the windows, casting Tate—holding Libby on his hip—in a golden glow.

Standing by his side, Val smiled, love sparkling in her gaze.

Jealousy, cold and hard, twisted Gabby's stomach and flattened her smile. She sipped her iced tea, but the chilled liquid did nothing to douse the fire burning inside her.

CHAPTER NINETEEN

SHE'D DONE IT!

Val sank onto the worn leather sofa, the fabric soft and familiar beneath her. What a day! If she could muster the energy, she'd pinch herself just to ensure she wasn't dreaming. Like she ever got a full night's sleep.

But hugs from her family had made it all worth it. Despite her doubts, her instructions had gone okay. Everyone, even Tate's parents, had listened, learned. Everyone accepted Libby. Everyone wanted to help keep her safe. The constant pressure that had weighed her shoulders for the past six months shifted. She wasn't alone.

This! With a dreamy smile, she took in the fire's gentle glow flickering across Tate's comfortable and very quiet living room. On a colorful padded mat, Libby slept, her small form curled against Hank, who lay ever watchful by her side.

Val inhaled, letting the scent of burning wood soften her fatigue. In a few hours they'd hit the sixty-day mark. Maybe at seventy, she'd stop counting. She reached for her glass, the deep red liquid catching the light. But after today, after seeing her parents interact with Libby, that shadow felt... smaller.

Lighter. The fear remained. It always would. But it didn't own her anymore. She'd spent too long waiting for the worst. Maybe it was time to start living for the best.

When she lifted her gaze to sip, Tate's watchful expression captured hers. Gratitude expanded her chest.

"Thank you for talking to my parents," she said, her voice barely above a whisper.

"You're welcome." Tate's gaze flicked to the flames. "I couldn't have pulled it off without your sister."

"Hannah's a force of nature. It's awesome knowing she's at my back." But it had been Tate who had pulled it off, and she yearned to show him just how much that meant to her. "I thought today went well."

A chuckle escaped him. "I have this inner sense that detects a 'but' coming. It serves me well in court."

With the warmth in his gaze mirroring the fire's glow, her grin widened. "I just bet it does. Hannah's been working on my parents for fourteen, no fifteen months, without success, which means she had help."

He raised his glass in silent acknowledgment. "Hannah had the inside track. I offered a way to shift the blame away from you."

"So you told them I left because of you?" Val's gaze dropped to her glass. "What did you say?"

"Does it matter?"

"No. What matters is you went to my parents—for Libby."

"And you." Although low, his words were clear, along with the tenderness in his gaze. "When I said we're in this together, I meant it."

Val nodded, afraid she'd be unable to speak past the constriction in her throat.

"Have you ever gotten mad and said things you didn't mean to?" Tate said. "You know, the crazy, illogical anger that churns your gut? Later, once your brain turns back on, you want to make up, but just can't do it? It's like the words just get stuck. That happens with me and Senior." Tate sipped his wine. "More often than I want to think about. Anyway, I figured it might be your dad's problem."

"I guess." But she couldn't remember feeling like that. "I get Papa believing you about an argument. But my continued silence? You must be an awesome attorney to move Papa past that."

"He wanted a reason to forgive you," Tate replied, his shoulders slightly slumped. "I gave it to him."

Her fingers curled around her wine glass when she wanted to curl them through his hair, feel the warmth of his flesh, the brush of his breath against her cheek. Tate's kindness and his generosity of spirit had first attracted her to him. With time, her appreciation for those qualities had deepened into love. Neither had faded. She'd tried to deny the truth. She couldn't stop the feeling.

The fire crackled and Libby stirred, her tiny lips pursed, her hand flexing against Hank.

Love and gratitude expanded Val's chest. Together, she and Tate would keep Libby safe, a far more important goal than her murky feelings. For now, that was enough. She swirled the wine, waiting for her emotions to settle.

"I hope someday I can do something as important for you," she murmured, knowing there was nothing that could repay his kindness.

"Team Libby," he said.

Except it was more than just keeping Libby safe. Val also benefited.

"And Gabby?" The name tasted bitter on her tongue, stirring a whirlwind of old emotions she'd tried to suppress. She loved her friendship with Gabby. Missed it. But even though she'd left Tate, she couldn't get over the fact Gabby had slid into her place. It was irrational, unkind, and unfair. But it was there, and she couldn't seem to shake it.

He took a measured sip, his eyes meeting hers with steady resolve. "The three of us had a great friendship. I don't know if Gabby and I would've worked out. But I knew I missed the camaraderie we once shared. A friendship like that is rare. Why not try to mend it?"

Val shook her head, her heart aching with unspoken feelings. "I can't go back."

Tate turned to face her, his gaze searching. "I'm not suggesting we go back. But we can move forward. We've grown, changed, experienced life."

She tried to smile, but the sadness in her heart made it wobble. "Experienced pain and loss."

He stood, the sofa creaking under his movement, and a pang of regret tightened Val's grip on her glass. She wanted a second chance, wanted him. But not at Libby's expense. Libby needed her father. If she and Tate tried again and failed? A shudder cooled her yearning for Tate. She couldn't risk it.

Tate returned to his seat moments later, holding his guitar with a gentle reverence.

Tears stung Val's eyes. Was he playing again? Were the man and the dreams she'd thought she'd lost surfacing?

He began to strum, the notes filling the room with a melodic warmth that soothed her. The cushions shifted with his motion, drawing him nearer to her. But it was his music that wrapped around her, calming the storm of emotions she'd been trying to contain.

"I always loved hearing you play," she said.

Libby stretched again, her tiny mouth opening in a contented yawn before she nestled back against Hank.

Grateful for a distraction from the buildup of feelings

inside her, Val focused on Hank's liquid brown eyes. "He loves her."

"We all do," Tate replied, a soft smile playing on his lips. "You were great with Mom."

Surprised, Val studied his features to gauge his feelings.

However, the melody had captured Tate's concentration.

"I always thought your mom was kind of...stuffy. But not with Libby. Today, all I saw was love and the same joy I feel when I cradle Libby."

The urge to snuggle her baby to her chest and listen to her faint snores almost drove her to pick her up. But Libby was happy with her new best friend.

"Momma, on the other hand, was totally predictable." The memory curved Val's lips. "I knew she'd suffer insta-love the moment she held Libby. And Papa too. He's a softy beneath that quiet exterior. But your mom surprised me. A very happy surprise."

Tate paused, letting the silence fill the room. He looked down, his fingers tracing the strings before meeting Val's eyes with a sorrowful smile.

"She never mentions it so it's not well-known, but Mom had trouble conceiving after I was born. I don't know why. I just know she underwent IVF."

The softness in his voice sent a shiver of dread through Val. Although she wanted to reach out, comfort him, she couldn't risk it. They were parents, not lovers.

Since he'd bowed his head over the guitar, she couldn't read his expression. After a few soft chords, he glanced up. His watery gaze lanced her heart.

An embarrassed half-smile softened the angle of his jaw. "I don't remember her early pregnancies, but the way she told me..." He shrugged and looked down at his guitar. "The memory still holds sadness. Guess that's why she used a story to explain it."

Anxiety crawled along Val's spine, and it was almost impossible to keep from snatching Libby and holding her.

"One winter evening, Mom finished reading me my bedtime story. I wasn't very old, maybe four or five. Her tears scared me. When she snuggled me close, I remember feeling so safe, like nothing could happen to me. But it was her words that stayed with me. She said, 'Life gives us the toughest trials to make us stronger.'"

Tate played another chord, letting the crackling of the fire absorb the last of its vibrations. "I learned later that she'd lost the second of her two baby girls that night."

Val sucked in a breath, the pain of another's loss crushing her chest in a vise. "No wonder her love for Libby is so intense." The thought of losing a child, losing Libby, gripped Val's heart. "Thank you for telling me. It helps me understand better. But it also sharpens my shame. I never meant to hurt you and your family with my silence."

"I didn't share the story to make you feel guilty. We're going forward, remember?"

"Yes." Val swiped at her tears. "With kindness and understanding."

"She'll be a great grandmother," Tate said over the soft melody he produced with his fingers.

"She already is," Val murmured. "And I'll be sure she knows how I feel and include her in Libby's care often."

"She'll like that."

His hands stilled. When he didn't look up, anticipation spiraled through Val. But she'd learned to be patient with Tate. After a few moments, he captured her gaze, something she couldn't name burning in their depths.

"I've been working on something new. The opening came to me after I held Libby for the first time." His fingers moved over the strings, crafting a melody that lulled Val into a calm she hadn't felt since before Libby was born.

"I put the lyrics to it yesterday. I call it "A Father's Promise.""

IN YOUR EYES, I see the morning light,
    A guiding star through every night.
    With every step, I'll be your guide,
    Forever here, right by your side.

YOU ARE the secret that unlocked my heart,
    Showing me love's a brand-new start.
    With every hug, you teach me grace,
    In your smile, I find my place.

I'LL WATCH you grow with each new day,
    Supporting dreams along your way.
    As you spread wings to soar above,
    I'll wait for you to find true love.

THE FINAL CHORD resonated through the room, and tears stung Val's eyes, blurring her vision. Tate frowned, setting his guitar aside with care. He came to her, catching her tears with the pad of his thumb, then he leaned toward her. His lips, warm and firm, brushed hers—a promise of something more. Val's hands clutched his shoulders with the emotions spilling over.

CHAPTER TWENTY

AND HE THOUGHT HE WAS OVER HER.

Tate shifted, the haze lifting from his mind. He blinked at Val's wide-eyed expression. Uh-oh. Did he pull her onto his lap?

Looked like it—right after he'd kissed her. Man, had he ever.

Based on her mix of wide-eyed surprise and smoky interest, she was still suffering from the same shock and awe exploding inside him. So what the heck did he say now?

She scrambled away leaving a cold unease in her wake. Worse, he missed her warmth. Missed it a lot more than that.

He rubbed his tingling lips with the back of his hand. "That was not planned."

She settled at the end of the sofa, crossing her legs and folding her arms. "It's the guitar. Gets me every time."

"You used to like me to kiss you," Tate said, hoping his heartbeat would return to a normal rate before he passed out. Earlier, a fire seemed like a good idea. He pulled his shirt away from his sticky flesh. Now, the heat felt stifling.

Oblivious to the drama rampaging them, Libby stretched

with a delicate grunt and then resettled in the hollow of Hank's shoulder. His traitorous dog narrowed its eyes like he'd become a threat—more like a bad example. Still, she was adorable. Did she always make those grunts and gurgly sounds or had they disturbed her?

He'd ask Val, but she was still tucked in her corner. If she crossed and uncrossed her arms one more time, she'd probably develop road rash. A grin tugged at his cheeks.

"At least I'm not the only one suffering after effects," Tate said, glancing her way.

Good thing Libby was still asleep. Her mom's frown would probably frighten her.

"Well, it wasn't all me." The slight quiver in Val's voice gave her away.

Although she was making a valiant effort to hide her frustration, the bite of humor painting her voice made him chuckle—so not the way to end a heated kiss. He touched his lips. She hadn't lost her mastery in that department.

Tate gentled his voice to bridge the gap. "Feel safer over there?"

Val's dark gaze sparkled with defiance. "Who said I felt threatened?"

Decision time. Did he lay it out here and now, or continue to suppress what was going through his mind? He snorted. Go for broke.

"The real threat is the feelings we're trying to hide."

"Sneaky little suckers," she said, a wry grin tugging at her bruised lips.

"They sure are." He stretched his arm along the top of the couch, wishing she were closer. "I had noble thoughts at first. I wanted us to be a family for Libby. I was lying to myself. It's not just for Libby. I want us to be a couple—a real couple. So, baby momma, what are our next steps?"

She narrowed her gaze and wagged her index finger at him. She looked adorable.

"There will be no additional steps," she said.

"For a while." He probably should have curbed his playful tone, but a guy had to take a chance once in a while. Besides, he was pretty sure she'd fallen into the self-deceit pit. He'd just emerged a little sooner. Then there was that touch of orneriness in his DNA. No doubt, Libby would inherit it. Maybe his little button could control it. But him? He'd never been able to stop pressing Val's buttons, seeing the tension and amusement playing across her face. Guess some things never changed.

"Exactly." She rubbed her hands together like she'd finished a task. "We're parents."

"Nailed that one." Tate's chest expanded with pride. "We have a beautiful little girl."

"Exactly. And she's sleeping two feet away from—" Val waved her hand back and forth between them. "This."

"She's six months old." Tate laughed, the sound causing Hank's head to shoot up. "My darling daughter has turned my dog into a stranger. Check out his warning look. I bet he's thinking, 'Wake my baby and we're going to have trouble.'"

Tate narrowed his gaze at Hank. "You're forgetting who buys the dog chow in this house."

Val giggled. "Do you always talk for him?"

"You saw his expression." Tate raised his palm in mock surrender. "Reading nonverbal cues is an art. It's a tremendous asset in court. So please, don't look at me like I'm certifiable."

"Hank is the perfect protector and playmate for Libby." Her gaze softened. "I can't believe how fast he bonded with her. Growing up, I had a pup named Bandit. I loved that dog. Now Libby has her best friend."

"I thought we were best friends." Tate got up and sat

beside her. Ignoring the warning look on Val's face, he placed his arm around her shoulder, pulling her close. "I was hoping you'd see me as your protector."

She prodded his chest with her finger, a playful challenge in her eyes. "And playmate?"

He grabbed her finger before she poked him again. "Can't say I'd complain." He studied her, weighing if he should be honest or wait. He'd already wasted over a year.

"I know we can't go back. But I want what we once shared —only better. I've been watching the way you mother Libby. Watching how you handled my parents. You're not the girl I dated in college." He held out his palm to her and she placed hers on his. The weight of her small hand caused a funny sensation on his insides.

"I admire the woman you've become." He rubbed his thumb over her hand. "I want you by my side, raising our daughter together. Not in separate households. Together."

Val stilled, her lustrous brown gaze flickering like she was trying to gauge his feelings, his words, him. The uncertainty in her gaze mirrored his own internal conflict.

"I'm afraid," she whispered.

Her words stung his mind and heart. "Of me?"

She shook her head. "Of what happens if our second chance fails. Libby needs a dad and I need a partner. We've accomplished that. But if we take the next step and fail..."

He stood, unable to remain idle. This was a case he had to make.

"We don't fail." He lifted the brass poker and shifted the logs, sending a shower of sparks drifting up the chimney.

"I've seen my share of divorced couples." He jabbed again. "Some were justifiable due to abuse. But most—most gave up. Gave up on themselves and one another."

He returned to the sofa, holding out his hands to hers.

When her cool fingers touched his palms, he guided her to her feet.

"I'm ready to make a commitment. Right now. No matter what comes up—even the smallest annoyance—we talk it out. It might be embarrassing, humiliating, and scary. For sure, it might be painful. But nothing's off the table. We talk. We listen. We learn. No running away. If you have a problem with me, tell me. Here. Now."

When she released his grip, disappointment almost choked him. But she didn't back away, just kept searching his gaze. When she traced his brow with her fingertip, a tickle shivered along his senses.

"You're very determined," she murmured.

"I have to be—for my daughter." He swallowed. "And for you."

"I love how much you love her," Val whispered. "I'm so thankful I didn't ruin that for the two of you. I'll always be grateful, just like I'll always carry that shame."

"Hey." Tate held her gaze, scrambling for the right words to express what lie in his heart. "No looking back. Focus on now, living our best lives with Libby. I believe in us. So, tell me your reservations."

When she dropped her gaze, he found her hands and squeezed, willing her to be honest with him and herself. But she was looking at Libby, a softness in her expression that twisted something deep in his chest.

"You always had a way with words," she murmured, barely louder than the crackling embers in the fireplace.

Tate rolled his shoulders to shake off the weight pressing down on them. "Didn't need words. Just the truth."

Val lifted her chin, eyes searching his. "And what's that?"

He hesitated, every instinct screaming for him to say something solid, something irrefutable. But all he had was *need*—for this, for them. "We could have this, Val. The three of us. A real life."

"What kind of life?"

Tate frowned. "A family. A home."

Val released his hands. "You mean a house, Tate. A nice one, I'm sure. Big yard, guest rooms for visiting relatives. Probably a country club membership thrown in for good measure."

His stomach twisted. "That's not fair."

"Isn't it?" She met his gaze now, eyes sharp but weary. "I know you, Tate. You love her. You care about me. But you get pulled into things, things you don't even realize."

His jaw tightened. "Like what?"

"Like your cases," she said, her voice low but determined. "Like the pressure to live up to the Carver name. Like expectations you never set but still follow."

His gut clenched because he couldn't tell her she was wrong. His cases were piling up because of his time with Libby. But he was managing it.

Val returned to her place on the sofa. "I love Libby's song. Love that you've found your heart for music again. But one song doesn't change everything. We can't pretend the past didn't happen. That I won't be standing in a house I don't belong in, waiting for you to come home from the firm at ten o'clock every night."

Tate dragged a hand through his hair. "You don't know that."

She tilted her head, something sad and knowing in her eyes. "I do."

A knot formed in his throat, tight and unrelenting. "Then tell me what you do want, because I'm standing here ready to give you everything I can."

Val looked down at their daughter, then back at him.

"Time," she whispered. "Not money, not houses. Just time. To dream, to love, to be together."

Tate swallowed hard.

For so long, he'd fought for what he thought was his future—cases, courtrooms, winning. He'd spent his whole life working toward something that didn't make sense anymore.

But this—Val, Libby, a future with *them*—it did.

His guitar glistening in the firelight drew him. But so did the weight of Senior's expectations, his own choices pressing hard against his ribs.

"I want that too," he said, his voice rough. "But I don't know how to change overnight."

Val held his gaze, something unreadable in her expression. "Then don't promise me forever, Tate. Just promise me you'll figure out what you really want before you ask me to believe in it."

"I'll show you," Tate said, determined despite the weight of her words. But he'd asked for honesty and she'd given it to him.

He returned the guitar to its case, slowing his movements to give him time to brace for the next phase of the conversation. He couldn't back away. This discussion had to happen for them to come out on the other side.

"What else?" he said. He sipped his wine to ease the hoarseness in his voice.

"I've wondered about..." She shook her head before meeting his gaze. "What about Gabby? She still loves you and she's trying. I sense her jealousy towards me."

Tate squeezed his lids closed against the throb in his forehead. "I never loved her like that. I should never have asked her to marry me. I know it now."

He shrugged and glanced at Val, hoping she didn't think less of him because of his confession. "I used her to help me get over losing you. I'm not proud of that. I love her—but never like a man loves a mate. I love her like the friend she's always been. I hope she finds a man who feels about her like..." He paused, knowing it was too much too soon, but couldn't stop himself. "Like I feel about you. Like I've always felt about you."

Val looked away, shaking her head. "I want to go back to work in the garage. "Will you help me with that?"

Work? Tate massaged his temple. He'd ripped out his heart for her. Instead of returning his feelings, she wanted to discuss work. She'd felt something when he kissed her. He saw it. Felt it.

If he had his way, he'd move her into his house today. Make it a home. Then he wouldn't be wasting precious moments with his family driving back and forth. But those weren't the words she was waiting for. He drew a deep steadying breath and nodded. Rebuilding their relationship was like preparing for a full trial, not a quick hearing. He opened the end table drawer and withdrew the thick packet of legal documents. He'd been hoping for a different outcome but had prepared for the worst.

"For now, you don't need to work." He opened the table of contents describing his legal obligations. "I had Xavier draw these up. He specializes in family law."

Val scanned the page and then looked up at him, confusion lining her pretty features.

"Marshall left to meet friends one night and didn't come home. When something like that happens to your brother, it changes you. I prepare for any circumstance." He tapped the documents. "Those papers outline everything I've drawn up for you and Libby. It covers her support, health insurance, life insurance, Libby's educational fund, housing, and transportation, plus unexpected expenses. Xavier's good at his job, very thorough.

"Read it over and let me know how you want me to set up

funding. We can deposit it into your account or set up a trust fund, whichever makes you comfortable. Call Xavier and make an appointment or pick another attorney. I'll pay the fees. I want you to feel financially secure."

"Tate, I—"

"You're the mother of our child. I need to know she'll always be cared for. There's also a provision should something happen to you. Make an appointment to make sure you understand and agree with the terms."

"I don't know what to say. I mean...thank you." Val bit her lip like she had more to say and she wasn't sure how he would handle it. "I still want to return to work. Papa needs me in the garage. I want to help my family."

What about our family? He swallowed the words. A good negotiator understood how to give and take.

"Welding is dangerous," he said, trying to curb the defensive tone in his voice.

"I have a very important little one depending on me." Val's gaze had narrowed and a little v formed between her brows. "I never take my responsibility to her for granted."

No, screamed in his brain. It was too dangerous. Libby needed her mother. His gaze fell on Hank and his little peanut. He had to make this work and fighting Val wouldn't help.

"You have my support." The words scraped his throat, raw as his feelings. "We'll find a nanny."

"Momma won't be happy about that."

"Neither will Grams Connie." Tate tried to mimic the hint of humor in her tone, but his heart wasn't in it.

"They both have lives and families," Val said.

Although true, Tate resisted agreeing. It just seemed—too soon. "Leaving Libby with a stranger—" He hesitated the reality of what he'd said pounding his brain. "Even one—" he gritted his teeth. "Even one you've vetted and trained..."

"Will be challenging for all of us."

How could she be excited? They were talking about leaving Libby with a stranger. A month ago she'd lost her mind about leaving Libby with him.

"Part-time?" Tate cringed. He felt like a little kid begging for a later bedtime.

"I've thought about this," she said.

Although he loved the warm glide of her fingers on his forearm, the gesture didn't reassure him. His office had space. He could set up a crib, take her to the firm with him.

"I'll start one day a week. If Momma or Grams Connie—" She shook her head. "That is too hard to say. Is the name negotiable?"

Who cared about stinking nicknames? They were talking about leaving Libby. And he was losing his mind. Libby had two loving grandmothers. One of them would come through.

"Mom was very clear about Libby calling her Grams Connie," he said, surprised his voice sounded so calm. "Talk to her all you want. I'm out of this one."

"Maybe it's a name that grows on you with time. Anyway, I'll talk to the grandmothers to see if they're available. If they're busy—"

"If one of them can't watch her, I'll take her to the office," Tate said, filtering through the logistics. It would work. Senior might sputter and cause a scene, but he'd get over it. And Max? He owned the smaller share in the firm. Gabby might object, but she'd flex—in time.

"I can't see Grams Connie—" He frowned. The name *was* ridiculous. "Mom might give us a hard time about hiring a nanny. She's wanted a little girl far too long. Be prepared to referee grandma time. Mom might have a hard time sharing." *Please, don't share, Mom. Please.*

Val's laughter sounded in the room. His frown melted. He'd always loved the bell-like quality to it. Always loved the way her smile gave him a light airy feeling. In the meantime, he was being a grouch. And grouches made poor negotiators.

"Our ray of sunshine has many guardians," Val said.

"Thanks for being so understanding with Mom. I know my family can be—"

"Pretentious?" She raised a brow.

"Not as much as Senior."

"I'm feeling generous after that kiss," she said.

The little vixen had the audacity to wink.

His unexpected laughter drew another side look from Hank. "I appreciate your patience," Tate said. "Is there anything else I can do to make your transition easier?" Besides kiss her senseless and coerce her to move in, create a real family. So much for being a patient man.

He hesitated. Based on the shallow wrinkle in her brow, something was on her mind. How much more was there? The discussion wasn't painful. It was brutal, and he'd earned nothing—except for her honesty.

"I want to stay in the cottage," she said.

Tate's breath whooshed from his lungs like she had punched him. Although he followed up with a cough to hide his disappointment, he doubted his ruse worked.

"We have a child together, but we're not married," she said, her words rushed. "You know the Glen Falls gossip line, and Libby's going to grow up here."

"Then marry me." *Way to go, Carver.* Just blow every chance in your life in one fell swoop. Too bad. It's what he wanted. She might as well hear it now.

This time her gasp cut through the silence. However, she made no attempt to hide it. She moistened her lips. "Not until you show me."

He'd agreed to every demand. Wasn't that enough? Tate swallowed his objection. "Can't blame a guy for trying," he muttered, dredging up a wry smile with no humor behind it. "You can set the pace—as long as we move forward."

Her brow arced.

"Got it," he said. "I was born and raised in the Show Me State, too."

"Thank you," she said.

With that fake demure grin on her face, he was surprised she didn't curtsy too.

"What about you?" Val asked. "Anything else I should know?"

"Probably." Tate hesitated. He'd told her he wanted her. Told her he'd never stopped loving her. He couldn't just ditch his career overnight. But they were so close to reconciliation. Don't ruin this chance—Libby's chance for the family she deserved. So no more secrets.

"Okay," he said, hoping his voice didn't betray his nerves. "But don't interrupt. Hear me out until the end. What I'm going to tell you has changed over time."

Val crossed her arms in front of her. "I'm not going to like this, am I?"

"I don't care much for it either," Tate admitted. "But this is full disclosure. Secrets have already cost too much."

Val's features tightened, but she nodded.

"When I got the results from my paternity test, I um... didn't know what was going on with you." Tate cringed at the involuntary pause, but confessing his feelings was harder than he expected. "You'd kept Libby a secret," he said. "And I knew I had to be part of her life so... I prepared to fight you for her." Man, it sounded even worse out loud, but he couldn't stop now. "I didn't know what you'd do next, but I wasn't going to lose more time with her."

Although Val remained silent, her intense frown made every word harder. Based on the narrowing of her gaze, her thoughts were on fast-forward, which didn't give him a warm fuzzy feeling.

"Xavier drew up a custody suit," he said. "Since you agreed to visitation, I didn't file."

"I'm not stupid." Tension stiffened her features, but she didn't seem poised and ready for a battle. "I expected that move. That's why I agreed to move back to Glen Falls."

"I was hoping it was for me," he admitted.

"Oh, it was. Just not for the reasons you'd want." She huffed out a breath. "This straight-forward approach is not for the faint of heart."

Her words removed some of the sting, but Val had always given as good as she got. "I had two choices. Take her and run or move home. I wasn't going to let you take her back to Glen Falls with me in North Carolina."

Tate swallowed the blow. "I underestimated our loss of trust."

Val held his gaze, her eyes probing for a hint of deceit. The room seemed to hold its breath with him, the only sound the soft crackle of the fire and Libby's gentle snores. Libby. His reason to stand firm, regardless of the obstacles.

"We've both made mistakes." Val glanced at Libby and her expression softened. She held out her hand to him. "To our future?"

Tate took her hand, noting the strength in her grip. "We have a beautiful daughter. She deserves all the love and stability we can provide." He kissed her knuckles to convey his commitment. "I want to be there for her and for you."

"For Libby and for us," she said.

Tate laced his fingers through hers, his heart stuttering in his chest at the way they fit together. "We'll build a strong family."

They had to. Because it wasn't just for Libby anymore. He couldn't lose Val again.

CHAPTER TWENTY-ONE

"GOOD MORNING, LIFE!"

Val opened the lacy kitchen curtains to revel in the bright sunshine. Even Mother Nature was celebrating her return to the family business. She stepped into the golden puddles of sunlight dancing on the hardwood floor, her feet tapping with the building excitement galloping in her heart. Did she still have her welder's touch? She curled her fingers into a fist and shook it.

"Mommy's reclaiming part of her life!" She picked up Libby and danced in a circle. Libby giggled and Hank yipped, wagging his tail so hard he'd probably leave a bruise on her leg.

"I still love you and I'll miss you." But she wanted, needed to be creative, productive. "And your daddy made it possible."

She returned Libby to her playmat and her anxious guardian. Hank, the helicopter dog, wanted his baby on the floor near him.

"And I thought I was overprotective," she muttered.

Hank circled and plopped down beside Libby, who patted his broad back and voiced a response in gibberish.

She'd come a long way from the tired, nervous mother who had first entered the cottage. Mercy, and the dreadful pink nursery! But Connie had meant well and adored Libby. True to her words, Connie now asked about their needs before descending on her with an armful of goods—most of the time. At least she'd accepted Val's everyday tastes were okay and respected her working-class roots.

The low rumble of an engine tugged her to the present. She pushed the front window curtain aside, expecting her mom's 4Runner. Instead, a sleek, deep-red Audi Q7 gleamed in the driveway, the metallic paint dazzling against the cottage's weathered sidewalk.

"Stay with her, buddy."

Hank raised his head and thumped his tail once. Libby crawled to his side and fluffed his ear.

Outside, Tate's mother stepped out of the Audi, radiant as ever in a tailored navy blazer and heels that somehow didn't sink into the gravel. She swept up the porch steps, her pumps clicking against the wood, and enveloped Val in a light hug.

"Val, darling!" Connie breezed past her, practically glowing. "I hope I'm not intruding. I know it's Debbie's day, but I couldn't wait another moment. I have the most wonderful idea!"

"Morning, Connie." Val closed the door behind her, struggling to keep the anxiety from bleeding into her voice. "What... idea?"

"A hug from my granddaughter and coffee." Connie flashed a playful grin. "Then I'll tell you." She paused, her face lighting up at the sight of Libby, who had pushed herself up to stand with Hank's help. "Oh my goodness. I can't believe she's already trying to stand. My little darling is much farther along than my boys."

"Your bias is showing, Grams Connie." Cringing at the

awkward name, Val hurried toward the kitchen. "Let me grab you a cup."

By the time she poured the coffee, the sound of tires crunching the front gravel filtered through the room. Momma, right on time. Val typed a text to Papa.

GRANDMOTHER DELAY. Hope to break away in five.

"MORNING, SWEETHEART!" Momma greeted, her practical sneakers squeaking on the polished floor. "Hi, Connie. I didn't know you'd be here."

"Debbie! Look at our angel standing like a little ballet dancer," Connie said. "You're just in time. I was about to share my idea."

While Connie held Libby's hands to balance a few steps, Momma settled into a chair at the kitchen table.

Val focused on pouring coffee in the mug instead of the time on the microwave. Why did they have to review an idea on her first day of work? "So what's this big idea? You've got me curious now."

Libby dropped to the ground and crawled toward Hank, so Connie joined them at the table.

"I've been thinking about something special for Libby." She crossed one leg elegantly over the other. "Libby will always have access to the best care, of course, but other families aren't as fortunate. I've been doing my homework on MCADD. Scientists need more research funding. So, I thought, why not a gala? A fundraiser for MCADD!"

Val froze mid-sip. "A gala?"

"Yes, darling," Connie said, her face animated with enthusiasm. "A formal event to raise money and awareness. We could host it at the country club and have dancing, auctions, and education. It would be perfect."

Val rubbed over the burn in her chest. She'd have to add toast to her breakfast. Her morning joe was eating a hole in her stomach.

The word gala pulsed in her mind like Libby's cries in the dead of night—persistent and impossible to ignore. Although a noble idea in theory, the image of a country club gala turned her heartburn into a blowtorch. No way did she want to walk into the club in her navy sheath, the only nice dress she owned, surrounded by people dressed in designer apparel.

"I know it might sound overwhelming, but it's important. After Marshall's accident..." Connie's voice softened, her expression turning serious. "I've learned how precious life is. I can't bring back my son, but I can make sure other families have hope. And who knows? Maybe we'll fund something that helps Libby's future."

The mention of Tate's younger brother tugged at Val's heart. Libby babbled in the background, a gentle reminder of how much Val had to be grateful for and Connie had lost.

"That's a wonderful idea," Momma said. "There might be other families here in Glen Falls affected by MCADD and not even know it."

Connie's face lit up. "Exactly! I want you both involved. Debbie, you'll bring a fresh perspective, and Val, your insight will be invaluable."

Although Val couldn't suppress her building anxiety about the idea, Connie's words had flattered her mother. Momma's life hadn't been easy, raising four children on a mechanic's wage. Now, her cheeks glowed with excitement. Val didn't have the heart to dampen her enthusiasm.

"I'd love to help. But I've never been part of anything like this before," Debbie said. "It sounds... exciting! Certainly more interesting than cars and car parts," she added with a laugh.

Despite her building discomfort, Val forced a smile. She'd always assumed her parents felt the same way about the economic gap. Was she wrong?

"Well, don't feel pressured." Connie leaned back with her coffee. "We'll start small—just planning a few details. And don't worry about hair or makeup. I'll take care of that. We'll have a girls' spa day. You'll both look fabulous!" Connie tapped a lacquered red nail against her lips. "My only regret is I can't dress Libby for the event. I love shopping for baby clothes."

Though meant to reassure, Connie's words only tightened the knot in Val's chest. Fancy dresses, country clubs, speeches —it all felt too big, too much.

"Hannah would be crushed if we used a different hair stylist," Val said.

"That's perfect!" Connie said, never missing a beat. "This will be the perfect time to showcase her talents. I'll talk to Rolen, my stylist in the Bluff. He's always looking for new talent."

Val shot a nervous glance at Momma, but she was smiling like it was a fabulous idea. But it was only a good thing if her sister agreed.

She made a show of checking her phone. "Gosh, Papa will be wondering what happened to me."

"Don't let me hold you up. And don't angst about the gala." Connie picked up Libby, nuzzling her chubby neck and making her giggle. "I was nervous as a cat in the bathtub at my first event. But this is an opportunity to enhance our darling's future. And maybe for our great-grandchildren."

Val swallowed hard. She couldn't say no to that. And she didn't have time to learn more details. She was already late for her first day of work.

Suppressing the urge to race through the three stoplights in downtown Glen Falls, Val tapped the steering wheel to ease the vice squeezing her chest. Fifteen months had passed since she'd held a torch. Did she still have the skill? She'd been hefting Libby, but that wasn't the same as pulling her weight in a busy garage. Papa depended on her. Reeser Garage needed a good welder. She owed her family so much. She couldn't let them down.

However, the minute she walked beneath the red and white Reeser's Garage sign and inhaled the familiar scent of motor oil and grease, the tension drained from her stiff spine and a smile tugged at her lips.

She was back!

Inside, the clang of tools and hum of conversation welcomed and grounded her after the whirlwind of the past few weeks.

"Welcome back, honey!" Papa's booming voice called across the garage, drawing a few chuckles from the other mechanics. He crossed the shop floor in a few long strides, pulling her into a bear hug.

"I missed you," he said, squeezing her tight before stepping back.

The hands that had comforted her after her first skinned knee, had steadied her when she was learning to roller skate, and had comforted her after her first heartache, rested on her shoulders. His steady gaze looked her up and down like he was making sure she was a living breathing human and not a figment of his imagination.

"I'll tell you this—the part-timer we hired?" Papa snorted. "Couldn't hold a candle to your skills."

"Thanks, Papa." And thank goodness, she'd regained her senses and come home. She couldn't imagine Libby growing up without the love of her grandfather. She placed her hands on her hips with just enough sass to keep from tearing up. "I hope you let him down easy."

Papa chuckled, the sound music to her lonely ears. "I was nice—mostly." His expression turned serious for a moment. "Just be careful, okay? I've never doubted your skill, but accidents happen, and Libby needs her mom."

Val folded her arms, cocking an eyebrow. "You sound like Tate."

"And I bet you set him straight."

"I did."

Papa grinned, clapping her on the back. "Atta' girl. Now, let's get you back to work."

He motioned for her to the far stall, where her equipment had been stored, waiting for her like she'd been gone a few days instead of months.

Val ran her hand over the workbench, her fingers brushing against the familiar grooves and scratches on its surface. Against the wall, tools hung on the pegboard or rested in bins on the floor, everything in its place. Papa handed her a pair of gloves and she tugged them on, the familiar fit empowering.

While she adjusted the tank's gauge, Papa crouched beside her, checking the regulator. The faint hiss of gas from the valve filled the silence.

"So, how's it going...between you and Tate?" he said.

Val twisted the valve shut. "Papa, are you snooping?"

"Of course I am," he said his tone teasing and unapologetic. "A dad is always a dad. Do you still care about him?"

She straightened, grabbing the wire brush and testing its bristles against her palm. "Okay, this is getting personal."

"Wrong answer."

Val leaned against the workbench. "Yes, Papa. I still care about him."

"I knew it." Papa's scowl faded into a knowing grin. "The

man is embarrassing, following you around like a love-sick puppy."

"Shh." Val held up her hand. "Don't let his clients here you say that."

"I've never seen him work a courtroom. I'm just saying when it comes to his heart, he's an open book. He better stay away from the poker table. He'd be cleaned out in a minute."

Val's laugh escaped before she smothered it with her palm. She loved this place. Loved working with her family. Even loved the teasing.

"How long are you going to punish him?"

"Papa! That's harsh. It's not punishment." She busied herself with the tank, readjusting the gauge to avoid Papa's knowing look.

"So if the feelings are still there, what's the holdup? You've made a beautiful baby." He removed her helmet from the shelf and handed it to her. "You guys kind of added a trailer before the hitch, but isn't it time to give my granddaughter a family?"

Val fingered her helmet. If she pulled it on, Papa would get the hint. However, she wanted his opinion, needed it. The stakes were too high to make a mistake. She'd made too many of them and Libby's happiness hung in the balance.

"It's not Tate I'm worried about," she said, relieved to say the words that had circled her mind since her return. "It's how he was raised."

Papa leaned against the wall, crossing his arms over his chest. "You're worried about the garage-country club divide again, aren't you?"

Val shrugged, still focused on the tank. "It's not nothing, Papa. You don't get how wide the gap is."

"Sure I do. But keep one thing in mind." He leaned in. "What other people think doesn't matter. You're a good welder. Best I know. And a fine mother. You love him, right?"

Although the knowledge had hovered at the back of her mind for weeks, saying it out loud felt like standing at the edge of a drop-off.

"I never stopped."

Papa exhaled, tipping her chin up with a calloused hand, just like he'd done since she was little. His love was steady, grounding her in a way nothing else did.

"Then keep it simple, honey. He loves you and Libby. That makes him a good man in my book."

She wanted to believe that. Wanted to grab onto it and hold tight. But love wasn't the problem.

"It's not about love, Papa. It's about life." Her voice dropped, roughened by old wounds. "I need more than promises. I need him to be all in—not just fitting me into the empty spaces of his day."

Papa nodded, taking that in. Then he huffed, shaking his head. "If you love each other, you make it work like me and your mom did. Why do you think she works in the office?"

"But you built your life and the business together. Tate's following the life his parents built for him. The one that doesn't have room for a wife who works with her hands." She turned back to the tank, gripping the wrench tighter than necessary. "I won't be a trophy wife who gets trotted out for firm dinners. I won't let him come home at nine o'clock every night, too tired to see the family he claims to love."

Papa studied her for a long moment before pushing off the wall. "Then don't."

She blinked. "That's it?"

"That's it." He smiled, but his eyes held the same steady conviction he'd taught her to weld with. "Stand firm. He'll figure it out."

The tension in her back and shoulders eased—just a little. She hoped Papa was right.

"There's another thing," she said, thrilled to have his ear

again. "Tate's mom wants to host a gala for MCADD research. A fancy one, at the country club."

Papa's brow furrowed before his face softened. "Sounds like a good idea. Kids will benefit, right?"

"Yeah, but it's...big. And intimidating." She fiddled with a loose thread on her glove. "I told Connie I'd help. Momma's going to help too. She's excited about it."

"Your mom's gonna love it. And I'll be there, too."

"You will?"

"Of course," he said, his tone firm. "I'd do anything for my granddaughter—and for the other kids out there who need help."

The warmth of his words settled over her like a blanket, and Val found herself smiling. "Thanks, Papa."

"Anytime. I'm just happy to have you here." He motioned toward a half-disassembled truck in the next bay. "But you didn't come here to talk about love. That Ford needs a new exhaust system. Let's see if you've still got the magic touch."

Val laughed and turned to her tools, but she still wasn't looking forward to the Connie Carver Show.

CHAPTER TWENTY-TWO

Why'd he have to fall in love with a welder?

Tate leaned back in his chair, the documents of the water rights case scattered before him. The black-and-white text blurred into images of the Reeser's garage. He couldn't shake the memory of a welder case he'd represented in the Bluff—a careless moment with a container explosion had left his client with severe burns and a lifetime of scars. The image flickered like a warning light, and his finger hovered over the call button for Val. His gut twisted. What if—

No. He shook his head, lowering his hand. Calling her wouldn't help. Val could take care of herself. She'd made that clear enough. But the unease didn't budge the stubborn ache lodged under his ribs.

Turning back to the case file, he tried to focus, but the words mocked him. Was his dream to build a life with Val and Libby more like an illusion than a promise? They went through the motions well enough. Every evening, he drove to the cottage after work. Val would either cook or they'd share takeout. He played with Libby, bathed her, read her a story, and tucked her in. But the second he switched off her light, the harsh gavel of reality dropped.

Before he could sink into the sofa, Val had him out the door, always with an excuse—work, errands, a new clinical trial to review, early mornings. Polite, sure, but the truth loomed in the unspoken: would they become a family and if so, when?

Family. The word tasted bittersweet. What kind of family man didn't even have a home for them? His house—large and comfortable—had space for a wife and daughter, and a fenced-in yard for Hank. But without their presence, the structure felt as hollow as an empty tin. Even his dog had abandoned him for Val. If it weren't for his infrequent escapes to Uncle Rob's cabin, he'd have lost his mind.

Good thing he'd returned to music. It anchored him. In the last month, he'd written four songs, each steeped in heartbreak. Uncle Rob thought they had potential—enough for Nashville, even. Considering he'd sacrificed work time to be with Libby, Senior could force him to test Nashville's potential interest. Because he had, in fact, neglected his cases. His clients hadn't noticed, or at least hadn't voiced concerns, but he noticed. At present, he needed a 36-hour day.

A soft knock broke through his thoughts. The door opened and his mother stepped inside, looking poised and polished, as usual. "Got a minute?"

"Sure." Tate massaged his strained eyes.

If he looked at another document, he'd probably worsen his vision. Besides, Mom's visits always promised entertainment, though rarely peace.

"Family meeting." She gestured toward Senior's office, her gold and diamond bracelets clinking together. "I stopped by the Bluebird Café this morning. I've got a dozen of Tiffany's blueberry muffins, still warm. Grab some coffee and let's go."

Tate masked his groan. A family meeting with muffins?

That couldn't bode well. He grabbed his mug, anyway, knowing the bad news would at least come with a sweet distraction.

In Senior's office, the scent of leather and old books clashed with the too-cheerful spread of muffins on the conference table. Although he'd give anything for a break in the manicured garden outside the bay window, he picked up a muffin and bit into the moist cake.

Mom settled into a chair, smoothing her skirt with a deliberate motion. "Before you protest, I've already run my idea to host a gala to benefit MCADD by Val and Debbie Reeser," she began with a bright tone. "It's going to be a fabulous black-tie event at the country club."

The sweet taste of the muffin curdled on Tate's tongue. Just what his budding relationship with Val didn't need—an event to highlight every difference between them. But once Mom got going, there was no stopping her. At least she'd asked Debbie Reeser to help. Plus, the money raised would benefit MCADD.

"Debbie Reeser?" Senior grumbled, shooting his mom a sidelong glance. "They aren't members. Besides, the town's mechanic and his family won't fit in with my associates."

Tate set down the muffin, swallowing to keep his tone even. "The people of this town are the reason Carver & Stanford Law exists. Since the gala would help children from every walk of life, everyone should be welcome."

Senior leaned back in his chair, his fingers steepled together. "That's a nice sentiment, son, but it doesn't reflect reality. People get along when it's convenient. The moment interests diverge, alliances fall apart."

"Libby's doing beautifully," Mom said, her attempt at redirection obvious. "I was with her this morning. She's standing already! Can you believe it? She's going to be a fast learner, just like Marshall."

Tate froze at the mention of his brother. The air thickened, the unspoken loss hanging over the room like a shadow.

"You were such a cautious child." His mother's tender squeeze pulled him to the present, but her laugh rang hollow in the silence. "Thank goodness for that. I was so inexperienced."

"Like that Reeser woman," Senior said, his tone sharper, but there was a tremor in his voice Tate hadn't noticed before. "Did you know Val was so scared after Libby's diagnosis, she couldn't sleep?" He nodded. "Gabby told me that. You know what exhaustion does to judgment?"

"Val's one of the strongest people I know." Although he wanted to rant and rave, Tate kept his tone calm, even. "Gabby hasn't been around Val in over a year so her perspective may be off."

"Are you willing to risk Libby's life on that assumption?" Senior snapped, his voice cold. "We lost Marshall. I won't risk another Carver."

The words struck like a blow, knocking the air from the room. Mom shifted in her seat, her confidence visibly shaken.

"I think you're overreacting," she said, though her voice lacked its usual strength. "Val taught us all how to—"

"And we listened like she was an expert," Senior said. "But Gabby sees what we refuse to. She's fond of Libby, and she loves you, Tate. She's willing to forgive you—despite the way you humiliated her by calling off the engagement."

"I don't love Gabby," Tate said, his temper threatening to give way. "Not in that way."

"Love will come later," Senior said, his tone cool and void of emotion, like marriage was merely a transactional agreement. "Love grows. Gabby's well-educated and understands responsibility. She's steady, reliable—the kind of partner you need. The kind your clients expect. My granddaughter needs a good role model, not someone working in a garage and playing house in a run-down cottage."

Tate rose, the scrape of his chair breaking the heavy silence. "We're done here."

Mom caught his arm. "The gala?"

"It's fine," he said, his voice clipped. "Thanks for including Val and Debbie."

Tate walked back to his office, his footfalls heavy with his father's words. Gabby had managed the practice for over four years. Not one time in her tenure could he remember her having a personal discussion with Senior. So why now? Had Senior raised the stakes, pulling strings Tate hadn't realized existed? And using Marshall's name? That wasn't a memory. It was a warning.

He'd never known Gabby to go behind someone's back. But he'd hurt her. And he'd noticed changes in her. Sometimes she acted like nothing had happened between them—almost like she expected a kiss. At other times, she was distant and almost hostile. It gave him emotional whiplash.

But something was up between Gabby and Senior. Although Gabby's reaction confused him, nothing about Senior's behavior surprised him. His father would do anything to keep his vision of their family intact.

CHAPTER TWENTY-THREE

THE BLUEBIRD CAFÉ'S MORNING RUSH HAD SETTLED, leaving behind the hum of conversation and the soft clink of coffee cups against saucers. Gabby curled her fingers around her mug, grip tighter than necessary. Steam curled upward, fragrant and warm, but she barely noticed.

She hadn't planned to see Tate this morning.

And yet, here he was—standing at the counter, waiting for his coffee, his presence unraveling the control she'd spent years perfecting.

Why did he still have to look like the boy she'd once loved and the man she still wanted?

Tate turned before she could look away.

His brows lifted—surprise, hesitation. He didn't turn away, didn't ignore her. He also didn't rush toward her. That part stung. They were supposed to be easy.

She forced a smile, lifting her mug in invitation. "Sit with me?"

A beat of hesitation—so small most people wouldn't notice, but she did.

Still, he pulled out the chair across from her, setting his

coffee down. She hadn't seen him look so down since after Val left. For a moment, she almost didn't want to play the game.

Almost.

She traced a finger along the rim of her cup. "You look tired."

Tate huffed a quiet laugh, shaking his head. "Thanks, Gabby. Always a confidence booster."

"Just an observation." She let her smile slip into something softer, something that reminded him of who they used to be. "Long night?"

Tate leaned back, stretching long legs beneath the table. But he wasn't warming up to her. Not really. He also wasn't shutting her out.

"Something like that." His gaze flicked to her, unreadable. "Long nights are the new normal these days."

Gabby took a slow sip of coffee, considering her next move.

She could push, make a joke about how easy life could be if he'd just come back to her—where things made sense. But the words tasted bitter before they even reached her tongue.

Instead, she aimed for something lighter, safer.

"Maybe you need a break from the whole serious, responsible thing." She let her fingers brush against his on the tabletop—just for a second. A calculated move.

Tate didn't flinch. But he also didn't move toward her.

Strike one.

Gabby leaned in, dropping her voice to a softer, more intimate tone. "Your father is just looking out for you, you know."

Tate stilled.

Not a full-body shift. Just a fraction of a second, but warnings jangled along her nerves. She'd pushed too far.

His gaze sharpened. "How do you know that?"

Gabby forced a laugh, waving a hand like it was nothing.

"Come on, Tate. I'm the practice manager. Of course I speak with your father."

She needed to stop talking. Now. But she couldn't. Because he was looking at her now—really looking.

She backpedaled. "He just... he cares about your future. About making sure you don't throw away everything you've worked for."

Another mistake.

Tate's gaze narrowed on her. "I never said anything about throwing anything away."

Too sharp. Too smart. He'd caught the slip, and she had nothing to soften the blow.

She sighed, shifting gears, leaning forward like they were lovers again. "You know what I miss?" she murmured, resting her chin in her palm. "Back when things weren't so complicated."

Tate wasn't fooled.

His gaze stayed guarded, but something flickered in his expression—not longing, not attraction. Something else.

Doubt.

Not about Val. About her.

She was unraveling. Losing control of the discussion and the plan. This was supposed to be simple. Tate belonged with her. It was better that way, cleaner, safer. But the weight of that belief rattled, an old printer ready to fail.

Was she fighting for him... or just running from everything else?

She let out a small laugh, reaching for her coffee. "You ever wonder what would've happened if things had gone differently?"

Tate's jaw ticked. "No."

Flat. Final.

She'd lost him—at least in this round.

The regret coiled tight, but she kept her smile in place.

Let him think she was fine. Let him think she hadn't just lost ground.

Tate glanced at his watch, already reaching for his coffee. "I've got to go."

Gabby nodded, keeping her expression light, unaffected. Under the table, her hands clenched. He was slipping away.

But was she pushing him?

BACK AT HER OFFICE, the silence pressed in, thick and unmoving. She straightened her planner with trembling hands, flicking lint from her keyboard. The Bluebird logo on her coffee cup might as well have been a neon sign blinking *FAILURE*.

She should have played it better.

She handled herself. That's what she did. What she was supposed to do. Say just enough. Keep the emotions in check. It was how she'd survived growing up—the calm one, the responsible one, the one who cleaned up the messes no one else wanted to deal with.

And yet, today...?

Control had slipped through her fingers like sand.

Tate's sharp gaze. The moment she slipped. The way his entire demeanor changed.

She'd felt his stare when she passed his office. Heard the soft click of his door, shutting her out.

She lifted her coffee to her lips, but her hand trembled. The sip went down cold, bitter. Irritable, she tossed the cup in the trash.

She wanted Tate. She had to get him back. Didn't she?

Her gaze fell to the minute chip at the edge of her mahogany desk. The answer should have been simple. It used to be simple.

But doubt curled around the edges of everything she thought she wanted.

A life with Tate meant freedom. A clean break. A way out of her family's suffocating grasp. No more late-night phone calls from her mother, slurring apologies she didn't mean. No more pretending her father cared for anyone except appearances.

Tate was her escape.

But what if... he wasn't the right one?

What if she was just running?

A sharp breath hissed through her teeth.

She'd spent so much of her life holding everything together, smoothing over the cracks in everyone else's lives. And here she was, actively breaking her own.

Because no matter how hard she tried to pull Tate back to her, no matter how much she convinced herself that he was the answer—

She was the one sabotaging it.

Gabby rested her face in her hands, forcing back the heat behind her eyes. Tears didn't fix things. She knew that better than anyone.

Instead, she pressed her fingers to her temples.

She'd spent months convincing herself that Tate was still hers to have. That with just the right push, she could erase Val from the picture.

But she couldn't erase what had already happened.

Tate had changed. Val had changed.

And maybe...?

Maybe she was the only one still clinging to something that had never been real in the first place.

Pressure built beneath her ribs, tight and unyielding. The truth had sharp edges.

If she wasn't fighting for Tate, then what was she fighting for?

Her breath stalled, the only sound in the office the low whoosh of the heat pump.

She was fighting for herself.

Not for love. Not for Tate. For a way out.

But a terrifying thought crept in, curling around her ribs, squeezing until it hurt.

What if there was no way out at all?

CHAPTER TWENTY-FOUR

VAL WANTED TO BELIEVE IN THE FAMILY TATE KEPT talking about. Wanted it so bad, her chest ached. But life had taught her that wanting didn't mean getting. And the laptop case stashed behind Tate's seat whispered a warning her heart didn't want to hear.

"How'd the morning go at your grandmother's" Tate asked.

Despite the little voice wondering if the question was more of distraction, a smile tugged at her cheeks. "Perfect. Libby chatted up Granny while Hannah styled her hair." The image sent tears stinging her eyes. "I took a picture of the two of them. I'll show you later." She pressed a palm to her chest. "It still warms my heart. I don't know how I did it, but I captured the perfect moment when they were looking at each other. The four generation photos came out good too. But none of them beat that moment. I'm going to have it blown up and hang it in the living room."

"Some day she'll thank you," Tate said. "I never knew my great-grandmother but Grandma was special."

"Ma ma ma ma," Libby chirped from her car seat.

"I hope the ride doesn't put her to sleep," Val said, keeping her voice light. Tate looked like he hadn't slept in days.

"It's not that long of a ride." He turned onto a two-lane road winding through the hills. "You're going to love the cabin,"

Val angled her visor to catch a glimpse of Hank's ears twitching beside Libby, alert for animals beyond the glass. She exhaled, soaking in the view.

Autumn stretched across the hills in a riot of color. Scarlet and amber leaves shimmered beneath the late sun, dappling the asphalt in golden flashes.

"This is why I love southern Missouri," she murmured, letting the stunning scenery runaway with her imagination. The evening was going to be so much fun: a hike in the fall foliage, dinner by the fire, and maybe Tate would surprise her with a new song.

"Glad you were able to get off early." She rested a hand on the console between them.

Tate yawned and reached for her hand. His touch, warm and familiar, unraveled something in her. She hesitated. She wanted this life—Tate, Libby, the cabin and dog. But the uneasy twist in her belly said something was off. And that terrified her.

When they turned onto the dirt lane, Hank whined and Libby squealed.

"I guess that means she's ready for that hike you promised," Val said, trying to keep the hope from slipping out as fear.

But Tate was quiet. Too quiet, after pleading with her to come.

The cabin appeared between the trees like something out of a painting—wood and stone nestled in golden leaves.

Tate pulled to a stop. "I just need thirty minutes to wrap up some work."

Val's seat belt clicked open, but her fingers stilled.

Work. Of course.

The same laptop. The same folders.

"Hey, Button." Tate kissed Libby's temple. "Daddy bought you a new carrier and Mommy's going to give it a test drive."

Val stepped out, her boots hitting the dirt with a finality she wasn't ready for. "I thought *you* were taking us on a hike."

He popped the hatch. "You can take the short path to the stream. It's marked."

He handed over Libby and a hiking backpack carrier. Hank barked, tail wagging furiously. Libby giggled and pumped her legs.

Val adjusted the straps and whispered against Libby's hair, "It's okay, sunshine. We've got this."

Tate helped settle the carrier against her back, brushing a kiss against her cheek.

"Thanks for understanding. I'll be done when you get back. Then dinner and that lake hike. You're going to love it."

She nodded, repositioning Libby's weight.

Tate reached for his laptop. That was the tether he'd never be able to break. Not when she left. Not even now, when she was standing three feet away with his daughter on her back.

She lingered, waiting for him to glance up and remember this wasn't about a deadline. This was about them. About Libby.

He didn't.

The tightness in her chest squeezed harder.

"Come on, Hank."

The dog barked once and trotted ahead.

Val followed, boots crunching through the fallen leaves. She kept her eyes on the trail, even when everything inside her screamed to turn around. He hadn't even watched them leave.

Six months. That's how long Libby had been breathing air. That's how long Val had been back in Tate's world.

She knew he was trying. But every time she let herself believe in the man who played guitar lullabies, the one she'd fallen in love with—that other Tate showed up. The lawyer. The Carver son.

Hank splashed into the stream, droplets catching the fading sunlight. Val slowed, letting the woods seep into her bones.

Tate should've been here.

She didn't want a fairy tale. Just a real chance. Tonight, she'd wanted more than good intentions.

Libby yawned, her tiny cheek warm against Val's neck.

"Guess we better get back, sunshine."

They returned to a sky painted in indigo. The scent of smoke and something faintly sweet—his cologne, maybe—greeted her. Inside, the fire crackled. Tate slumped on the couch, asleep. Papers on the table. Laptop still open.

Val shifted Libby in her arms. Should she wake him? Lecture him?

Instead, she stepped close. Stray strands of hair clung to his forehead. She brushed them back before she could stop herself. The warmth of his skin beneath her fingers shivered up her arm cracking something inside her.

She pressed Libby's body closer, letting her warmth and the steady rise of her little chest steady her. After a moment the jittery feeling subsided. She laid Libby in the portable crib and turned to Tate.

"You were supposed to be here with us."

He stirred, blinked up at her. "I fell asleep."

She didn't argue. Just picked up his guitar and held it out.

He hesitated. Then took it, tuned, and strummed.

The melody was raw, unpolished. A song without lyrics, aching with emotion.

"That's new," she said.

"It came to me last night."

"You left the cottage at ten. Said you had a brief."

His fingers stilled, then resumed. "I did. The song came after."

"What time?"

"Two a.m.," he said with a faint smile.

"You haven't been sleeping?" she said trying to keep the judgment from her tone.

The music faded.

"Why not, Tate?"

He set the guitar aside. "Two reasons."

Her heart thudded.

"Gabby knew about my meeting with Senior before I told anyone."

Val's brows drew together. "You're sure?"

"I ran into her at the Bluebird and she slipped. I knew it the minute it happened, but didn't confront her. But the way she backpedaled? Nailed her."

Silence pressed between them.

"Senior's up to something," she whispered.

He nodded. "And Gabby's part of it."

Val wrapped her arms around herself.

"And the second reason?"

Tate exhaled and ran a hand down his face. "I don't know who I am if I'm not the Carver heir. But I'm working on that. What I can't figure out is what I have to offer you. And Libby."

The look of misery on his face brought tears to her eyes.

"If I walk away from the firm..." He ran his hand across the guitar and then looked up at her. "Music doesn't come with health insurance."

Val met his gaze. "Team Libby, remember?"

He looked away.

She reached for his hand. "It's not about what you can offer. It's what we can build."

His fingers curled around hers.

The fire popped. Shadows danced.

And for the first time, Val let herself hope that maybe, just maybe, Tate choosing her didn't mean he had to carry the world alone.

CHAPTER TWENTY-FIVE

She just wanted it to be over.

On Gala Day, Val shifted into park and hobbled onto the driveway in her paper flipflops and her terry robe with her name embroidered on the back. Leave it to Grams Connie to adhere to every stinking detail. But it was also Tate's mother who had found the perfect nanny. With Grace in charge of Libby's care, Val could actually breathe—most of the time. That hadn't stopped her from checking on her daughter.

If she pressed the nanny cam app one more time, her index finger would probably drop off. However, the day with the nanny had gone smoother than her day at the spa. She'd never been a spa kind of gal. Long waits made her flesh jitter. A day of waiting? So not her thing, especially with Libby at home with the new nanny.

On the upside? Momma deserved a pamper day, and Val loved watching the bond strengthening between Libby's grandmothers. Her time with her sister? Priceless. If Hannah landed a better salon, the day would be totally worth it—except for the fake eyelashes. Who wanted to peer through paintbrushes?

The warmth of the cottage, with its pine scent and soft glow, welcomed her home. She set her keys on the rustic wooden table, her gaze finding Tate striding from the nursery to the living room. Her heart accelerated. When was she going to get used to her heart palpitations every time she saw Tate?

"Welcome back," he said, moving toward her. He hesitated for a fraction of a second before leaning in to press a light kiss on her lips. She smiled, noting—as always—that brief pause, as if he wanted more but held himself back.

"You came home early," she said, aggravated that she'd given herself away.

His brows raised. "And you would know because—"

"Nanny cam," she admitted, wondering if the foundation the makeup artist had applied concealed her blush.

"How often?"

She narrowed her eyes. He was enjoying the interrogation too much. "How often did you check before coming home early?"

"I'll show you my stats if you'll show me yours!"

His laugh, as warm as the roaring fire, filled the room.

Val backed up to the fireplace. Although the plush terry robe had bundled her in warmth, its thick fibers could not ward off the November chill.

"Thanks for coming home early. How's our girl?"

Tate's face softened. "Grace said she didn't nap today and was a little fussy." His smile widened. "But for Daddy? She devoured her dinner, turned the bathroom into a water park during her bath, and fell asleep before I finished the first page of her favorite book."

Val laughed, placing her bag on the table. "Sounds like you two had quite the evening. I have a damaged finger from punching the app, and of course, she's sleeping peacefully."

"Still not warming up to the nanny?" he asked, raising an eyebrow.

"Grace is lovely, qualified, and very aware of Libby's condition," Val admitted, biting her lip.

"But..." Tate drew out the word playfully, making her grin despite herself.

Val held up two fingers. "One: she's as cold as the frogs we used to catch down at the creek. Two: Libby's been with a stranger all day and now we're leaving for the evening."

"Nothing's going to happen to our daughter with you constantly monitoring the cameras and Hank by her side." But a deep groove in his forehead had reversed his smile.

"I'll feel better once Hank starts speaking human," Val sighed, resisting the urge to ruffle her meticulously styled hair.

"By the way, you look amazing." Tate's gaze lingered on her. "I like that shade of lipstick, but I bet it's a surefire way to stain my shirt."

Her cheeks heated. "Well, we wouldn't want that."

His smile didn't erase the lines creasing his face and the shadows beneath his eyes. She drew her finger along his cheek bone. "You look tired. Rough day?"

"There are two kinds of days at Carver Law: boring and exasperating." He wrapped his hand around hers.

"I've got time to listen if you need to vent."

"Libby took care of that for me." He grinned. "She always does. So how was spa day?"

"Momma loved all the attention." Val infused her voice with a cheer she didn't feel, hoping to lift his spirits. "I can't believe how she and your mom have hit it off. Who knew they'd become best friends?"

"Any time Mom felt down, she'd come back with a new hair color or sparkles on her nails. Froufrou is her thing. If your mom enjoys it too, they'll be best grandma friends."

"They're already planning a shopping weekend in St. Louis before Libby's birthday," Val said.

"That sounds exactly like Mom."

Although the low rumble in his throat didn't achieve his usual chuckle, it was a start.

Feeling the need to unwind, Val headed to the kitchen and poured two glasses of wine from the bottle his mother had left. Handing one to Tate, she leaned against the counter. "So, what at Carver Law has dimmed your spark this evening?"

He took a sip, his shoulders sagging. "It's my water rights case. The Isles and Jones families have been neighbors for years. Yet, they keep butting heads. The legal action has destroyed their friendship." He studied the contents of his glass like it held the answers to his questions. "Days like today make me resent my chosen profession."

She touched his hand, pulling his gaze to hers. "Maybe it's time for a change."

A shadow flickered in his gaze before he glanced at the closed nursery door. "Working on it. But I need to support a very special little girl and her mother."

"I"—Val thumped her chest—"can support myself."

He grinned. "Sassy as ever."

"You bet your fancy Italian shoes."

His eyes widened in faked shock. "You don't like my shoes?"

"It's the price that makes me stutter."

"I can go barefooted tonight."

Despite the cute waggle of his brows, her brain circled the word friendship like Hank preparing his bed before laying down.

"It's strange how things come between friends." She ran a finger over her glossy silver nail polish. "Gabby and I were inseparable through school. Remember skipping study hall to meet at the cave near your uncle's cabin? Our big topic was parental control, but we could talk about anything."

Tate's gaze grew distant. "I remember always wanting to kiss you down there in the dark."

"But you didn't because of Gabby." Val swirled her wine, watching the liquid catch the light. "She was there today. I tried to talk to her—like old times. It felt forced, weird. She's still hiding something."

Although she liked the warmth and weight of his big arm around her, the action didn't dispel the chill of her memory.

"People change," he said.

"Like the Isles and the Joneses?" She pressed her elbow into his side. "Maybe you should invite them to lunch at the Bluebird Café instead of meeting across a conference table."

"Or sit on the porch and strum old songs. It worked for me with Libby's song." He winked, making her heart stutter. "Maybe I'll get lucky again."

"Maybe," She laughed, avoiding the glint in his eye. "I'm sorry. Here I am, unloading my troubles after a spa day when you've had a tough day on the job."

He set his glass down and pulled her closer. "Hey, we promised not to bring work stress into the cottage, remember?"

She gave in to temptation and rested her head against his chest, letting the steady beat of his heart calm her. "And I vowed to leave the past behind. Seems we're both struggling with our intentions."

Hank lifted his head from his spot near the fire, ears perked, and then resettled with a groan.

"Poor guy's exhausted," Val said, glancing over. "He never leaves Libby's side when Grace is here."

"They'll be okay. Hank just needs a nap. Plus, we have the nanny cam." Tate checked his watch. "I better get a move on. The gala starts in an hour."

Val brightened. "No problem. I can fix this. You give the speech tonight and I'll stay home. Hank needs time off."

"Oh no you don't." Tate wagged his index finger at her. "I'm not going alone. It's bad enough I have to wear that monkey suit." He tugged at his collar. "I'm already starting to itch."

"Poor baby." She played an imaginary fiddle. "My heart bleeds for the golden boy who is used to such events. Try navigating in heels for two hours while wearing these." She batted the fans attached to her eyelids for emphasis.

Tate squinted. "Are they heavy?"

"Kind of. Mostly, they mess with my vision. I can't see up."

He moved in close, his breath warm on her flesh. "Can you take them off?"

Only if he'd take off his shirt. Stunned by her thoughts, Val stepped back and tightened the tie on her robe. The makeup had poisoned her brain. She was a responsible mother. He was a long way from leaving the life she despised.

"The makeup artist threatened to find me if I touched her masterpiece before the gala."

"Whoa!" Tate slipped into his jacket. "Pressure. So you'd probably veto sneaking out after an hour? That's about my pumpkin time for a circus. Besides, Mom's the event pro. I swear she thrives on them. The fancier, the better."

"You're forgetting. This circus has a purpose," Val said. "Raising money and awareness for MCADD is important."

So she would put on her gown and give the speech—

Firm, warm lips captured hers. Tate. Before she could draw away, he deepened the kiss. Worries about nanny cams, heels, and public speaking evaporated with the rapid beat of her heart, the curl of her toes into the rug. Heat washed through her body, and her fingers curled into his back muscles.

When they finally parted, her short breaths mixed with his.

She pushed against his shoulders. "Go home and shower."

His grip intensified with his gaze. "My home is here with you and Libby. When are we going to make that happen? I've done everything I can to show you I'm here for you and Libby. We can make this work. It doesn't have to be all or nothing."

She studied his chest, unable to maintain eye contact, unable to speak the words he needed. Despite the slight tremble in her fingers, she loosened his tie and the tiny button beneath it.

"My doubts haven't gone away," she whispered, her voice hoarse. "How long can you keep this up? You're exhausted."

"I wouldn't be if I lived here."

But they both knew that wasn't true. Their trial at the cabin had illuminated the facts. She'd been so hopeful, but hope was starting to fade.

The click of the front door closing jumpstarted her thoughts. Was she asking too much? Libby needed Tate and so did she. But at what price? It might work for two years, maybe ten. But he couldn't sustain the pace, which meant she and Libby would lose out. Hank's cold nose nudged her hand.

"I know boy." She stroked his broad head. "We do it for Libby."

But even after one hour and forty-five minutes, doubts continued to plague her. While Tate held open the Rover's door, Val eased into the bucket seat, her fingers smoothing the lavender silk chiffon of her gown. She pulled the seatbelt away from her dress, praying the tough belt wouldn't snag the fabric. With a little luck and no clumsy spills, she could return the designer dress Connie had insisted on buying for her and use the money as an MCADD donation. If she survived the night.

The thought of Val Reeser—hands-on welder—adorned in an Elena Marquette erupted into a laugh, though amusement and anxiety tinged it.

Tate glanced over from the driver's seat, his eyes warm and concerned. "Everything okay?"

Val took a deep breath, pressing her palms against the silky fabric of the gown. "Oh heck no! I mean, look at me!"

His big hand found hers and squeezed. "I am looking. You look amazing. Mom was so pleased with herself for picking that dress. I know you aren't a fan of galas and ball gowns, but thanks for letting her do this for Libby. You and Libby have made her happier than I've seen her in years."

Val bit the inside of her cheek, swallowing back her frustration. He meant well. Connie meant well. And she *was* grateful. But...

She exhaled, staring down at the shimmering fabric pooled in her lap. "Your mom is wonderful, Tate. She's kind and generous, and what she's doing tonight—raising money for MCADD? It never would've occurred to me. I'm grateful just to be a part of it." She swallowed, rolling her shoulders like she could shake off the weight pressing against her chest. "It's just... hard to feel grateful while pretending to be someone else."

Tate's gaze softened. "You're beautiful."

She glanced down, her cheeks warming. "Thank you. But that's not what I mean." Her fingers smoothed over the intricate beading, delicate in a way nothing in her life had ever been. "I weld metal for a living, Tate. I drive a fifteen-year-old Honda and buy my work boots secondhand when I have to. This?" She lifted a hand, gesturing to the gown, the car, the whole *moment*. "This isn't me."

Tate bumped the turn signal, his mouth twitching. "Well, I still don't know who Elena Marquette is."

A surprised laugh escaped her, easing some of the tightness in her chest. "She's a famous designer—based in Missouri."

He smirked, tapping the wheel. "So technically, you have more in common with her than I do."

Val shook her head, but the tension eased. Tate might not fully get it, but at least he *saw* her. And maybe, for tonight, that was enough.

Tate turned onto the long drive leading to the country club, the streetlights casting a warm glow.

"A famous Missouri-based designer meets the finest southern Missouri welder," he said. "The perfect match."

Val couldn't help but laugh.

"Tate!"

"What?" he asked, a playful smirk tugging at his lips.

Her laughter faded into a wave of unease.

"Stop the car!" She pointed ahead, her finger trembling.

Tate jerked the wheel to the right and hit the brakes, sending Val's weight pressed against the seatbelt.

"What is it? Are you sick? Did you get an alert from Libby's app?"

Val blinked, steadying herself. The unfamiliar sight at the top of the knoll loomed unchanged.

"Does it—" She swallowed hard, a lump forming in her throat. "Does the club always look like that?"

The Rover's dome light gave the moment a surreal feeling.

"I have no clue what *that* means," Tate said, his deep voice edged with confusion.

"It's just... the country club. It looks like Tara from *Gone with the Wind*."

Tate chuckled. "No clue what that means either. Mom's on one of the club's committees. They probably spruced up the place for the gala."

"Those columns and porticos aren't new?" Val said, curiosity replacing her shock.

"No, but they weren't that white before. And I heard her talking about cleaning out the pond. Just don't tell her I said that. It's a reflection pool."

Val's giggle escaped before she could stop it. "Rude! But you impersonating your mom? Classic."

Tate waggled his eyebrows. "Anything to make you smile."

Although meant as a joke, the tenderness in his gaze touched her heart. "Thank you for making me forget how out of place I feel."

Tate lifted her hand and brushed warm lips across her knuckles. "I love you, Val. I'd do anything to make you and Libby happy."

Anything, but leave the firm. But for some reason. the issue between them didn't burn as bright. Her thoughts fogged and her fingers curled. She was Cinderella. His musky aftershave intoxicated her. She pulled him closer without a care to his expensive midnight blue tux.

His breath mingled with hers. Her lipstick would smear. Who cared? She'd wrinkle her gown. So. The slight rasp of his clean-shaven jaw tingled along her fingertips. His lips parted and she was lost in his warmth, his passion, him. When she couldn't draw enough air, she pulled back and nibbled the side of his mouth, cheered by the slight curl to his lip.

Libby would be sleeping when he took her home. She'd ask him in for a nightcap. Wasn't that the usual line? But tonight was the perfect time to talk about their future, to reveal what was truly in her heart, and push him to act—for Libby, for them.

When she pulled back, the ambient light sparkled off his gaze and shadows danced across the angular planes of his face.

"We could skip the gala and just make out in the car like old times." He moved in for another light kiss, teasing her, making her want more.

"We aren't kids anymore." She laughed, trying to regain her composure. "Besides, Tate Carver Esquire, we have an important gala to co-host."

His forlorn look almost made her second-guess her decision.

"Can't charge a guy for the idea," he said.

Five minutes later, Tate led her into a ballroom glowing with twinkle lights. Elegant floral arrangements bursting with seasonal blooms perfumed the space, with the herbal scent of goldenrod and the honey-like scent of asters mingled with traces of aftershave and perfume.

"If this doesn't loosen wallets, I don't know what will," Tate murmured near her ear.

His warm breath sent a flutter of desire, skipping across her collar bones exposed by the gown's sweetheart neckline.

"Are you cold?" Tate pulled her closer. "Want my jacket?"

"And mess up that handsome tux?" She winked. "Remind me to tell you later just how gorgeous you look in your monkey suit."

He grinned, his gaze taking her and her gown in. "I'll sleep in the stupid thing just for another sexy smile like that."

Val straightened her spine and her mouth. "Protocol, counselor. Protocol."

Though she rarely clung to anyone, Tate's sturdy presence comforted her during the meet-and-greet part of the evening. Couples she'd seen at the garage, now dressed in their finery, greeted her. Did they even recognize her from the welder who had fixed their car? They didn't seem to notice the quiver in her voice or the tremble in her hand.

However, she needn't worry about her shaky hostess skills because Connie had mastered Events 101. Dressed in a vibrant emerald-green gown, Tate's mother floated through the crowd, welcoming attendees and suggesting large donations. Unlike his gracious wife, Senior and his partner stood like soldiers at the head of the donation table.

Val greeted her minister's wife and then opened her rhinestone encrusted bag to check the time and the nanny cam. Libby was safe, but the stress and her uncomfortable shoes were draining Val's energy.

She edged toward the front entrance. "If my family doesn't get here soon, they'll miss my speech. Do you think something's happened to them?"

Tate glanced at the entryway, where a waiter stood with a tray of champagne for late arrivals. "Your parents wouldn't miss your speech. They're just smart." He winked. "Come in time for the good stuff and then leave early."

Five horribly long minutes later her parents, her sister, and her brothers and spouses entered the ballroom. While Val's shoulders sank in relief, Tate raised his arm. Momma's grin washed over Val, warm and soft as her favorite nightgown. Unlike Tate and Senior dressed in expensive tuxedoes, the Reeser men wore their best business suits. Despite their lack of black ties, they still cut a sharp image escorting their wives through the crowds. Hannah? Val's fingers curled around her clutch. Her sister had drawn every male gaze in the ballroom. Hannah, her personal style showcased, wore a vintage gown with a modest V-neckline to frame the graceful arch of her neck.

And Momma? Val pressed her hands to her chest. Dressed in a cobalt-blue designer gown rented from an online site, Momma sparkled brighter than the elegant chandelier glittering overhead.

Despite her shoes, Val hurried to meet them.

She hugged Momma close. "You look stunning."

Momma smoothed her hands down her thighs. "I do clean up pretty good, don't I?" she whispered.

"Are you ready for the big speech?" Papa asked. "Because you look great."

Papa looked handsome as ever in his charcoal-gray suit. And her brothers? She hadn't seen them in anything other than their heavy-duty jumpsuits with the Reeser insignia since Ruger's graduation.

Tate extended his hand. "Thanks for coming. I see the ladies have champagne. Mr. Reeser, Brett, Ruger, can I get you a drink?"

"How do you think Sis talked us into dressing up for this show?" Brett said.

While Tate walked to the bar, Val swallowed the lump of pride in her throat. She loved her family. How had she ever left them for so long?

"Thank you for coming. I was so nervous." Val blinked back tears before her makeup had a chance to run. "But with all of you here…I think I'm ready."

"Hey, Sis," Ruger's mouth stretched in his devilish grin. "Do you want us to whoop and whistle or just—"

She punched his shoulder, happy to focus on something besides opening a vein in front of every inhabitant of Glen Falls. "A polite clap will do."

"You're no fun," Brett said.

"What I need is a picture of me with Mom and Hannah," Val said. "Granny will love seeing us all dressed up."

"I can't believe you got that dress from an online rental service," Hannah murmured while Brett snapped the photo.

"Connie sent me a link," Debbie said. "The woman is amazing. There she is. Come on." Momma herded her sisters-in-law to the left. "I want to introduce you."

Val slipped her hand around Papa's arm. "Thanks for coming. It means a lot to us."

Papa patted her hand, his eyes shining with a pride that always made her feel taller, an approval she'd missed.

"Wouldn't miss it for the world." He tapped his chest. "I've got the family donation right here. Do you want to take it?"

"We have a donation table. Senior is manning it." She turned and hesitated. Gabby, dressed in a soft blush pink dress stood between Senior and Max Standford, Gabby's father and the second senior partner in the firm.

"Can you wait until after my speech? I'd like to walk you over." She leaned closer. "I need your strong arm until I speak."

Papa patted her hand and pressed his arm close to his chest. "Right by your side for as long as you need me."

By the time Tate returned with three beers for Papa and her brothers, Connie had approached the podium. Val's heart raced, and she whispered a little prayer for the poise Libby's Grams Connie projected.

Connie raised her hands and the room quieted.

"Good evening, everyone. It's truly an honor to be here tonight in support of a cause so close to my heart. But before we move forward, I want to take a moment to introduce someone who embodies exactly why we're all here.

"When I heard my granddaughter, Libby, had MCADD, panic engulfed me. I remember being plagued with the fear of the unknown and endless questions circling my mind. But more than anything, I remember watching a mother— one who had already sacrificed so much—stand strong for her daughter, even when the ground beneath her felt unsteady.

"This incredible woman has never asked for recognition. She has never once sought credit for the quiet, relentless fight that so many parents like her face every day. But if there is anyone who deserves to be heard tonight, it's her.

"She is not just a devoted mother. She is a fierce advocate, a tireless protector, and the reason Libby is thriving today.

And I can tell you, without hesitation, that my granddaughter could not have been born into better hands.

"So tonight, it is my privilege to introduce someone whose strength, love, and determination inspire me every single day. Please join me in welcoming Valinda Reeser."

Val blinked, Connie's words processing like cold molasses through her mind. Connie thought she did a good job? Had said the words in front of her friends and neighbors. Tears filled Val's eyes and she blinked to dry them. But Connie's praise kept repeating in her thoughts, bolstering her confidence. She was a good mother, and she'd be a good speaker for Libby and for all the mothers who were worrying about their babies.

"Are you ready?" Papa's low voice sounded near her right ear.

Another firm hand squeezed her left arm. Tate.

"You're going to be amazing," he murmured, guiding her to the podium.

Val walked forward, confident in her mission. Near the podium, Tate and Papa stopped, and she continued toward Connie, who embraced her.

Surprised by her tiny mother-in-law's strength, Val returned her fierce hug.

"Thank you," Val whispered.

"They're all yours now." Connie nodded, her smile wide, tears glistening in clear blue eyes so like Tate's. "Tell them how much their support means to Libby."

Val turned to face the audience, her hands steady on the sides of the podium. Although eager faces filled the room to capacity, only the soft clinks of glass filled the silence. Her friends and neighbors waited, the wealthy who wrote the big checks and the ones who earned them. Everyone had come to help.

She drew in a slow, steady breath and ditched the speech she'd prepared. Tonight, she'd recite the words in her heart.

"Good evening, everyone. I'm honored to stand here tonight—not just as a guest, but as a mother, as a member of this community, and as someone whose life has been forever changed by the work we're supporting tonight.

"When Libby was born, I'd never heard of MCADD. I didn't know something as small as skipping a meal could turn lethal. Like so many parents, I thought newborn screenings were just another box checked at the hospital. They aren't."

Val paused for emphasis and found Tate and her family standing proudly to her right.

"That's the thing about MCADD—it doesn't care where you come from. It doesn't care about your last name, what kind of house you live in, or what's in your bank account. It affects families everywhere—in big cities and small towns, in households just getting by and in those who have never worried about money.

"Tonight, when I look around this room, I see what makes Glen Falls special. I see families like mine—hardworking, steady, showing up no matter what. I see families like the Carvers—successful, generous, committed to making a difference. Where we come from doesn't matter. We want the same thing: to give our children a safe and healthy future."

The next thought popped into her head along with a smile.

"When I first walked into this room tonight, I had this old, familiar feeling—like maybe I didn't belong here. I've spent a lot of my life thinking there were two kinds of people: the ones who have the power to make a difference and the ones just trying to get through the day. But standing here now, I know that's not true. Because the only thing that matters tonight isn't our backgrounds, our bank accounts, or where we grew up. It's what we choose to do with the chance we have to change lives."

She pointed to the life-size image of a smiling Libby with Hank.

"My daughter is healthy today because someone, somewhere, cared enough to make MCADD screening possible. But there are still parents out there who don't know they need to fight for this, still babies who won't get diagnosed in time. So tonight, do more than listen. Act. Make sure no parent ever has to hear the words, 'If only we had caught it sooner.'"

Although she couldn't remember a word she'd said, relief nearly melted her into a puddle at the bottom of the podium. Until she noted the hands: one covered in callouses and one soft and pristine.

Both outstretched for her.

"I'm so proud of you," Papa said.

Near tears, she wrapped her arms around his big strong shoulders. "Thanks, Papa. Thanks for making me strong enough to do this."

When she turned, Tate leaned in, his signature scent infiltrating her senses, making her forget the shouts of congratulations. "If you ever question where you belong, remember this moment. Because you are exactly where you're meant to be. And I'm honored to walk by your side."

She turned to him, but the crowd surrounded her with congratulations and encouraging handshakes. Backing away, Tate placed his palms together and gave her a bow before the enthusiastic crowd swallowed him.

Later, when her well-wishers had thinned, Hannah handed her a glass of champagne. "You totally nailed it, but that wasn't the speech you practiced when I styled your hair."

Val sipped her bubbly. "You know me. Living on the edge."

"Well, it worked for this crowd." Hannah tipped her chin toward the donation table. "Check out the line."

"This night is unbelievable." Val pressed her palm to her chest. "I mean me, the person who was losing her stuff, made a difference."

"Of course you did," Hannah said. "You're my sister."

"I hope Papa didn't already donate. I wanted to go with him."

"I don't think so. He was near the bar talking to Ed Salisbury about a piece of equipment. We should all go up together." Hannah lowered her voice. "But that would be overkill. Afterall, we must protect our good name."

"Be careful," Val said. "Senior is your goddaughter's grandfather."

"Don't remind me. But I love Connie. That woman is a class act—despite her husband."

Val turned in a slow circle. On the other side of the room, Connie, her hands animated in a conversation, stood with Momma and Brett's wife. Tate and her brothers stood to the right of the bar, but Papa wasn't with them. When Hannah's friend from the salon joined them, Val excused herself and moved toward the donation table, thanking participants as she threaded through the crowd.

"Val?"

The tension in her shoulders relaxed and she turned to Papa. "There you are. I was afraid I missed your donation."

Papa patted his pocket and lifted his elbow. "Not a chance. You and I are representing the Reeser family contribution."

Although the crowd thinned, only the glittering *Donate Here* sign was visible along the opposite wall. She'd hoped to catch Tate's eye. Her pumps had worn a blister on her little toe, and if she had to live another thirty minutes wearing false eyelashes, she might reenact one of Libby's tantrums.

When the owner of the Bluebird Café and her husband shifted to the left, a sigh of relief whispered past Val's lips. At least Gabby had left her position. Now, only Senior manned the donation table.

"Val, Paul." Senior's booming voice captured her attention. "We've had a lot of donations tonight."

Gooseflesh pimpled her exposed arms, which aggravated her. She'd addressed the entire ballroom and survived. She could handle Tate's dad. After all, he was her daughter's grandfather—a pretentious grandfather, but still a blood relative.

Papa stepped forward, the gray wool of his jacket brushing against her arm. In his hand he held a check with the Reeser logo at the top. "You really know how to put on an event. This was impressive." He placed the check on the table and thumped it with his forefinger. "We're happy to make our contribution."

Tate, a few feet away, waved, distracting her.

"Well, now, that's generous," Senior said. He turned to Greg Lawson, owner of Glen Falls Hardware. "Didn't your truck just come out of Reeser's shop? Maybe you ought to start paying your mechanic a little more—then he could afford a better donation for his own granddaughter."

The words hit like a slap, casual enough to sound offhand but deliberate in their precision.

Val stiffened. A flush crept up her neck while Greg shifted, glancing between Papa and Senior with an uneasy chuckle.

"Paul does good work," he muttered before stepping away, clearly wanting no part of whatever game Senior was playing.

Papa's exhale sounded beside her. A silent warning—*don't make a scene.*

Senior made a show of slipping his own donation into the collection box, then gave Val a small, knowing smile. "I suppose some men take better care of the people they claim to love."

Val's stomach clenched.

He didn't say Tate's name, but he didn't have to.

It wasn't just an insult. It was a reminder.

No matter how much time passed, Senior would always see her as the girl Tate left behind—the one who'd chosen a life that didn't measure up.

Her chest burned, a simmering rage bubbling beneath the polished surface of her borrowed sophistication. Senior had taken something generous, something given in love, and reduced it to a dig at her father's success—and a fresh stab at her own choices.

She bit her tongue, forcing herself to look away before she did something reckless.

Then she saw him.

Tate.

Not alone.

Gabby stood at his side, clutching his arm, her smile wide and bright as the diamond on her finger.

Champagne sloshed in Val's stomach. "Déjà vu," she murmured, her voice hollow. Tate and Gabby together—just like at his graduation.

"Thanks for hosting the party," Papa said, jerking her attention back to the table. "I'm sure the amount raised will help the kids."

Val turned, forcing her feet to move, stepping away from the table, from Senior's cool indifference, from Gabby's smug smile. Papa squeezed her arm, a quiet reassurance that should have settled her. But instead, it nearly shattered her.

He wouldn't say a word about the slight. He never did. That was the Reeser way—work hard, hold your head high, and don't let the rich folks in town make you forget your worth. Her throat tightened.

"I better find your mother," Papa said, his voice as steady as ever. "We've got a full schedule tomorrow."

Val nodded, but her mind was still stuck on Senior's casual dismissal, on the way Gabby curled against Tate like she belonged there. She turned toward Papa, desperate for something real to hold on to.

"Would you mind giving me a ride home?"

Papa's eyes widened, but he nodded. "Always have room for one more Reeser."

She tightened her grip on his arm. Tonight had given her a glimpse of a dream—one where she could belong in this world, where she and Tate could find their way back.

But dreams were illusions. Reality was the weight of Senior's disdain, the way Tate's world had already moved on without her. And tonight, she was done pretending otherwise.

CHAPTER TWENTY-SIX

Had Val walked out without a word again?

Tate pushed open the cottage door, the hinges creaking in the silence. Hank scrambled across the hardwood, nails clicking in a frantic rhythm before his sturdy body slammed into Tate's legs. A chuckle rumbled in his chest and he bent to rub the dog's smooth head, the familiar press of warmth easing the tension knotting his shoulders. At least someone was happy to see him.

Then, his gaze lifted.

Val stood in the doorway, one hand braced on the frame, her expression unreadable. No welcoming smile, no softened stance—just cool detachment, like a stranger deciding whether to let him inside. The warmth in his chest didn't just fade; it curdled, leaving behind the raw, hollow ache of what he'd lost.

"It's late," she said, her voice quiet but firm. "I was just going to bed."

"I won't stay long," he said, stepping forward, but he was going to have his say.

She didn't block him, but she didn't invite him in either,

her slippered feet pivoting toward the living room in reluctant retreat. He followed her to the couch, where she curled into the farthest corner, legs tucked beneath her. The fire crackled in the hearth and shadows danced across the room in rhythm with the tension stretching between them.

"Any problems with Grace tonight?" Tate asked, keeping his tone neutral.

Val shook her head, her gaze on the flames. "She knows I monitor the nanny cam."

Tate sat on the edge of the couch, his elbows resting on his knees. Silence. Really? After she'd left the gala without him?

After waiting as long as he could stand, he turned to her, softening his voice. "You could've told me you were leaving. I looked everywhere for you."

Her head snapped toward him, and her gaze, dark with frustration, locked on his. "I didn't see a point in staying somewhere my family wasn't welcome."

Tate blinked, her words hitting him like a sucker punch.

"Excuse me?" he asked, lowering his voice to keep Hank from whining again. "I checked on your brothers a couple of times —they were having a good time with their friends."

"I wasn't talking about my brothers," Val said, her tone clipped. "I was talking about your father."

Tate scrubbed his hand over his face. What had Senior done now? "Senior can be a jerk. That's not a secret."

"I've come to expect that from him," Val said, her voice flat. "I didn't expect you to stand there and say nothing."

His gut twisted, a slow, ugly squeeze. Her family had seemed fine, smiling, enjoying the event. The only hiccup? Right before her speech. He'd walked her to the podium with Paul. She'd been pale, nervous—but once she started speaking, her words had been so heartfelt they nearly brought tears to his eyes. He hadn't noticed anything else. Had he missed something?

She stood, walked toward the fire, and turned on him, her hands fisted at her hips. Firelight caught the hard lines of her face, and his stomach sank. Whatever had set her off—it was big.

"I said nothing... when?" he asked, wary.

"When your father belittled Papa," Val's voice rose, raw and steady. "And my family. A week ago, that would have crushed me. But I'm proud of them." She paused, her gaze narrowed. "Papa has worked twelve-hour days to provide for my family. While he wore tattered clothes and patched boots, we never went without. He built a reputation in this town on hard, honest work. So I expected you to react. But you didn't notice the insult because it's normal for you. That's when I knew."

Panic coiled in his gut, a slow, creeping fear he hadn't felt before. "Your dad's a great guy and an even better mechanic," he said, scrambling for a positive approach until he learned the details. "He's also a great dad and grandfather."

Val folded her arms. "One thousand dollars is a lot of money for my family. Brett and Ruger have kids to support. Hannah and Jeremiah want a house. Someday Momma and Papa hope to retire. They were proud to support the benefit, and I was proud of their support."

"I didn't see the donation, but I'll be sure to drop by the garage and thank them."

"No need." Although her voice held steady, her eyes glistened with unshed tears. "They don't need your approval and neither do I."

"Look, Val." He swallowed past the thickness in his throat.

"No Tate. I need to say this," Val said. "When I moved

here, I resented you and your family. But I was willing to make sacrifices to create a home for Libby."

She swiped at a tear and Tate's heart twisted.

"You told me I was where I needed to be. You were right. I am in a good place," she said, tapping her chest. "I don't have to fit into your world with the fancy clothes, foreign cars, and big homes. I like who I am. Your mom was right too and her words helped me own my value. I'm a good mother. When she gets older, Libby will see that. She'll be proud of me, like I'm proud of my parents. But our homes will always be separate."

Tate's lungs burned for air. "Val." His voice came out hoarse. "I've done everything possible to let you choose. The cottage. Your job. The nannies. Everything. I know my work is still an issue, but I thought it was getting better. I thought you were choosing me."

Val shook her head, and whispered, "I thought I was too. But I can't keep choosing someone who won't stand up for me."

"It's just Senior." Tate hated the desperation creeping into his voice. "Mom doesn't feel that way and neither do I. You know that. I'll speak to Senior."

She nodded, and hope sparked in his chest.

"If you're so committed to me, why was Gabby clinging to you and showing off an engagement ring?"

Tate stood. So, she'd seen it. He should've known.

"It's not what it seems. I was going to tell you, but I didn't get a chance. I called off our engagement just like I said. But Gabby didn't want a formal announcement and I didn't see a point in humiliating her. Tonight?" He raised his hands, trying to make her understand. "She said she wanted help with her mother. I had no idea it was a show like we were still engaged."

Val held his gaze, the pain in her eyes cutting deeper than any words could.

"This isn't working for me." Her voice broke, cutting him to the bone. "I love you, Tate. But love isn't enough when respect is missing."

The crack of the fire punctuated his ragged breathing. He lifted his hand to reach for her. Her gaze narrowed, the flat steady stare drilling into him. His fingers curled in defeat. She'd already made up her mind.

CHAPTER TWENTY-SEVEN

CAREFUL TO ENSURE THE HEAVY OFFICE DOOR DIDN'T SNAG her tulle and organza gown, Gabby entered the firm. At least at one a.m. the office staff were not present to witness her shame. Anger, an emotion she worked hard to suppress, bubbled in her empty stomach.

How had she been blinded with desperation? Tate loved Val. His actions tonight had made his feelings clear to her and everyone else who attended the gala. She blinked back a tear for her loss, and for Val and her heart-felt speech, and moved forward.

Her heart pounded with the rhythm of her blush pumps clicking against the polished law firm floors, the sound too loud in the otherwise quiet space. She gripped her matching clutch and sucked in a deep breath. You can do this. For a little girl she barely knew. For Tate. For a friendship she missed. For yourself.

The door to the conference room stood ajar, and Senior Carver's sharp, commanding voice carried through the crack.

"This suit is non-negotiable, Max," Senior said. "Tate's too weak to do what needs to be done, but I won't let him ruin everything this family has built for some mechanic and her kid."

Gabby froze just outside the door, her breath catching. Time to stand up for herself and for her friends—if she still had them. She placed her hand against the cold wood and shoved.

Silence. Senior, his face red and eyes blazing, stood at the head of the table. Her father sat across from him, calm but tense, his hands folded in front of him. Both men turned toward her, their expressions a mixture of irritation and disbelief.

"What's the meaning of this intrusion?" Senior demanded, slamming his hand on the table.

"Gabriella," Father said, his tone edged with warning. "This isn't the time."

Gabby stepped into the room, ignoring her wobbly knees and lifting her chin. "It's exactly the time. I'm finished. I'm not going forward with my part."

"You're already in it," Senior said, trying to glare her into submission.

"Not after tonight!" She hated it when her voice came out sharp and shrill, but it couldn't be helped. "Not after hearing Val's speech. Seeing Tate—" But she couldn't say the words. It was bad enough she'd witnessed his love for Val. She didn't have to point it out to Senior and Father.

"She abandoned my son in front of the entire town!" Senior drained his bourbon and slammed the heavy glass against the desk with a thud. "Made him the laughingstock of Glen Falls. I'm done waiting. This suit will shake some sense into him."

The hard, determined creases in his face combined with his harsh tone stilled her breath in her chest. He was going to go forward with the suit—without Tate.

She glanced at Father, but he was still staring at his hands.

She focused on Senior. "You can't go forward with the suit without Tate..."

"It's for his own good." Senior poured an inch of bourbon into his glass. "Marshall understood how the real world worked. Tate's always been a dreamer. He'll resist. But once the dust clears, he'll see this is best for our family and my granddaughter's future."

"What he gets is he's in love with Val Reeser," she said, emphasizing each word so this narrow-minded man would understand. "I saw the way Tate looked at her when she addressed the audience, saw the panicked look on his face when he couldn't find her. He's probably with her right now."

Senior straightened in his chair. "He thought he was in love with a music career too. But I made him see he couldn't make a living with it. Now, look at him. He's a pretty good lawyer—when he's thinking straight."

Gabby's vision cleared, like she'd removed reading glasses that were too strong for her. Tate had been thinking straight all along. Senior had used her as a mere pawn in his outrageous plan. Even Father, an excellent family attorney, knew the suit wouldn't work—not without Tate. Yet, he was going along with it—just like she had.

The clasp on her clutch bit into her flesh, but she didn't loosen her grip. She'd enabled them, just like she'd enabled Mother. But it stopped now! Despite the shame heating her cheeks and the pitch in her stomach, she slipped Tate's engagement ring from her finger.

Time to create her own path. A path where she honored herself and her friendships. First and foremost, Tate and Val were her friends—at least they had been.

Gabby placed the diamond solitaire on the desk's polished surface, its sparkle thwarted in the soft light. "The charade is off. If necessary, I'll testify in court. Tell them the whole thing was a sham."

Senior pushed his chair back and rose to his full height, towering over her. "You think you can walk in here and tell me how to handle this?" His voice boomed, vibrating through the room. "You're nothing but a spoiled little girl. Leave before you embarrass yourself."

Gabby flinched but stood firm. "I've already embarrassed myself enough by trying to do what you wanted." Her voice cracked, but her words carried strength. "I won't do it anymore. Val is a good mother. Far better than any of us. Besides, this isn't about protecting Tate or Libby. This is about control. You're punishing Tate because he chose a partner who doesn't fit into your perfect family picture."

Senior took a step toward her, his finger jabbing the air. "Don't you dare speak to me like that!"

Father stepped between them. "That's enough," he said, his voice sharp, commanding. "Let me handle this."

Senior's glare darted between hers and Father's before he stepped back. "You'd better handle her," he said, his voice still low and dangerous. "Or I will."

"Gabriella, my office," Father said, his jaw set, his tone clipped. "Now."

Gabby spun around to face him, braced for battle. "You're really going to let him do this? You're going to jeopardize your license and this firm by helping him drag Val through a custody suit based on lies?"

"Max?"

Father raised his hand to Senior and then turned back to her. "You don't understand the full picture."

"Oh, I understand just fine," Gabby said. "The suit has nothing to do with Libby's safety. It's about him"—she jabbed her finger in Senior's direction—"controlling Tate and punishing Val. And we were going along with it. Me, out of desperation and saving face, and you because of the good ole boy system. Is that system worth everything you've built?"

"Do you have any idea what's at stake here?" Up close, fatigue lined Father's features. Her mother's addiction was taking its toll on him too. "This firm, our reputation, our entire future—"

"You mean *your* future and his. Not mine. And certainly not Mother's."

Father stiffened, his expression darkening. "Leave your mother out of this."

"No," Gabby snapped. "Mother and her addiction have imprisoned both of us."

"She was getting better," Father said, his voice a harsh whisper. "For the first time in years, she was herself again. But the second Tate broke things off, she started spiraling. She was supposed to help at the donor table at the gala. Do you know where I found her? Passed out in the backseat of our car! I arranged for a driver to take her home.

"Now, pick up that ring so we can fix this. Your mother will be okay tomorrow," Father said, his voice softened with his returning control. "Once she hears your wedding is still on, she'll continue planning for it. She told me tonight the country club would be the perfect venue for your wedding."

"She's an alcoholic, not blind." But there was no emotion in her tone. Control had returned with her final decision—a decision she should have recognized the day Tate left for North Carolina.

"Now, if you gentleman will excuse me, I have plans to develop for my life." Gabby stopped on the threshold. "I'll draft a personnel ad for a new office manager. I've always wanted to travel."

Senior chuckled, slow and smug. "You're threatening me? Sweetheart, by the time I'm done, everyone in this town will know exactly what you did. That you strung Tate along, tried to force him into marriage when he never loved you." He sat back, smirking. "That you're nothing but a bitter, jealous woman who can't stand to see him with Val."

Gabby's stomach turned and heat crawled up her neck. He was going to paint her as the villain. And worse—people would believe it.

Father steepled his hands and met her gaze. "You know what, Senior? Maybe you have a point."

Her breath caught. No. No, not him too.

Father straightened the black silk bow tie at his throat. "I've been too soft on you, Gabby. Paid you twice what most office managers make. Covered for you when you needed time off for Alexa. I wanted you to succeed, but I see now I've only coddled you." He shook his head. "If you don't understand the importance of loyalty, maybe it's time you learn it from someone else's firm."

Her heart plummeted. "Father—"

"No." His voice was calm but firm. "You made your choice. Now, I'm making mine."

Senior's smirk widened as Father pulled out his phone, tapping something on the screen. "Karen can take care of the ad for your position when she draws up the termination paperwork first thing Monday morning. You'll have your severance by the end of the week." He met her gaze, unreadable. "You're smart, Gabby. You'll land on your feet. But not here."

Senior lifted his glass. "Tough lesson, kid. But necessary."

Gripping the edge of the conference table to steady herself, Gabby swallowed hard. This was real. She'd stood up to them, done the right thing—and lost everything in the process.

But as she turned to leave, the familiar weight that had pressed her into submission for years, lifted. No more lies. No more playing a part in their schemes.

She was free.

Even if she had no idea where to go next.

CHAPTER TWENTY-EIGHT

SUNDAY AFTERNOON BROUGHT IN FRIGID TEMPERATURES and a wintry mix of snow and sleet. Tate slowed the Rover, his mind still spinning from his decisions like his tires on the slickened asphalt. If Val still loved him, he had a chance—a slim one, but he'd take any opening he could. When he arrived at Uncle Rob's doorstep last night after his altercation with Val, he'd been a sorry mess. Uncle Rob, as always, offered a safe haven.

This morning his path lay as sharp as his headache from sleep deprivation. He'd never try to control Val like Senior exerted control over him, but he could be her friend. He could be a good parent to Libby, and he could be a better man —but first he had work to do.

When Juanita told him his parents had left early, he turned toward the office. Mom was probably out with church friends but Senior? The man inhabited three places: the house, the firm, and the courthouse, a life he'd been imitating —until now.

When he wheeled into the parking lot and parked by Senior's black Benz, his heart thudded in his chest. It wasn't rapid. It didn't skip a beat. It pounded as steady as Val's voice. *I love you, Tate. But love isn't enough when respect is missing.*

Last night Val had lost respect for him, and he'd lost respect for Senior. For so long guilt had kept him silent. His family had suffered a devastating blow with Marshall's death. However, fifteen years had passed since the accident. While he and Mom had struggled, they'd emerged on the other side. Grief, bitterness and loss had consumed Senior—still did.

His grandfather, the firm's founder, had built the practice to defend working people, to protect their rights and ensure they weren't trampled by big-city lawyers or corporate greed. But Senior had lost the firm's vision and become a bully, wielding control like a weapon. Today, Tate would serve as the reminder.

Inside the building, Tate opened the heavy door to Senior's office.

"Did you find her before she bolted with my granddaughter?" Senior didn't bother lifting his face away from the document on his desk. "That woman isn't stable enough to raise a child."

Ignoring the bait, Tate stepped inside, letting the door swing shut with a solid thud. "Val and Libby are at the cottage," he said, his voice calm, devoid of emotion. "Glen Falls is their home. They aren't leaving."

Senior lifted his head, the heavy fall of his white hair shifting over his furrowed brow. However, there was distance in his gaze, like his thoughts were elsewhere.

"Hmph." He touched a photo of Marshall with a trembling finger. Then he shook his head and refocused on Tate. "Are you finally ready to measure up to your responsibilities? Something you've been neglecting lately. You've been so busy trying to please that woman you haven't settled the water rights between Isles and Jones."

Tate crossed the room and planted his hands on the edge of the desk. "I have a meeting with them tomorrow."

Senior scrolled through the firm's scheduler. "You'll have to hold it in your office. I've already booked the last opening for the conference room."

"We're meeting for breakfast at the Bluebird Café."

Senior ran his hand through his silver mane, his gaze narrowing. "We adhere to protocol at Carver Law, you know that! Is this your way of rebelling against the rules your grandfather established?"

"Not at all," Tate said. "This is me acting as my clients' counselor and friend. I've known the Isles and Jones families since I was in grade school. They've forgotten about their friendship. I'm going to help them find it over biscuits and gravy."

Senior's jaw tightened, his eyes narrowing. "Don't screw it up. You've been pretty lax lately. Don't think I haven't noticed. Leaving early, coming in late looking like you were out with *her* all night. But you better think long and hard about your caseload and your responsibilities to your daughter. Libby needs stability—Carver stability. Something that woman can't provide."

A sharp pang of pity knifed through Tate. Was there anything he could do to help this bitter shell of a man? He drew a steadying breath. Senior needed more than he or his mom could provide.

Tate placed the envelope on the desk. "That's my resignation. It's effective tomorrow at close of business—after I settle the water rights case."

Senior's face darkened, and for a moment Tate worried his dad might be having a stroke or heart attack. "You think you can walk away from this? From everything I've built? You're walking away from your legacy and your daughter's future."

Tate squinted. He didn't even recognize the man in front of him. "I'm not Marshall. I can't replace him. I never could."

Senior stood, pointing a trembling finger at Tate. "What would you be without me? I stopped you from throwing your life away on music. Don't think I've forgotten that ridiculous phase of yours."

"That wasn't a phase."

"No?" Senior sneered, his voice laced with sarcasm. "You wanted to run off and become some kind of starving artist, like my brother Rob. Look what that got him."

"Are you talking about happiness?" Tate turned but hesitated at the threshold. Heavy grooves lined Senior's face. All he had was his bitterness and his loss. "I hope someday you can revive yours."

CHAPTER TWENTY-NINE

VAL LOVED HER JOB. LOVED THE METALLIC ODOR. LOVED being a part of the family business. Just not today. Although she knew she'd made the right decision, she'd never prepared for the horrible emptiness losing Tate caused.

"Are you coming in tomorrow?" Papa called as she hung up her helmet.

She forced a thin smile. "Same time, same station."

Zipping her coat, she trotted to her Honda parked behind the garage. If she hurried, she'd have more time to play with Libby before dinner and bath time. Maybe she should order carry out from the Bluebird Café. The last thing she wanted to do was cook. She ducked her chin against the stiff breeze filled with the scent of the approaching winter.

"Valinda Reeser?"

Val straightened. Kathy Larson, one of the firm's assistants, stood near her Honda. "Hi Kathy. Papa's just closing up. But if you have an engine problem, he'll probably check it out for you."

Val shivered. What was with Kathy's smirk?

Kathy thrust the envelope at Val. "You've been served."

Val blinked at Kathy's retreating form. Served?

Another chill caused her teeth to chatter. Enough already. She tossed the envelope on the passenger seat and started the car. She would not let whatever that envelope held ruin her evening with Libby. Right now, she wanted to hug her daughter and soak in a hot tub. After Libby was snug in her bed, and Val finished dinner, she might—and right now that was a giant might—open that ominous-looking envelope.

Still, the stupid thing taunted her on the drive home like a snake ready to strike.

"No more." She pounded the steering wheel.

Instead of Grace's tan Kia, Momma's Forerunner and Connie's Audi occupied the gravel drive. Val cut the engine and stepped out, ignoring the body aches from a sleepless night and a long day at the garage.

"This too shall pass," she muttered.

But she could sure use a snuggle with Libby. Her cheeky grin always lifted her spirits. Inside, Libby's babbles drifted through the entryway, mingling with soft laughter. Val halted. Momma sat cross-legged on the living room floor, waving a toy rattle at Libby, who was sprawled on a brightly colored gym mat. Not the one Val had bought. No, this one was new —bigger, shinier, and clearly from someone with a more generous budget. Connie waved from the couch, her mani-cured nails wrapped around a steaming mug of tea, looking as composed as ever.

Val dropped her bag by the door along with the envelope. "Am I interrupting something?"

"Not at all, honey," Momma said. "You're just in time."

"For what?" Val kicked off her boots and walked further into the room.

When the grandmothers exchanged a knowing glance, the hairs on Val's forearms lifted. Thank goodness she hadn't opened the envelope. A person could only handle so much drama after a major breakup. Val dropped to the floor and kissed Libby, savoring her baby scent. Libby squealed and all of Val's troubles dissipated. If her little dumpling was safe and sound, nothing else mattered.

"We're having a Family of Sisters meeting," Connie said, as if this explained everything.

Val cocked an eyebrow at Momma, who merely laughed and shook Libby's rattle. "Connie's idea. She said we needed a support system for when the men in our lives lose their minds. Hannah's included too, but she couldn't break away. I promised to fill her in later."

Val huffed out a breath. She welcomed their support, but she no longer had to worry about losing her mind over a man. She'd lost her heart, but she'd ended her drama with Tate Saturday night. Soon, her heart would get the memo—or not.

"And I stand by that need," Connie said, her eyes dancing with a light Val couldn't identify. "If we don't stick together, who will? Besides, I have something important to discuss."

Val lifted her chin toward the new gym mat. "Will that explain the upgrade?"

Connie waved a dismissive hand. "I know, I promised to check with you first. But I couldn't resist. Libby needed a bigger one—she's growing so fast. You should've seen her legs dangling off the old one. But that's not why I'm here."

"She's been plotting this all afternoon." Momma leaned in and whispered like they might be overheard by—Hank? "Said it couldn't wait."

"Why don't you start with when and who?" Val lifted Libby onto her lap. "I'm having a hard time imagining Papa losing his mind. Brett and Ruger?" She turned her palm back and forth. "Possibly. But Papa's steady as the earth. I don't think I've seen him mad except—"

"When you came home to tell us about Libby." Momma

arced a brow. "Look what that caused—precious time with you and Libby."

"Well, Senior's been wallowing in darkness too long, but you won't catch him admitting it. He's still hurting." Connie blinked hard, her eyes moist with unshed tears. "Marshall's death...it shattered something in him. And to be honest, it put too much weight on Tate to fulfill promises that were never his to carry."

Val scooted to Connie's side and hugged her. At first, her arms didn't seem to fit around Connie's thin frame. Then, Connie turned and the awkwardness dissolved. The expensive jewelry, designer clothes barrier dissolved, leaving two women trying to erect a safe, loving cocoon around Libby.

"I like your idea of a sisterhood," Val said, her voice catching with emotion. "We all need someone at our sides."

"And someone to share insights." Connie wrung her hands. "That's why I'm here—to help you understand my husband and my son."

Libby's gurgling broke the silence while Connie collected herself.

"Senior expected Marshall to take over the firm, to carry on the family legacy. Not because he didn't love Tate," Connie hurried to say. "But Tate and Senior had different visions."

"Tate never felt like his dad understood his love for music," Val said.

"I tried to tell both of my sons to find their own way, something that gave them purpose, joy." Connie shook her head, distance in her gaze, like she was remembering past conversations. "When we lost Marshall, Senior never let go of passing the firm to his son—even if that son didn't want it."

"Tate shouldered those expectations without complaint," Momma said, her tone soft, empathetic. "Because that's the kind of man he is. You did a fine job of raising him."

"Thank you." But Connie's once cheerful expression

remained sad. "Responsibility has hampered his happiness. And now Senior's using guilt and Marshall's absence to justify...other things."

A shiver raced along Val's shoulders. Hank, who had been snoozing in his bed beside the fire, stood and walked to her. She held out her hand, welcoming his comfort. "Is that the real reason for this meeting?"

"You're scaring me, Connie," Momma said.

"It scares me too. After Gabby told me what he was up to, I spent all day yesterday counteracting it. I've kind of cut myself adrift." Connie reached for Val and Debbie's hands. "I've put up a roadblock, but I guess...I needed support—from you."

Val glanced at her bag with the envelope lying on top of it. This was bad.

"Earl is going forward with the custody suit." For a moment, Tate's cheerful, fearless mother cowered. "It's Senior's way of keeping Tate and Libby close. Tate can make his own decisions. But I won't stand by and let Senior do to Libby what he did to my sons."

"A custody suit?" Val handed Libby to Momma and then stood on shaky legs. Memories of Kathy's unpleasant smirk when she handed her the envelope resurfaced. Senior's lackey had delivered the papers to take Libby from her.

"Val?"

She continued walking to her bag, shaking her head. But denial wouldn't cut off the viper's head. When Val returned, Momma's narrow gaze followed her while cradling Libby in her arms.

"With all due respect," Momma said. "Your husband needs a reality check. Libby's not a pawn for him to move around. I've got her back. And I can promise Paul and our boys will stand up too. He can't win. I don't care how much money he pays to push through this ridiculous suit."

Val scanned the documents in the envelope and then tossed them on the sofa near Connie.

"They served you today?" Connie picked up the papers. "Who gave you the envelope?"

"Kathy Larson."

"I think Senior is moving forward without Tate. But I can't confirm it. I haven't talked to him since the gala," Connie said. "I know he was upset when he couldn't find you. If Senior knew, he kept it to himself. But he had this smug look on his face, and he and Max had a late-night meeting after the gala."

A sharp knock rattled the front door.

Connie and her mother exchanged a glance, but neither moved.

Val stood, her head pounding from the tension threading through her shoulders and walked toward the door. Was it Kathy Larson again, delivering more bad news?

She yanked the door open.

Gabby.

"I just—I need to say I'm sorry," Gabby blurted, her breath clouding in the chilly air. "For everything."

Val stiffened, gripping the doorframe. Gabby, with her wide, pleading eyes, stood like she expected an invitation inside. Like she hadn't been the one who helped set this disaster in motion.

"I'm not ready for that," Val said, keeping her voice low. "Not when I'm holding proof of what your family's done."

Her former friend's face crumpled. "I tried to stop them last night after the gala," Gabby said, her voice hoarse. "Wearing Tate's ring was a sham. He didn't know about it. I never meant to hurt you, but I did. And I can't change that. All I can do is try to make things right."

When Gabby turned away, Val exhaled. Thank goodness

she was leaving. A clean break, just like before. No more history between them. No more hurt.

But then Gabby hesitated. Her fingers hovered over the knob, shoulders stiff like she was bracing for something.

"There's something else," Gabby said, her voice uneven. "Something I learned at the firm."

Val followed her inside the house. "What now?"

Gabby hesitated, her mouth twisting in indecision.

"Just go," Val said, waving toward Connie and her mother. "We're having a family discussion."

"Then you better listen to what I have to say." Gabby's gaze darted around the room. "Your lawyer needs to subpoena Senior's case files. He's been gathering evidence against you, Val."

Heat prickled along the back of Val's neck. "What kind of evidence?"

"Not fabricated," Gabby rushed to say. "But... selective. He's twisting things, picking apart records to make you look unstable. I overheard him and Father talking about it. He's got files on everything—when you paid rent late in Sunberry, the time Libby missed a pediatric appointment. He's pulling together anything that makes you seem like a struggling single mom."

Val's stomach churned. She *was* a struggling single mom, but that didn't make her unfit. It made her real. It made her human.

Across the room, Connie let out a slow, measured breath, but Val could see the tension creeping into her frame. "So he's stacking the deck before the hearing even starts."

"If he takes this any further, he'll cross a line." Gabby hesitated, her gaze shifting to each of them. "I know you don't trust me but let me help. I can tell you where to look, what to request. I'll testify if you need me to."

Val stared at her old friend—the girl who had once known

all her secrets, the woman who had betrayed her with that same knowledge. And yet, she wasn't wrong. If Senior was willing to twist the truth to win, Val needed every advantage she could get. Even if it came from Gabby.

"I'm sorry our friendship has come to this." Val clenched her fists, willing herself to stay strong—for Libby. "I don't trust you anymore. I wish I could, but I can't. Not after this. But if you've got information to help keep Senior from tearing my life apart, I'll take whatever you've got."

Gabby nodded, a flicker of relief crossing her face. "I'll send you a list of what to subpoena." She hesitated. "And Val?"

Val lifted her chin, waiting.

"I really am sorry."

Val didn't answer. She couldn't—not yet.

Gabby turned and left, the front door clicking behind her.

Connie groaned. "I wish I could say I'm surprised, but I'm not. This is classic Senior. If he can't win outright, he'll maneuver the game until the odds are in his favor. I just never thought...he'd use the strategy against family. This has gone too far."

Val swallowed but the burn in her throat persisted.

"You're not fighting this alone, Val." Momma shifted Libby onto her lap. "If Senior wants a war, he'll get one. Paul and the boys won't stand for this."

Val wanted to believe it, wanted to hold onto that certainty, but her chest still felt hollow.

Then Connie stood, straightening like a woman preparing for battle. "And neither will I." She pulled a thick folder from her bag and placed it on the table. "I came prepared."

Val frowned. "What is this?"

"Your war chest." Connie folded her arms. "I know Tate set up a trust for Libby, but this is for you. You may need it to fight Senior, and if you don't, then it's for your future and Libby's."

Val hesitated before flipping open the folder. She blinked at the account balance, her heart slamming against her ribs.

"Connie, I can't—"

"You can, and you will." Connie's voice remined firm, unwavering. "Senior fights with money. I'm making sure you have enough to fight back. If you run out, I'll get more."

Val's throat tightened. "Why?"

Connie's expression softened, and the kind woman behind the expensive clothes and polished demeanor shone through.

"Because I know what it's like to lose a child," she said. "It changes you, makes you desperate to hold on to what you still have. I want to make sure you and Libby never have to worry. Call it grandmotherly guilt."

Momma reached for Connie's hand. "That's generous of you."

"It's not just generosity," Connie said, her voice quiet. "It's about healing. Senior's grief drives him to control, but mine drives me to give. I've seen what happens when we don't have support, and I don't want that for you or Libby."

Her words circled Val's thoughts, but her tough, no-nonsense look convinced her. Val nodded. "Is that why Senior's pushing so hard?"

"He doesn't know how to let go." Connie took her empty cup to the kitchen and returned to her seat. "Grief makes people do crazy things. I got help, but Earl refused. Always the tough guy. He could beat grief on his own terms. But you know what? He wasn't strong enough to face the loss of a son and his dream."

Momma kissed Libby's curly head and then looked up with tear-filled eyes. "I judged your husband too harshly. I don't know what it would do to me to lose a piece of my heart."

"I've tried to talk to him," Connie said, pointing at the documents in Val's lap. "I was praying he wouldn't go through with it. But when he served you, he served me too."

"Move in with me," Val said. "This sofa is not bad. You can have my room and I'll sleep out here."

"Thank you." Connie's eyes misted. "Just knowing I'm welcome here is enough. Besides, my son has a three-bedroom home—unless he's aligned with his father. But I don't think that's true."

Val groaned. "I pray you're right. If he did that...I don't know if I'd ever trust him to even visit her."

"I don't think Tate knows," Connie said, but creases of doubt lined her forehead. "At least the son I raised wouldn't do such a thing. But sometimes Senior can be so strong. It's difficult going against him."

"I understand," Momma said. "I let Paul's anger sway me."

"But we're united now," Connie said, retrieving her phone.

"And women's bonds can work small miracles. Now go take a long bubble bath. I'll call a food delivery service for a nice dinner from the Bluebird? It's chicken-fried steak and potatoes night. Then I want that sweet baby. It's my turn to snuggle her."

Val fought the urge to take her daughter and run like she did last year. But that scared young woman no longer existed. This time she had options. This time she wasn't alone.

CHAPTER THIRTY

TATE BACKED THE ROVER INTO HIS DRIVEWAY AND OPENED the hatch. Although his heart had been eviscerated, a flicker of hope still burned. Val had been right about handling the Isles and Jones families. A plate of biscuits and gravy and several cups of coffee had ended their dispute. Although the approach wouldn't work for everyone, it had worked with two old friends who had lost sight of what's important. Now, if only he could work out the rest of his life.

The interior of his cold, silent house swallowed him like a tomb. It wasn't a home—at least, not for him. He belonged at the cottage with Val and Libby. He squeezed his eyes shut, forcing down the yearning to hear Libby's jabber, to feel her chubby arms around his neck. Val had promised he could see her whenever he wanted. Problem was, he wasn't sure he could visit without breaking down, without begging.

Shaking off the ache, he turned on his gym playlist and threw himself into packing. Two hours later, sweat dampened his t-shirt, but he'd emptied the master closet and even vacuumed the shelves and carpet. A clean house improved sales, and he needed to sell fast—enough to float him for a year while he figured out if he could make a living with music.

The sharp rap, rap, rap at his front door yanked him from his thoughts.

Hope leaped in his chest before good sense kicked it down. Tate shut the fridge, abandoning the shriveled apple in the drawer. Val tucked Libby into bed by seven o'clock. It was almost nine.

Senior?

Tate snorted. No way. Senior had probably already reassigned his cases and hired a new associate.

He swung open the door and froze.

Mom stood on his stoop, three Gucci bags lined up beside her. She held out an expensive bottle of wine.

"I need a place to stay. I brought wine. Thought you could use it. I know I can."

"What—" He barely got the word out before she breezed past him, dropping her expensive coat onto the sofa.

He sighed. "Looks like the Carver Crazies are widespread."

Connie waved a hand at the boxes stacked in the hallway. "What's all this?"

"Preparing to sell the house. Uncle Rob's letting me stay in his loft at the cabin. It's a good place for me right now. I can think, compose my music."

She opened the cupboard, pulling down two wine glasses. "Glad you haven't packed the kitchen. Wine? It's a good one. Took it from your father's collection."

Tate smirked but said nothing. Mom had a story to tell, and something told him he wasn't going to like it.

She poured them each a glass. "I'll buy your house."

"No way." Tate shook his head. "If you want it, it's yours—but I'm not selling to you."

"Why not?" She arched a brow. "I have my own money. Not as much as I used to, but enough."

"Have you eaten?" He opened the fridge and grimaced. "Not much here."

She lifted a Bluebird Café takeout bag from her tote. "Our leftovers. I think there's enough to feed you. Debbie, Val, and I talked more than we ate."

Uh-oh, this day was getting worse and worse. Tate turned away, concentrating on the food like he was hungry. Just the mention of Val's name bombed his stomach. When the microwave dinged, he grabbed a fork and braced against the counter. "Should I eat before we talk?"

Connie sipped her wine. "How's your appetite?"

Tate snorted. "Not great since the gala. I had breakfast with the Isles and Jones families. They worked out a water rights agreement."

Connie's brow lifted. "A meeting at the café instead of the firm?"

"Val's idea." He stirred the gravy over his steak.

"She's a remarkable young woman." Connie's voice softened. "After meeting Debbie, I see where she gets it. Libby's in good hands."

Tate choked down a bite and then filled a glass with water. This conversation required a clear head.

Connie set her glass down. "Your father moved forward on the custody suit."

Tate froze mid-swallow, his stomach twisting.

"That's not possible." He eased his grip on the glass before it exploded in his hand. "I closed that case. I told the court I wasn't pursuing custody."

"Your father refiled." Mom's exhale filled the silence. "As the grandfather."

"That won't work," Tate said, ignoring the cold wave of

anger rolling through him. "The judge will have to throw it out because he doesn't have standing."

"You know your father." His mother's usual carefree tone had given way to a slow and careful cadence. "Gabby told me he's arguing his case to anyone who will listen. He's pulling favors, calling in debts. He's not letting this go."

Tate's pulse pounded in his ears, making it difficult to think. But even a lay person would understand the suit would fail. "This could ruin him."

"It might." Mom nodded, her face unreadable. "I don't think he cares."

Tate pushed back from the counter and paced the kitchen. "He's been practicing for years. Why would he do this? He knows I won't let him take Libby from Val."

"He never got over losing Marshall. And since finding out about Libby, it's gotten worse. I tried to get him professional help. Offered to go with him." She shook her head. "He refused."

"I thought something was off. I knew he wasn't himself, but I put it aside because—" He huffed out a breath. "Because I was dealing with everything with Val and Libby. And then when I resigned... I should have seen this coming."

"He's a very sad man." Connie turned her glass on the counter. "And deteriorating. He lashes out more, even over trivial things. I had to talk the house staff out of quitting twice. He's not thinking rationally, and this..." She motioned vaguely, as if at the whole mess. "...this is him grasping for control."

Tate turned to her, resolve solidifying in his chest. "I'll shut this down before it ever reaches court. But I can't save the firm, Mom."

She nodded, then set her wine glass down, turning the stem between her fingers. "Let me buy the house."

"Mom—"

"I don't know how long I'll need a place—maybe forever. Regardless, we both need somewhere to land. I'll buy it, and you can stay here too. At least until you figure things out."

He wanted to argue, but she wasn't wrong.

She met his gaze, something unreadable in her expression. "You and Val are a good pair. But Libby is your priority. You have to maintain an amenable relationship with Val even if you aren't a couple."

"I was trying to give Val time. Give myself time." His voice cut through the silence, quiet and rough around the edges. "I can't be the man she and Libby need when my own life is up in the air. And now this."

Tate's hands curled into fists. His life was far from settled, but one thing was certain— he wouldn't abandon the people who mattered. Not Mom. Not Val. And definitely not Libby.

CHAPTER THIRTY-ONE

VAL SLID INTO PLACE, BRUSHING HER FINGERS AGAINST THE Bluebird's worn vinyl booth. Memories, warm and comforting, washed over— nights spent in this very spot with Gabby and Tate, sipping milkshakes and sharing fries, their laughter filling the air. It felt like a lifetime ago.

Across from her, Gabby cradled a cup of tea. She looked up, offering a faint smile, and gestured toward the empty space beside Val. "Crazy how nothing here ever changes, huh?"

Val turned her head, taking in the retro checkerboard floor and the faded posters of rock stars long past their prime.

"Not even the booth," she said, giving in to the grin tilting her lips. "How many nights did we sit right here?"

Gabby's smile widened, this time genuine. "Too many to count. Talking about boys and dances."

"Unless Tate was with us." Val's smile turned wry. "Then it was just dances."

"He had no patience for our crushes."

"Probably because we wouldn't shut up about how dreamy Greg Madison looked in his football uniform."

"Dreamy?" Gabby lifted her gaze to the cracked ceiling overhead. "You called him a linebacker with a mop for a head."

"I may have been harsh, but you thought he was cute."

"We were young," Gabby said, a flicker of nostalgia in her eyes.

The moment hung between them, the shared memories softening the tension that had lingered so long. Val leaned against the booth, the brief fun moment gone.

"Thanks for warning us about Senior's intent," Val said, the issue still raw in her mind.

"I—I had to. I couldn't let him hurt you like that—for nothing."

Val nodded, sensing there was a lot more Gabby hadn't said, but not wanting to push it. Besides, she'd extended the invitation to clear her own conscience.

"I've been thinking a lot about our friendship. How close we were. And I realized... I owe you an apology."

Gabby stiffened in her seat, her eyes wide. "An apology? For what?"

"For how things ended between us." Val tightened her grip on the warm ceramic mug. "When Tate and I got together, I didn't think about how it might affect you. And after everything fell apart...I didn't explain my feelings. Didn't give you a chance to explain yours. I just ran and shut you out."

Gabby tilted her head, her gaze steady. "I'm the one who should apologize. I made things worse."

"We both messed up. But I forgot something very important. I was your friend first, and I let you down. I want to own that."

Gabby stirred her tea, her gaze darting side to side. "I don't know what to say."

"Say what's on your mind," Val said. "No filters."

Gabby hesitated, then met Val's gaze. "Why did you leave him? Tate, I mean. You two were...everything. Why disappear without a word?"

Val traced a coffee ground floating in the bottom of her cup. "Immaturity. A lack of self-confidence. A lot of little things. But if I had to point to one moment, it was Tate's graduation from law school."

"What does that have to do with anything? You didn't even go."

Val exhaled, her voice soft but steady. "I saw you with him and his parents that day. You looked...like you belonged. And you did. You were polished and perfect, and my boyfriend was a lawyer while I was a welder. A good one, sure, but still a welder."

Gabby opened her mouth, but Val held up a hand. "Let me finish."

The painful memories thickened Val's throat, but she'd made a promise to herself the day she'd scheduled the meeting.

"You should have seen the look on his parents' faces. They were so proud. My parents had a similar glow when I graduated from tech. Anyway, you were part of that picture. His parents never looked at me that way. And I didn't think they ever would."

"Val, that's not—"

"I realized I'd just drag him down," Val interrupted. "And I'd be miserable because I'd never measure up—not like I wanted to. I was proud of what my family built. It's not a fancy law firm, but the garage is a good business. We offer a service our neighbors need. It's honest work, and I'm proud of that."

She paused, waiting for the slight tremble in her voice to stop. "When I was with Tate's family, I lost that pride. I felt like I was playing a part in someone else's world. I didn't want to live that way. That's too much for a young marriage to sustain. Tate and I both deserved more."

Gabby was quiet for a moment, her tea forgotten. "Out of the three of us, you always seemed so sure of yourself. I couldn't imagine going against the rules my parents dictated. But not you. Weren't you the only female in your welding class?"

"I was."

"I always admired your bravado, and now I learn you were questioning your decisions all along—like me? I had no idea you felt that way."

Val shrugged, her smile as bitter as her now cold coffee. "It's not exactly something I was ready to admit back then. I'm still working on me"

"Do you still feel that way?"

Val hesitated, then shook her head. "Sometimes, but it's different now. I know the problem isn't me—it's Senior. He's the one who made me feel like I wasn't good enough."

"He's got a way of making everyone feel small. Some people mellow with age. He's gotten worse." Gabby pushed aside the napkin she'd shredded. "I should have kept my mouth shut. I was never into gossip. But I was desperate to hold onto an escape. To have a life of my own—away from Mother and the responsibility of cleaning up." She dropped her gaze, sending a chill up Val's spine. "I told him how scared you were when Libby was diagnosed."

Val's throat tightened. The betrayal stung fresh and raw. Gabby had taken one of the worst moments of her life—her panic, her helplessness—and handed it to the man who already saw her as unworthy.

Warm, trembling fingers pressed against hers. Val swallowed. Her friend wanted forgiveness. But this was too much to ask. The hurt too deep. The fallout too dangerous. Not just for her, but for Libby. Gabby's actions had threatened her baby.

"I was wrong." Gabby's hoarse whisper roared in Val's ears. "I'm ashamed of myself for betraying your trust. I was just...so desperate."

Desperate? She had the nerve to talk about desperation. Gabby had never held her baby wondering if she were holding her for the last time. Gabby had never walked the halls wondering if someone—someone she loved—would take away her precious daughter. Gabby had facilitated that event.

Air raked in and out of Val's lungs. One, two, three...By the time she counted to ten, her breathing had resumed a normal rhythm. Air tainted with cooking oil and fried onions filled her lungs.

"Val?"

The catch in Gabby's tone scraped at Val's resistance. Gabby had hurt her, yes. But Val had hurt her friend, too. And she didn't want to continue to raise Libby with anger in her heart.

Val lifted her gaze, taking in the tears streaking Gabby's face.

"I just wanted to be loved the way Tate loves you. The way you both love Libby." Gabby's grip tightened, her desperation clear. "Forgive me. Please."

Val forced a tight smile, focusing not on the betrayal but on the friendship they'd shared.

"Okay," she said, the word not quite forgiveness but not rejection either. She wasn't there yet. Maybe in time.

Removing her hand from Gabby's grip, she gulped her water. "What about you, Gabby?" The words felt tight in her throat, but she couldn't talk about the past for one more second. "What do you want? For your life, I mean."

Gabby blinked, clearly caught off guard. "What do I want?

Besides marrying your baby daddy?" she added with a wry smile.

Val swallowed her gasp of surprise but couldn't manage a smile.

"I've spent so much time trying to make everyone else happy—Father, Mother, even Tate—that I forgot how to make myself happy. I don't even know where to start."

Val chewed her lip. And there it was, the reason she'd befriended the poor little rich girl suffocating under the responsibility of her mother's addiction. A girl might get a pass, but not a woman.

"Then maybe it's time to figure it out," Val said, removing the judgment from her tone. "Not what your dad wants or what your mom needs—what you want. For you."

Gabby stared at her, something flickering in her eyes—hope, maybe, or determination.

"Thank you for that." Gabby pressed her palm over Val's hand, her gaze filled with gratitude and something else. "I don't know if you're right. But I think it's time for me to try."

"We were good friends," Val said, her voice rough with emotion. "I know we both need healing time. But in the future, I think we should try to put this behind us. Maybe another lunch?

"I'd like that," Gabby said. "Once we're past the crazy."

The moment lingered, soft and unspoken, and for the first time in years, the distance between them didn't feel so insurmountable.

CHAPTER THIRTY-TWO

WHAT JUST HAPPENED?

Gabby sat outside the Bluebird Café, her roadster struggling to warm the chill from its cold leather seats. The scent of her jasmine hand lotion mingled with the aged interior, a contrast of exotic and decay, much like the life she was leaving behind.

Her fingers drummed against the steering wheel, Father's words looping in her head like a chant carved into stone.

"Stanfords stick together, no matter what." But they hadn't. Not for her.

Mother had disappeared into a bottle while Gabby cleaned up the mess, covered the lies, and kept the world from seeing the cracks. And Father? He'd turned a blind eye, so long as the family's name remained untarnished. The only person who had ever truly stood by her had been Val. And she'd rewarded her friend with betrayal.

And for what? A broken engagement. A mother slipping back into addiction. A hollow life carved from someone else's expectations.

She flexed her hands around the steering wheel, remembering Val's quiet apology—as if she had something to be sorry for. Val had lived up to her own standards, walked away from Tate with her dignity intact. Gabby had spent years walking in a direction that wasn't even hers.

Out on the sidewalk, two older women hugged before stepping into the café. Like normal people. Like people in charge of their own destiny.

A new resolve curled in her mind.

Father will explode. He'll call me selfish, disloyal.

And for the first time, she didn't care.

Her hands tightened. *So what's it going to be, Gabriella Stanford?*

Stay silent. Stay trapped. Stay the obedient daughter. Or take back her life.

She exhaled through her nose, steadying her hands as she prompted her phone to dial Father's private line.

"I'm on my way to the office," she said when he answered. "Clear your schedule so we can talk."

A pause. Just long enough to send her pulse racing.

"It's about time," Father said. "Karen can't handle the firm."

The air in her lungs turned thick and sharp. Of course he thought this was about the firm. About his future. Not hers.

She wet her lips, but her throat remained dry. "I'm not returning." The words felt like steel in her mouth. "We need to discuss... arrangements before my departure."

Silence. Not long, but enough.

"Not at the firm," he said at last. "Meet me at the house."

Her finger hovered over the End Call button. She'd spent her life waiting for someone to choose her. Now, she was choosing herself.

Two hours later, Gabby stepped onto the thick Persian rug in her father's home office, her heels soundless against the expensive fibers. Father, his face drawn with fatigue, stood behind his desk, looking older than he had the week before.

She squared her shoulders. Not her problem anymore. Still, guilt tugged at her heart. This wasn't about punishing him. This was about saving herself.

He gestured toward the wingback chair opposite his desk, then closed the door with a soft click.

"Tate is going up against Senior," he said without preamble.

Gabby held his gaze, unflinching. "Tate is doing the right thing."

"He's embarrassing his father."

"He's standing on his own." Her pulse slammed against her ribs. "That's what I'm doing."

Father's expression darkened. "So what now? You think walking out on the firm and your mother is going to fix the situation?"

No. But she could regain her self-respect, stop her continual spiral downward.

She met his gaze, unflinching. "Senior's plan was doomed the moment Tate and I ended things. If I had stayed, I would have ended up just like you and Mother—in a loveless marriage built on obligation instead of love."

His voice went flat. "Grow up, Gabby."

Her father was always controlled, always precise with his words. But something inside him wavered now, something that hadn't been there before.

"I supported Senior because I understood the importance of holding on to what I've spent a lifetime building. And do you know who could destroy it all in an instant?" His breath hitched. "Your mother."

Gabby stiffened and then studied Father's face for a sign of deceit. "What are you talking about?"

"Your mother didn't start drinking because I didn't love

her. She started drinking the night Tate's brother died." He swallowed hard. "Because she was driving the car that hit him."

The walls of the office warped and tilted, forcing Gabby to grip the chair to keep herself upright.

No. No, that wasn't possible. Mother driving?

"She called me," Father continued, his voice hollow, like the words were being torn from him against his will. "She called me that night after her bridge party. She didn't have a problem then. You know Alexa. Just a little bit of a thing. And she was always watching her weight so she hadn't eaten."

"What are you saying?" But the words, cracked and hoarse, didn't sound like hers.

Father pounded his fist into his palm. "She didn't see Marshall... until it was too late. She panicked. Kept driving. And I... I made sure it never touched her. Never touched us."

A broken sound escaped Gabby's throat with the tortured twist of her stomach. She'd spent her entire life protecting her mother. And all this time, Father had been protecting her too.

"You covered it up." Her voice came out thin and fractured. "And you expect me to keep doing the same?"

His shoulders sank as he lowered himself into his chair, the fight draining from him. "You're a part of this family. That means you do what's necessary."

Gabby stood and forced air into her lungs, but the weight of the room pressed down hard.

"I've spent my whole life doing what's necessary for this family." Thank goodness, she'd talked to Val. Already thought through what she wanted—or more importantly, didn't want —in her life. "I'm finished living a lie."

Father's expression flickered—regret? Panic? He was too late.

Gabby turned on her heel and walked out of the office, her heart hammering against her ribs. She didn't look back.

Outside, she gulped mouthfuls of frigid air. At the second-floor window, Father stood, backlit by the dim glow of his desk lamp, his shadow cutting an imposing silhouette against the glass.

Gabby climbed into her car and gripped the wheel, her breath unsteady.

"You don't do what's necessary when it's wrong," she whispered.

The engine roared to life and she drove into the night. While darkened streets streamed by her window, the truth settled like a gavel. For years she'd blamed the problems in the Carver household on Senior's coldness, his rigid expectations. But Father's confession illuminated the cracks beneath the Carver legacy—the grief, the weight of an unanswered tragedy. Marshall's death hadn't just stolen a son and a brother. It had reshaped them all. It had turned Senior into a man desperate to control everything. Had made Tate the son who couldn't afford to fail. Had cast a long shadow over their town, one no one dared to step out from beneath. And she—she had been tangled in the dark edges of the story without even realizing it.

Her hands ached from her grip on the wheel. She needed to get away from Glen Falls. To think. To figure out what came next when every foundation she had once trusted had crumbled beneath her.

Her phone buzzed, illuminating the console screen. She glanced to the right, afraid to take her eyes from the road, expecting another call from Father. But the name flashing across the screen made her foot ease off the accelerator.

Ethan Brooks?

A friend—well, maybe more while he'd attended UMSTL and she'd studied at Washington University. Long before she returned to Glen Falls to do what was expected of her. Ethan had left Missouri, chasing his own ambitions, but now?

She hesitated, then pressed play on voicemail.

HEY, Gabby.

It's been a long time. I saw the firm's ad looking for a new attorney.

Thought maybe it was fate—me passing the bar, Glen Falls needing a

lawyer, and you... being the only person I know there. I don't know if you even remember me, but I'd love to catch up. Call me?

FATE? Gabby breathed, trying to relax the tension in her neck and shoulders. Maybe fate wasn't something handed to her. Maybe it was something she had to choose.

If so, she was ready to grab it with both hands.

CHAPTER THIRTY-THREE

Tate leaned against the railing of the park's pavilion, his chest swelling with love and longing. The late afternoon sun filtered through the barren trees, painting Libby, dressed in a puffy purple jacket and pink mittens, and Val in her down vest, in a golden hue. Behind the baby swing, Val smiled down at a chattering Libby and pushed. Libby squealed with delight, her mittened hands gripping the swing's chains, her chubby legs kicking.

Val's laughter mingled with Libby's delighted squeals, soft and carefree, a sound that tugged at something deep in his chest. She'd built this life for their daughter—piece by piece, sacrifice by sacrifice. She'd fought for her family, refusing to let Senior diminish her family's worth. Shown him through her example what it meant to take pride in where you came from, to stand firm in your beliefs even when the world tried to knock you down.

That's why he'd fallen in love with her, why he still loved the amazing mother and woman before him. She wasn't just his heart—she was his compass, showing him the way to be a better man, a better life.

But before he earned her love, he had to tell her the truth —all of it. Even the pieces that still clawed at his soul. Tate swallowed the lump of regret lodged in his throat. What he wouldn't do to replay the gala's tragic events and the aftermath. But he'd finally committed to the hard choices. Now, only execution lay before him.

The swing slowed, and she scooped his precious girl into her arms, kissing her cheek. His breath caught in his chest, waiting for her to notice his presence. When her expression hardened into a guarded expression, he knew she'd spotted him. Air whooshed from his lungs, leaving his knees unsteady.

Although he hadn't expected a warm welcome, he'd hoped — Still, he didn't blame her. He held out the manilla envelope, hoping she didn't notice the way it quivered in his hand.

"It's over," he said, meeting her steady gaze. "We both have something to be thankful for this Thanksgiving. Senior backed off. The case was dismissed, sealed, done." But he prayed she wasn't done with him.

She stared at the packet, and for a moment he wondered if she'd take it or throw it back in his face. She took it from him but didn't open it to verify he was telling the truth.

Her brow wrinkled in confusion. "That easy?"

He snorted. "Not easy. Just right."

Something shifted in her intense gaze—not relief, which he expected. No, this was something else. Something deeper, something that he couldn't identify.

"This ordeal made me take a hard look at myself," he started, determined to tell her the truth before she shut him down. "I felt guilty about living when Marshall died. His death broke our family, and I guess I thought it was up to me to fix it." He shrugged. "I made it worse. Enabled Senior to live a lie. Made Mom struggle with an impossible future. Hurt you and Libby."

The urge to touch her, connect, make her see his changes, curled his fingers in his pockets.

"I'm pursuing music now." He straightened, fighting the temptation to ask her to let him back into her life. "I'm choosing what's right for me. Music makes me feel better about the man I am so I can be a better dad for Libby." He toed the woodchips covering the playground. "Anyway, I wanted you to know what I was doing. When you're ready, you know how to find me."

A wry grin tugged at his lips. He was such a pathetic romantic. But his muscles refused to listen to his commands to turn around. He stepped backward, memorizing every detail about the woman and child who owned his heart.

When Val shifted Libby to her hip, every cell in his body wanted to scream, plead to call him back. But his precious girl just waved, breaking off another piece of his heart. Libby had learned bye-bye and he'd missed it. What else would he miss?

"Tate?"

He swallowed. Was the sound real or just his imagination living up to his fantasy? Fear paralyzed his limbs. Was she going to shut him down for good? Say she didn't want him in her life—ever?

Holding his breath, he forced his gaze upward until her face filled his vision. He narrowed his gaze, searching for hints of anger, rejection. She dropped the envelope on the picnic table at her side and held out her hand.

His brain scrambled trying to make sense of her actions. Hoping—

Her hand opened toward him. "I'm ready, Tate."

He touched his ear.

She stepped forward, her gaze direct, steady. Which was a heck of a lot better than his.

"I don't want to do this without you anymore."

In his head, her smile burst into one thousand glitters of light.

"Libby deserves more than that." She nodded. "We deserve more."

While his feet remained cemented in place, she stepped closer. Libby patted his chest.

"Dah, dah, dah," she jabbered.

Val's hand warmed his cheek. He blinked, and another tear oozed down his face. She was crying too, but her smile...?

"It's time we became a real family," she said.

He opened his mouth but nothing came out. They were doing this? Really doing this? Val didn't cry over nothing. His arm finally obeyed his command. Her skin, so soft, glided beneath his fingers.

Was this legit? Were her lips moving, because he couldn't hear anything over his heart pounding in his ears.

"Dah, dah, dah!" Libby batted at his shoulder.

He captured her little mittened hand and kissed it, his gaze never leaving Val's. "Are you sure? I don't have a lot to offer—a starving musician for now. But Uncle Rob keeps reassuring me Libby's song will sell."

"I fell in love with you, not your prospects."

Libby lunged forward with an open-mouthed kiss. A laugh exploded from his throat, releasing the fear and uncertainty he'd harbored so long.

"Thank you, sweetheart. Daddy needed some sugar from his girl."

Val withdrew a tissue from her pocket. When she dabbed at his face, her tender gaze warmed him, strengthened him the same as she always had. He hoped she always would.

He reached for Libby, his heart filling with joy when she held out her arms to him.

"Do you want to talk about it?" she asked, her tender tone stroking his battered heart.

"Not really." Tate breathed in Libby's scent, a blend of baby shampoo and possibly banana. "Let's just leave it that Senior's never been great at negotiations when it comes to family matters."

When he first approached the playground, he'd felt off-balanced, unsure. But now, with Libby clinging to him, strength grounded his weight.

"I had to end it with Senior," he said. "I couldn't be the father Libby needs and the man you deserve with him in the picture. I think Mom feels the same way. I'm done trying to live up to his expectations."

"When I couldn't talk to my family——" Val smoothed Libby's jacket. "It was terrible. I had this giant hole inside me I couldn't fill. I don't want to be the reason you're estranged from your dad. He only has one son."

"And that son needs to set boundaries. I've been examining the person I thought I had to be." He glanced at her, hoping for her understanding, but determined to tell the truth regardless. "I felt like I owed my parents something because I lived when my brother didn't."

"I never understood how Marshall's death affected you. That must have been hard living in his shadow."

"Marshall was more like Senior—smart, ambitious, the perfect son to carry on the Carver name. And when he died, I felt like it was on me to step up and fill that void. But no matter what I did, it was never enough. I wasn't enough because I wasn't Marshall." He paused, meeting her gaze. "It took me a long time to realize I can't make up his loss. I can only be me."

"You've thought a lot about this," Val said, her voice quiet, but filled with encouragement.

"I have to do what's right for me. For us. Senior doesn't have to agree with my choices, but I can't let him control them anymore." He nodded toward the picnic table and the manilla envelope. "There's something else in there."

Val opened the packet and thumbed through the contents and then stopped. Her gaze found his, a question wrinkling her forehead. "The cottage?"

"Mom told me about the war chest she gave you. That's a relief because I don't have the kind of money I used to. Without the firm, my cash flow is down to a trickle. But you've made the cottage a home," Tate said. "Libby deserves stability, and so do you."

She studied him for a moment, her gaze searching his. "I know about hard choices," she said. "I struggled with my decision to move back home."

"Was it the right choice?" he asked, holding his breath.

Her slow smile told him everything he needed to know.

"It was."

"How about mine?"

Her lips curved into a faint smile. "I like the sound of it so far."

"When I stripped it all down, it was easy. I can't live without you and Libby," he said, unashamed of the catch in his voice. "Can you forgive me, give me another chance to be the man you deserve?"

Val's eyes glistened, and she stepped closer, finding his hand and squeezing it. "I've already found the man I deserve. But don't stay angry with your dad. He needs help. Besides, Libby deserves his love too."

Tate shrugged. Although part of him acknowledged she was right, he wasn't ready to forgive Senior. "Maybe in time."

"You don't have to do this alone," Val said, her voice steady. "As for the money? Who knows? Libby may insist on a fancy education. I love my job, and I've already been thinking about working more days. The grandmothers are practically tripping over each other to negotiate their time with Libby.

But I don't need you to provide everything. I need you to be you."

Tate covered her hand with his, the warmth of her touch grounding him. "I need to be with you and Libby."

Libby babbled, and for the first time in years, he felt like he was exactly where he was supposed to be—home.

CHAPTER THIRTY-FOUR

HER MAN WAS COMING INTO HIS OWN.

Val didn't bother to suppress a chuckle. Who cared if Tate's first big appearance was at the regional fair? He'd always be her star. Even from their location sequestered in the backstage area, the sweet scent of funnel cakes mixed with kettle corn tempted her. She should have bought a snack before preparing for the show. But Tate had been too nervous to eat. Since the last time she'd attended the annual event, her tummy had revolted at the rollercoaster's jerky motions, and she hadn't pushed him.

"Hold still," Val said, adjusting Tate's collar.

He batted her hand away playfully, but a thin line had wiped away his usual smirk.

"You're fussing," he muttered, reaching for his guitar.

"Because you're nervous," she said. "You're sweating through your shirt, and the fan is running full tilt."

"I'm not nervous," he grumbled, tightening the strap on his guitar.

Her brother Ruger leaned against a nearby stack of amps,

his arms crossed. "Sure you're not, rock star. That's why you've been pacing like Dad at the DMV all morning."

Papa, holding Libby in his arms, joined in with a chuckle. "Don't let him get to you, son. Just remember you're not playing for critics or big-city producers. You're playing for your neighbors, and they already like you."

"And if they don't," Ruger added with a grin, "at least you've got Val to bail you out. You married into a crowd-pleaser."

Tate rolled his eyes, muttering something under his breath about helpful in-laws. The faint tug of a smile said far more than his words.

She smoothed a wrinkle on his sleeve. "You've got this. Just pretend you're playing to me and Libby."

The love glistening in his gaze still did crazy things to her heart.

He nodded, worry now shadowing his love. "That would be easier if I could close my eyes. But Rob told me to look at the crowd."

Val kissed his cheek; grateful this incredible man came home to her every night. "We'll be in the front row. Now, break a leg. Not really," she said. "Why do people say such ridiculous things?"

"You're up," called Uncle Rob from the break in the curtain.

Val and the family hurried to the front of the stage where an officer guided the VIPs to their designated area. People already filled the Stoddard County Fair bleachers. Some were familiar faces, others were strangers.

"Dad da," Libby chirped from the top of Ruger's shoulders.

With the late summer sun casting long shadows across the fairgrounds, Tate stepped onto the stage, his blue eyes owlish in the stage lighting.

"Let's give it up for our local boy turned singer-song-writer," the announcer boomed over the loudspeaker.

The crowd cheered, and Tate adjusted the microphone, scanning the rows of folding chairs. His posture stiffened and fear raced along her spine. Libby fussed, despite Ruger's efforts. Never taking her gaze from Tate, she reached for Libby, tucking her protectively at her side.

"Is something wrong?" Momma's warm hand touched her elbow.

Val followed Tate's gaze to the stage curtain. A figure moved in the shadows. A man. Silver-haired. "Senior," she whispered.

Val kissed Libby's sweaty curls. Senior wouldn't make a surprise appearance to heckle Tate, would he?

"No telling what's going on in Grampa's mind," she whispered.

But it couldn't be too bad, because Tate merely nodded and turned back toward the crowd.

To their right, two men in t-shirts shifted and Connie Carver dressed in...Val blinked, a smile tugging her lips. Dressed in a scarlet western-styled shirt with 6 inches of silver and white fringe under the arms moved toward a vacant seat in the VIP section.

"Hey, everyone." She wiggled into a seat between Val and Momma. "Give me my adorable grandbaby." She kissed Libby's neck, eliciting a sweet giggle. "Grams missed her girl."

"Was that Senior on side stage?" Val whispered.

"Stubborn old coot," Connie said, loud enough to nearly drown out Tate clearing his throat.

"Uh, hey, everyone." Tate nodded to the right and then the left before finding Val. "Thanks for coming out tonight. This is.... It's my first time playing like this. So, uh, go easy on me."

The crowd laughed, a few people shouting encouragement. Val whispered a prayer for his success.

"I want to start off singing a special song I wrote for my daughter." He adjusted his guitar strap, his voice gaining strength. "She turned one this past March. I think every dad knows this feeling—a wish to keep them safe forever."

The first notes of the ballad drifted into the warm evening air, silencing the chatter. His raw tone filled with love and honesty tightened a vice around Val's chest. A tiny hand patted her arm. She squeezed Libby's fingers and closed her eyes, letting the music fill her.

For three minutes, the melody carried memories of her time with Tate. The way his eyes crinkled in laughter. The tenderness in his smile when he cuddled Libby. The love in his gaze when he took her into his arms.

The final note faded, and the crowd erupted into applause, rising to their feet. Val's brothers whistled an ear-deafening sound, and Papa whooped and shook his fist in the air.

Tate smiled, visibly more relaxed now, and leaned into the microphone again. "Thank you. I couldn't have done this without all of you—my neighbors, my friends, and my family. Especially my parents, who took some time, but they've always been in my corner."

He paused, glanced to the side, and then found her.

"The biggest thanks go to my wife and daughter," he said, holding out a hand toward her. "They said 'I do' yesterday at the Stoddard County Courthouse."

The crowd erupted again, louder this time. Following his come-to-me motion, Val stood and turned, facing the crowd with a proud wave. The rest of his performance felt like pure magic. He played song after song of his new music and the crowd met every one with the same appreciation as she felt.

When Tate played the final chord and the applause died, her parents took a sleeping Libby to the car. Val meandered through the crowd to wait for Tate near the backstage entrance. Despite the festive fair lights, stars sparkled in a midnight sky. She closed her eyes, letting fond memories pass the time. Ten minutes later, Tate joined her, his smile still wide from the adrenaline rushing through his veins.

"What did you think?"

She opened her mouth to speak and a familiar voice cut through the quiet.

"Well, I didn't expect to be clapping at a county fair tonight," Senior said, stepping out of the shadows.

Tate straightened, his hand brushing Val's before he turned to face his father. "And?"

Senior released the button on his navy blazer and stuffed his hands in his trouser pockets. "Not bad. Not bad at all."

Tate raised an eyebrow. "Just not bad?"

A ghost of a smile tugged at Senior's lips. "Don't push it, son. You did good tonight." He cleared his throat, his voice softening. "Your brother would've been proud. I know I am."

The words hung in the air, heavy with meaning. Val shifted. This was an important father-son moment, she'd wait—

Tate caught her hand, holding it tight.

"Thanks, Dad," he said.

Senior glanced at Val, his expression still guarded, but the rancor had faded. "You've got a good family. Don't take it for granted."

"I won't," Tate said.

With a final nod, he walked away, his form disappearing in the soft glow of the fairground lights.

Tate turned to her, his voice quieter now. "Well, what'd you think?"

Val smiled. "I think you've found where you belong."

He slid his arm around her waist, pulling her close. "No ma'am. No thinking required on the subject. I know I'm where I belong."

———

IF YOU enjoyed the first story in the Glen Falls Romance Series...

You'll love where it all began—with the Clocktower Romance Series and the award-winning Murphy Family Saga.

An independent widow. Four fatherless children.
The Marine officer who ordered her husband's final patrol.

Will she risk her family's future for a second chance at love?

📘 **Download your copy of *Home to Stay*—NOW!**

———

💜 LOVE BEING FIRST IN THE KNOW?

Turner Town News, my monthly newsletter, gives you the inside scoop—exclusive updates, behind-the-scenes fun, and book news before anyone else.

📍 Subscribe at www.becketurner.com and get a **FREE reader bundle** featuring:

🔑 The **Clocktower Romance Character Map**—track your favorite characters, including the Murphy family, and find your perfect reading order.

🔑 An **exclusive prequel** to *Val's Last Second Chance*—the emotional story that leads into my next series.

Val's Last Second Chance is the series opener for my brand-new **Glen Falls Series**, releasing **April 22, 2025**!

———

Coming Up Next: **Home To Stay**

A CLOCKTOWER ROMANCE

HOME
TO STAY

BECKE TURNER

📖 ABOUT HOME TO STAY

Ava Robey's world revolves around her four kids, her late husband's memory, and the dream of opening Robey's Rewards, a furniture restoration shop in Sunberry.

But life gets complicated when Marine Major Ryan Murphy steps in—offering help she didn't ask for and stirring up feelings she didn't expect. Ryan's life has been built on duty and sacrifice, but Ava and her children make him long for something he's never had: a family of his own.

When a high-stakes business competition pits them against each other, sparks fly—and not just the romantic kind. Can they find common ground and a chance at love, or will their independent dreams drive them apart?

📕 **DOWNLOAD NOW** to experience a heartwarming story of resilience, healing, and finding home when you least expect it.

☞ Or flip the page for a **sneak peek** that ends with a twist you won't want to miss!

HOME TO STAY SNEAK PEEK

Talk about a crap storm. Ryan tensed. Time to look away, bolt for the door. He didn't move, didn't drop her hard stare. Didn't dare to. He'd faced down a lot of hostiles, but none with Ava Robey's intensity.

"Yes, ma'am. I can do that." He hoped his firm tone hid the yellow streak climbing up his spine.

She studied him like he'd become her latest target and then turned back to the range. He breathed. Next time he came across a teen fight, he'd keep on rolling. But what were the chances out of twenty thousand Sunberry residents he'd stop a fight with his Sergeant's kids? He gulped the coffee and burned a trail down his pipes. With that kind of luck, he should buy a lottery ticket.

No, he should've met his responsibilities. When he'd heard about Robey's death, he'd written a personal letter and asked to accompany the Casualty Assistance Calls Officer to notify her. But his responsibility to the family hadn't stopped. Mom told him Ava had moved to Sunberry. But he'd put off touching base with her, put off memories of the past. He owed Robey his life and now his widow— Ryan tracked her too slim frame while she prepared the meal. *Admit it, Marine.* The woman with tools had him wound tighter than a drill bit.

"I called after—" After what? Your husband was blown to bits? "after the funeral. I always got the answering machine or a kid. Probably Kyle. I left messages."

She didn't look away. But the pain in her golden eyes shone as sharp as the cramp in his gut. No more procrastination. He needed to help her out, ease the acid eating him from the inside out.

"That was a challenging time for me and my boys." The low timbre of her voice stripped the last scab protecting his conscience.

The urge to touch her and ease the memory curled his fingers into fists. "Yes, ma'am. That's why I called. I thought I could help. Take the boys to the movies. Fix your refrigerator. Whatever you needed."

She could mow down an entire unit with one of those looks. And he couldn't even defend himself because his tongue seemed to blow up in his mouth. The coffee might help, but his luck, he'd choke.

"I had a family to raise. I didn't need sympathy. I needed to pick up the pieces of my life and get on with it." She held his gaze again. "Do you understand?"

A raw edge still honed her glare, but the vulnerability he'd seen earlier had vanished. He'd known plenty of hard case Marines who had problems asking for help, namely his friend Schmidt. This was the first time he'd seen the same trait in a woman.

"A Marine is trained to take on whatever's thrown his way." He held her gaze but softened his tone. "But when he's down, he counts on his brothers to get him back on his feet. No man left behind. That's not just in theatre. It applies at home too."

His words curled his toes in his boots. *Way to go, Marine.* She wasn't a private straight out of bootcamp. She was a woman still mourning her husband.

"Thank you," she murmured.

He felt like throwing himself on his sword. She stared and he stopped bobbing his head like one of those bubbleheaded toys. He hated when he did that. It usually happened when he was in a tight spot—which was coming too often around Ava Robey.

Her distant look would probably haunt his dreams. Feeling that deep came from secrets a person didn't want to share. He knew because he had a few secrets too. Combat did that to a man. Loss did that to a woman. Mom had shown the same signs after his dad died.

"Marines serve and protect." He scrambled for something, anything to assuage the pain in her eyes. "That applies to families. As Sergeant's wife, you and your family are part of the Marine family."

Just the thought of losing the support of his Marine family sent a shudder across his shoulders. He couldn't imagine a life without them. Yet Ava didn't seem to know a life with them. He'd have to fill that vacuum for her. It was the least he could do for Robey's widow.

The timer on the range chimed and the haunted look evaporated from her features. When she opened the oven door, the savory aroma of bacon filled the kitchen. His stomach grumbled.

"I'm sorry. I should've returned your calls." She switched off the oven but didn't turn to face him. "At first I didn't want reminders of Josh. It wasn't you or the Corps. I needed time."

"I'm still here." This time he wouldn't let her down.

She faced him. "We're doing fine."

"Yes, ma'am." But she wasn't. Her boys were fighting and the farm was crumbling around her ears. A way to sugarcoat the truth would be helpful, but none came to him.

"You said you left Charlotte because of the oldest. There are lots of Marine families with teenagers at Lejeune. I could hook you up with a few. You know, like a support group of mothers."

As if on cue, the two younger boys entered the kitchen. She narrowed her eyes on him but didn't say what she was thinking. Which was probably a good thing. He'd pushed too hard. But he was trying to help. She had her hands full. Even an old bachelor like him could figure out that one.

The two boys fell into a rhythm and Ryan guessed this was the Robey routine. He'd bet his sidearm tonight was a subdued version of a usual night in the household—especially with three adolescent boys. Boys? They could be a handful. He'd had his share of experience coaching sports teams for the base kids, not to mention troops fresh from boot camp.

Ava added pancakes to a stack on a serving plate. If he remembered right, her family originated in Sunberry and later moved to Charlotte. He'd first seen her again at the Marine Corps Ball. She'd seemed taller. Probably wore high heels. Her toes had peeked out beneath her gown. Funny, what a guy remembered. She'd worn bright pink polish to match her dress. Robey kept her close that night—loving and proprietary to assure every man understood the beauty on his arm belonged to him.

Kyle barged into the kitchen, his dark hair wet against his scalp and anger simmering in his gaze. Ryan sipped his coffee. The kid had grit. No rounded shoulders or tail-between-the-legs for Robey's oldest. This one was all attitude. Ryan squared his shoulders. A hot-headed kid called for a smart man to be on the ready.

A cough broke the silence and Ryan turned toward the two younger boys. They exchanged a glance, a nonverbal messaging system. Kyle was testing boundaries and his brothers knew it. They also didn't like it. Ryan had figured Kyle, the oldest and smartest, held the alpha position when he'd first come across the boys and the ... situation they'd created.

Ava placed a plate piled high with browned pancakes on the table and the doughy scent caused Ryan's stomach to rumble. The big lab, resting on the rug along the wall, whined and repositioned. Whit brought over a platter of crisp bacon and Nate poured warm syrup from the saucepan into a serving pitcher.

The girl hurried to the table with a ratty toy that looked like she'd pulled it out of the dog's box. She pointed a chubby finger at him. "You're sitting in Grandma's chair."

With a mother's gentle touch, Ava smoothed the girl's long dark curls. "Mr. Ryan is joining us for dinner."

Although the kid continued to watch him, she climbed into her seat. Ava handed the pancake platter to him with a stand-down look that sent his heart rate hauling butt in retreat. Which is what he wanted to do. And he thought he had the chops to stand up to any fight—until he met Ava Robey. He forked three cakes onto his plate and returned the plate to her. Her house. Her orders. He owed her that. Owed her husband more.

Her solemn gaze held his, never wavering. So, did she regret asking him to share a meal as much as he regretted accepting her invitation? Maybe guilt drove her the same way it hammered him. Maybe she tried to work through the wounds of the past the same as any Marine who had seen battle. The same as Schmidt, hiding symptoms of PTSD.

She served one cake for herself, slipped one onto her daughter's plate, and handed the platter to Kyle. "Share your story, please."

With a sullen glance at first his mother and then Ryan,

Kyle extracted a rock from his pocket and placed it in front of his milk glass.

"Dad told me when he was deployed, I had to be the man of the house. No matter what, I had to hold up for my brothers. He didn't ruffle my hair or treat me like a baby. He made me look in his eyes and stand tall."

"Thank you, Kyle. Your father was proud of you." She gave the girl a reassuring smile. "All of you."

Ryan bit the inside of his mouth to keep his lips straight. This wasn't the time to smile or crack up. Ava would be all over him for encouraging her sons. He admired them. Based on the slight twitch of her mouth, she did too. Besides, the oldest boy gave an okay tribute.

She turned to the tow-headed kid. "Whit."

He placed a similar stone on the table. "One time when I was sick, Dad climbed into bed with me. He didn't worry that he'd catch something. He said a good man listens more than he talks. That made me feel good because I couldn't talk like the other kids."

Nate thumped his rock against the surface of the table. "Dad missed Father's Day at preschool because he was in Iraq. I hated it. My friends' dads came and talked about their jobs. My dad had a cool job and he wasn't there to tell my class, so I sat like a lump. When he got home, he came to my school. He showed his medals and talked about training. My class thought he was awesome. I'll never forget that day."

The girl shoved the tattered toy on the table, and Ava steadied Hope's milk glass to avoid a spill.

"Dude," Nate said. "Don't put that gross thing on the table."

"Mom!" Hope whined.

"It's fine, Hope," Ava soothed. "Tell us your story."

Ryan marveled at the girl's tiny hands stroking the raggedy toy's back. "I was iddy-biddy when my daddy was home. He bought me Piggy and said he'd be back in a jiffy. So, I named him Jiffy like Daddy told me. And I gave him a bath last night so he's not stinky like Nate."

Ryan covered a chuckle with a cough. Leave it to the cute girl to cause a revolt. While Ava calmed the war rumbling among the natives, he tried to frame a story suitable for Robey's kids.

Ava fingered the bare ring-finger of her left hand. "Your dad was always working to ensure everything around the house was in good working order before he deployed. He wanted us safe and cared for even when he couldn't be here."

And Ryan was supposed to pick up the slack. Although he'd kept track of her progress in Charlotte, the distance morphed into an excuse and only cowards hid behind excuses. Shame heated his face. He'd failed before, but he'd start to change that—as soon as he came up with a story to share. There'd been countless encounters. Sergeant Robey was his most trusted Marine. But that didn't mean he could share it with his family. Sweat beaded along his sides and the hard chair dug into his butt.

"Now for our guest." Ava seemed to stare right through him. "Mr. Ryan is a Marine. He was deployed with your father and agreed to tell a story about your dad."

Nothing like being in the crosshairs of five hostiles. The boys had no idea who he was when he broke up that fight. Now, they did.

He set down his mug. "Sergeant Robey was the best man in my unit. I depended on him for the hardest jobs and he always came through. Your dad was a hero. I owe my life to his quick actions."

"Like in the movies?" Nate asked, his eyes wide with wonder.

"Combat is not like the movies." The smell of enemy fire,

the cries of wounded men, and the taste of fear bombarded him.

"Dad saved your life?" Whit asked, his steady blue gaze knifing Ryan's insides.

Ryan sipped his coffee, but the situation required a stronger drink.

"How?" Kyle said.

Ava's gaze darted to his. She would stop the questions. All he had to do was give her a sign. He shook his head.

"Our unit was ambushed. I got hit in the leg and went down. Your dad came back for me. He ordered me to *hold on* and his words got me through."

A black wall clock ticked in the silence. Ryan's right eye stung. When he wiped at it, sweat slicked his fingers.

"Thank you for sharing your story with us." Ava's quiet tone cut through the silence. "Josh was a good father and a good Marine. Be proud he was your father."

Ava pushed her plate forward. "Now that we've honored him, I think you should tell me why you were late tonight."

Ryan released a breath. He'd underestimated Robey's wife. She was no pushover. Her narrowed gaze roved from son to son like a drill instructor assessing new recruits. She checked the swelling around Kyle's left jaw, moved to Nate's split lip, and ended at the cut opening Whit's eyebrow. When she sipped her coffee, Ryan had to cover a smile with his napkin. The lady had timing down to a science. She'd raised her family alone for over five years. That couldn't be easy. And he'd neglected his duty to assist a fallen Marine's family. Time to remedy that oversight.

"It's my fault," Whit was saying. "Derrick made fun of Talley's braces."

Ryan wiped his mouth. Now, he was starting to get this picture. The bully who had started the drama and the stepson Schmidt had complained about were the same kid.

"Talley?" Ava said. "Is she the new friend?"

"Yeah, she's cool," Kyle said. "She helped Whit at school."

Whit poured syrup on his pancakes. "She's sensitive about her braces. Derrick was being a dick."

"Language," Ava reminded.

"Derrick Schmidt's a fathead. Big football star. He sucks." Whit stabbed at the pancake.

Ava wiped her mouth with her napkin. "Who threw the first punch?"

"Dad always told me to stand by my brothers." Kyle scraped off a small pile of bacon strips on his plate. "The butt—"

"Language," Ava said.

"Whatever," Kyle said. "The bully called Whit a dimwit."

When Whit's face flamed with embarrassment, Ryan squeezed his fork. He hated a bully, especially one who preyed upon a trait that couldn't be helped. He'd noted the odd pattern of the kid's speech. The middle son must have a language issue. Except for his too-long blonde hair, the teen looked okay. His problem must be on the inside. Those always hurt the most.

"That's not nice," Hope said.

"Boys, we've had this discussion," Ava said. "Words don't start fights."

"He was asking for it." Kyle bit into a strip of bacon and moved it to the side of his mouth. "I told him to back off, but he kept coming. Big football dick going to show the poor kids how Sunberry High works."

"So, am I hearing that it was three against one?" Ava said.

"Try seven to four." Kyle's voice was more snarl than speech.

Ava's brow furrowed in confusion "When did this happen?"

"Right after school." Whit kept his eyes downcast. "Talley

stayed to help me finish a homework assignment. That's when she asked us to come over for a while. We weren't bothering them."

"And no one at the school saw this?" Ava said.

"They stopped us at the corner."

"Derrick drives a cool SUV with dark windows." Nate spoke for the first time. "We didn't know half the team was inside."

Ava pressed her fingers against her forehead. "Go on."

Kyle's anger had diminished with the telling of the story. "Talley might've said something. They got out."

"I hit him." Whit's words came out in starts and stops. "Couldn't help it, Mom.... I didn't care about... what he called me. He made Talley cry."

She gave Whit a slight nod. "So the three of you took on these boys?"

"Talley got in a few good kicks. She has some ridiculous karate moves." Nate moved his hands above the table. "Can we take lessons?"

Ryan scraped the syrup on his plate. If he didn't do something, he was going to start laughing. The Robey kids were too funny. No doubt, the household was utter chaos. Compared to their household, he led a boring, utilitarian existence. Maybe that's why they intrigued him.

"Right now, we need to get the story." She turned to Kyle with a stern look. "The *whole* story."

"After Whit hit Derrick, two of his friends jumped Whit from behind." Kyle chased down his food with a gulp of milk. "I was trying to break it up."

"Sure you were." A hint of sarcasm tinged Ava's words. She turned to Nate. "And you?"

"They were all over Whit and Kyle. I might have pushed one of the guy's head against the ground."

"We would've beat them if he hadn't come along and broke it up." Kyle nodded toward Ryan.

Ava raised her hand. "And that's all of it, the whole story?"

The boys exchanged glances and for a minute Ryan wondered if the trio would come clean.

"Talley was still fired up when we got to her house." Kyle turned away from Whit's glare.

"This wasn't the first time Derrick's made fun of her," Whit said.

"But this was the first time she'd had help," Ava guessed.

"Derrick kind of deserved it." Nate wrinkled his nose. "But his dad lost his mind when we hit his car."

Ava turned to Ryan with those big doe eyes and holy crap, his insides turned to mush. Now, he'd lost *his* mind.

She turned back to face the boys. "What did you hit the car with?"

"It was just tomatoes," Whit said.

Ava's chin dropped toward her chest and she mouthed the word *tomatoes*. That part had caught Ryan off-guard too. Kids usually threw rocks or sticks. But not this group.

"So you rescued them twice in one day?" she said.

"Colonel Schmidt lives behind me. There's common ground between us, but Schmidt sounds like a drill instructor when he's ticked." He shrugged. "I came out to see who was yelling."

"Thank you," she said.

The pancakes and coffee churned in his stomach. Sometime in the last twenty seconds she'd gone from ramrod stiff to soft and kissable. The woman was hot. A blind Marine could work that out, but that look. The gentleness in her hazel eyes and the hint of a smile on her lips generated something more than images of a few sweaty nights. A woman like Ava Robey made a man think about something with more substance.

But this wasn't the time to get involved with a woman, especially one with four children. Fact was, he wanted to help Ava and her sons. But he'd also agreed to help Schmidt in some lease competition. And untreated PTSD was more serious than a scuffle among a group of hormonal boys. A Marine's life was on the line.

———

Don't want to stop?

Purchase your copy and start the Murphy family saga today!

PLEASE LEAVE A REVIEW

Enjoyed *Val's Last Second Chance*? Your Review Means the World! 🤍

If you loved the story, would you take a moment to leave a quick review on **Goodreads, Amazon, or BookBub**?

Even one or two sentences—like *"I loved the characters"* or *"The ending made me tear up"*—makes a big difference. Reviews help other readers discover my books and help me grow as an author.

And yes—**you can copy the same review to all three sites**. I'm all for easy!

📖 WHERE TO LEAVE A REVIEW:

⭐ GOODREADS

- Click here to review on Goodreads

- Or visit Goodreads.com, search for *Val's Last Second Chance*, click the cover, and scroll down to "Write a Review."

⭐ AMAZON

- Click here to review on Amazon
- Or go to Amazon.com, search for *Val's Last Second Chance* under "Kindle Books," click the title, and scroll to "Write a Customer Review."

⭐ BOOKBUB

Click here to review on BookBub

Or visit BookBub.com, log in, search *Val's Last Second Chance*, and click the red "Write a Review" button.

————

Just five minutes and a few kind words can help *Val's Last Second Chance* reach new readers. Thanks so much for your support—it means everything. 💕

👉 **Flip the page for a tasty Turner kitchen recipe and a little something extra...**

EASY LEMON CAKE

Made with lemon cake mix and lemon pudding

INGREDIENTS:

CAKE:

- **15.25oz** box lemon cake mix, like D*uncan Hines Lemon Supreme*
- **1 5oz** box Instant lemon pudding mix, *(not ready made, not cook n serve)*
- **1 tsp** lemon zest
- **½ cup** water
- **½ cup** lemon juice, *fresh*
- **4** eggs large
- **½ cup** vegetable oil

Lemon Glaze:

- **½ cup** confectioner's sugar
- **1 tbsp.** cream, *or milk*
- **½ tsp.** lemon zest

**Note: One large lemon will provide fresh juice and zest for this recipe.

––––––––

INSTRUCTIONS:

1. Preheat the oven to 350 F. Generously spray a 10 cup bundt pan with baking spray.
2. In the large mixing bowl, add the dry cake mix and lemon pudding powder and mix on low speed for 30 seconds.
3. Add the lemon zest, ½ cup water, 1/2 cup lemon juice, and 4 eggs. Mix on low-medium speed for 1 minute.
4. Add ½ cup oil and mix again.
5. Fill the prepared bundt cake pan with batter.
6. Bake for 35 mins.
7. Cool for 10 mins then flip over onto a cooling rack to cool completely.
8. Prepare lemon gaze and drizzle over cake.
9. Enjoy! 🍰

ACKNOWLEDGMENTS

To every mother caring for a child with a chronic illness or disability—this story is for you.

You juggle so much more than meets the eye. The extra planning, the quiet worries, the middle-of-the-night alarms, and the fierce love that drives it all. Your strength doesn't always get the recognition it deserves, but it's there in every choice you make, every boundary you set, and every ounce of care you give.

In *Val's Last Second Chance*, Val's love for Libby is rooted in that same deep well of determination—the kind of love that will move mountains, challenge fears, and redefine what it means to start over. Libby's MCADD diagnosis may be invisible to most, but for Val, it shapes every part of her day—and every decision about their future.

To the moms navigating life with MCADD: I see you. I admire you. Your everyday courage is what makes hope possible.

If you'd like to learn more about MCADD (Medium-Chain Acyl-CoA Dehydrogenase Deficiency), visit the National Institutes of Health's resource at https://www.ncbi.nlm.nih.gov/books/NBK1424/.

Thank you for showing the world what love in action really looks like.

BECKE TURNER BOOKS

THE CLOCKTOWER ROMANCE SERIES

Welcome to Sunberry, North Carolina—a charming fictional town where friends feel like family and love is always just around the corner.

———

THE AWARD-WINNING MURPHY CLAN

Meet the Murphy family—beloved by readers for their heart, humor, and unforgettable journeys.

- *HOME TO STAY* (The beginning, Ava and Ryan Murphy)

- *MURPHY'S SECRET* (Whit Murphy's romance)

- *MURPHY'S CINDERELLA (Kyle Murphy's romance)*

- *MURPHY'S CHOICE (Nate Murphy's romance)*

- *MURPHY'S STANDOFF (Marriage in crisis, Ava and Ryan Murphy*

- *MURPHY'S RESCUE (Hope Murphy's romance)*

SUNBERRY FRIENDS & NEIGHBORS

More love stories from Sunberry—featuring familiar faces and new favorites.

- *CAROLINA COWBOY*

- *LOVING TROUBLE (companion novella to CAROLINA COWBOY)*

- *THE PUPPY BARTER*

- *A SUNBERRY CHRISTMAS*

- FLIGHT WITHOUT WINGS

📦 3-BOOKS COLLECTIONS– MORE ROMANCE, MORE SAVINGS!

📚 Love a Deal? Don't Miss These 3-Book Collections!

Save more and fall deeper in love—each bundle includes three heartwarming stories.

THE CLOCKTOWER ROMANCE COLLECTION

- *HOME TO STAY*
- *CAROLINA COWBOY*
- *MURPHY'S SECRET*

THE MURPHY MEN COLLECTION

- *HOME TO STAY*
- *MURPHY'S SECRET*
- *MURPHY'S CINDERELLA*

THE MURPHY BROTHERS COLLECTION

- *MURPHY'S SECRET*
- *MURPHY'S CINDERELLA*
- *MURPHY'S CHOICE*

THE FEEL GOOD COLLECTION

- *HOME TO STAY*
- *THE PUPPY BARTER*
- *MURPHY'S CINDERELLA*

———

WELCOME TO GLEN FALLS!

A brand-new town, a fresh start—but the same heart you loved in the Murphy Family Saga.

The Glen Falls Romance Series introduces new characters, emotional journeys, and the charm of small-town Missouri.

- VAL'S LAST SECOND CHANCE

Thanks for reading—your next great love story is waiting!

ABOUT THE AUTHOR

Becke Turner, Author of Sweet, Small-Town Romance

Becke Turner grew up in Salem, Illinois, but her path to writing took off at the University of Miami, where she ran a small writing business to finance taxi rides to her horse. Inspired by authors like Zane Grey and Julie Garwood, she wrote her first manuscript while raising her son.

Her career began in acute care nursing at Barnes-Jewish Hospital and The Ohio State University Wexner Medical Center. She later moved into healthcare policy, developing programs to enhance molecular diagnostics and prevent Medicare fraud as a government contractor. Becke retired in 2017 to write full-time.

Now living in Blythewood, South Carolina, with her husband of over fifty years, Becke is the proud mother of two and grandmother of five.

She writes sweet, small-town romances featuring strong women, found families, and second chances—perfect for readers who cherish home, healing, and the quiet power of love.

Want FREE exclusive material?

Turner Town News, my monthly newsletter, gives you the inside scoop—exclusive updates, behind-the-scenes fun, and book news before anyone else.

Subscribe now and get a **FREE reader bundle** featuring:

The **Clocktower Romance Character Map**—track your favorite characters, including the Murphy family, and find your perfect reading order.

An **exclusive prequel** to *Val's Last Second Chance*—the emotional story that leads into my next series.

Val's Last Second Chance is the series opener for my brand-new **Glen Falls Series**, releasing **April 22, 2025**!

Visit me anytime at www.becketurner.com

Home to Stay

Written by Becke Turner

Cover Design by Special-T Publishing

Edited by By the Book Editing, Beth Belmanno

Published by Special-T Publishing, LLC

ISBN - 978-1-953651-32-7

Library of Congress Control Number:

First Edition

First Printing --

Manufactured by Amazon.ca
Acheson, AB